THE ARSENIC BOX

G.H. FRYER

PICKETT &PROSE

PUBLISHING, LLC
COLORADO

Cover Design by Naomi Pickett. Cover art: Beauty Portrait by Alexander Krivitskiy. Photo by Moussa Idrissi.

Pickett & Prose Publishing, LLC

First Edition: June 2022

Library of Congress Control Number: 2022937345

ISBNs: 979-8-9861578-3-2 (Paperback), 979-8-9861578-1-8 (ebook) 979-8-61578-0-1 (Hardcover)

Look, Daddy, I did it!
(Waves to the urn on the mantle)

THE
ARSENIC
BOX

CHAPTER ONE

The sun had set hours ago, but Geoff Otto drove through the streets of Fort Collins, the kaleidoscope colors of neon signs and streetlights casting harsh colors upon the busy streets. Fort Collins was one of those university cities that craved all the luxuries of a metropolis but fought hard to keep its Wild West roots. He snorted aloud at the thought. It was a losing battle.

Geoff checked the time on his wristwatch; he was going to be late. He shifted in his seat as he adjusted his trousers. Geoff was not in the best of shape. He had a round belly and a pasty complexion, and much of the hair on his scalp had left him long ago. What he lacked in looks, though, he made up for in temperament and drive. He was slow to anger yet protective of the life he had spent decades working towards. Being the senior partner in an established architectural firm in a city that couldn't stop growing lent him a great deal of power. With that power came politics and the occasional rabble-rouser who wanted to push him off his throne. Power was not easy to keep hold of. It required constant nurturing and pruning, drafting designs, and cultivating relationships. He'd had a particularly trying day at work today in regard to weeding out a certain problem and was glad to have a pleasant diversion to take his mind off of things.

The lights of the city were fading as he drove north. The next town up was Wellington, a small farm town that had been fashioning itself as a bedroom community for Fort Collins proper. The constant growth of the two towns had brought them so close together you almost couldn't separate them, but for now, a little unspoiled countryside remained. That was where he was heading, back into the country roads where the city lights and the daily grind of business couldn't reach. He chided himself slightly as he realized he was dressed so inappropriately for the occasion. He would be lucky to not ruin his trousers and loafers.

As the city fell behind him, the road ahead grew dark. No city lights brightened the road, so he leaned forward to see better. It wouldn't be the first time a fox darted across the road or an owl swooped along the edge of his vision. He was meeting someone special tonight. Geoff fiddled with the links on his cuffs. He knew he had no reason for butterflies in his stomach; nonetheless, here he was, a grown man nearing retirement and as nervous as a schoolgirl. Following the familiar directions, he would turn off this county road or that one. He had been here enough times that he knew the way by now.

Eventually, he pulled over to the edge of the road. Once he turned off the headlights, he could barely discern the house's shadowy form. He grabbed the flashlight he'd brought with him and unfolded himself out of the car. Spread out before him was an untamed meadow covered in tall grasses, nettles, and wildflowers. A slight breeze blew through and set the grass to whispering all around him. He wouldn't be able to live here, so far removed from the bustle of the city, but his clandestine companion felt differently.

Geoff sighed as he stepped into the tall grasses that snagged at his clothing and made his way towards the derelict mansion. He'd done his research ages ago and knew what a beautiful example of Art Deco architecture the place was. It once boasted curved walls of glass and broad expanses of smooth white plaster that were the epitome of smart modern style from the twenties. The entrance had been grand and elegant: bold double doors with vintage geometric designs, covered in chipping paint. The underbrush was treacherous, and he tripped multiple times on detritus hidden within the grass. Eventually, he made his way to the porch, the steps forming a curved fan like a seashell.

One of the double doors was already open, but not enough for him to pass through. *She must already be here*, he thought. He pushed the stiff door open farther, and a pile of twigs and dried leaves rustled as he pushed them out of the way. He stepped into the dark, derelict mansion and was swallowed up by richly stained floorboards and peeling wallpaper. Outside, the wind was gentle and teasing. The black sky was sprinkled with stars, and the city a few short miles away cast a ghostly glow on the horizon. In the distance, two beams of light drew closer. When Geoff's car was nearly caught in the growing beams of light, the light extinguished. Tires crunched on the gravel road as a vehicle shrouded in darkness crept by.

Once Geoff stepped inside the decaying manor, the sounds from outside were muffled. He trod among the leaf litter and broken furniture, musing about how well this place was constructed. New construction was never so solid. He entered the conservatory at the other end of the house, and once he stepped into the remnants of the once opulent sunroom with his red face and forehead beading with sweat, he smiled.

The conservatory, like the rest of the house, was in shambles. It had been a very long time since anyone had loved the place. The cracked tiled floor was littered with leaves and the occasional skeletal remnants of small animals. The drapes that covered the tall, broad windows were sun-bleached and threadbare. The several seating areas and furniture remained where they had been abandoned so long ago. In stark contrast to the dreary decay all around him, Geoff couldn't help but smile at the vision before him. Stretched out comfortably on one of the frayed chaise lounge chairs was Verity Georgeson, an eccentric counterpoint to the current taste of what it meant to be a modern woman. Her fair skin made her easy to spot even in this dim light. Her auburn hair was twisted into a full smooth bun at the base of her neck, and her legs were stretched out and crossed at the ankles.

She looked up from the book she had been reading by the illuminated screen of her phone. When she saw him, she smiled warmly. Geoff found it impossible not to reciprocate when faced with her genuine smile. Her dark mossy green eyes sparkled, the corners creasing lightly. She was in her early forties, but she had a glow of youth about her. Geoff knew her more deeply than most and knew she had suffered through more than her fair share of trauma. The damage could be seen in her eyes when she didn't know anyone was watching her.

When he approached her, she closed her book and set it down before rising to meet him. They embraced warmly. *What a contrast*, he thought. A grumpy old man and a vigorous young woman. They were destined to meet. Her vision for this place and his connections would bring this old wreck back to life. A light flickered in a nearby window, and Geoff reflected fleetingly on the early summer storms that frequented the Colorado front range.

"Sorry I'm late, Verity," he huffed.

"It's okay. I wasn't worried." She gave him a wink.

"But I'm here," he added with a smile, "with good news."

"The good news can wait until you tell me what's wrong."

Geoff sucked in a breath. "How do you do that?"

"Do what?

"Always know when people are . . ."

"Distracted?"

"Yes."

Verity's smile turned slightly sad. "An acquaintance once told me I was empathic." She laughed.

"I believe it," he mumbled.

Verity held the large man at arm's length and gave him an unusual look. "I don't need to be an empath to see that you look less than your usual self." She plucked burs out of his silk tie as she straightened it. He dropped his head to watch her slender fingers work efficiently and patiently at the burs. Her patience was a rare quality that most people lacked these days.

He wrapped his hands around her waist. "What's happened?" she asked.

Geoff looked into her green eyes and saw concern.

"Oh, it's nothing." He sunk into the threadbare chaise she had been sitting on and pulled her down next to him.

"Liar."

"It's nothing you need to worry about."

"The same thing you've been concerned about?" she asked. He nodded. "Is there anything I can do to help?"

"That's kind of you, but no." He sighed. "I'll manage. Besides, you're not here to listen to an old man grumble." He leaned in conspiratorially. "You're here for better things."

"All right, then, tell me your good news," she said with a soft laugh. Geoff leaned back, stuffed his hand into the inside pocket of his suit jacket, and withdrew a single folded piece of paper. Verity's eyes grew wide and expectant.

"Did you get it?"

Geoff relished the anticipation in her face and could imagine what a joyful child she must've been.

"I don't know if I should show you," he teased.

"Oh, come on now, don't be horrible." Verity laughed.

He thought about it some more, but only in jest before he handed the folded paper to her. She took it gently from his fingertips.

Somewhere nearby, a tiny twig cracked, and Verity's head swiveled towards the sound.

"What is it?"

"It's nothing," she answered as she turned back to stare at the gift in her hands. "I just think we have a four-legged guest nearby." She unfolded the paper. The astonished smile on her face was all he needed. "I can't believe you finally managed to get it."

"*We* managed to get it," he corrected. "This was as much you as it was me."

"Geoff?"

"Yes?" he asked. She had been staring intently at the formal document with an ornate blue border and gilded accents. He smiled. He knew what she was looking at. "As long as we stay true to the era, they will gladly put this house on the registry."

Verity leaned over, wrapped her arms around his generous neck, and squeezed him tight. "Thank you so much, Geoff."

"It has been my pleasure, Ver. You really have something here. There is no one other than you who would've been able to see past all this rot and still be able to dream of what it used to be."

"I was just lucky enough to have your ear for my crazy idea."

"It's not crazy. It's magnificent and bold."

"It's ludicrous, you mean," she said, and he gave a big belly laugh at that.

"Yes, I suppose it is a little ludicrous, but if you can be patient with me, then I can assure you that by the time we are done with this place, it will be a beacon of opulence." He pressed his lips against hers, and her hands teased the back of his neck. "Someday, this place will be beautiful. I look forward to the journey with you."

"Thank you, Geoff. You are an amazing man."

"Enough already," he grumbled, but his cheeks reddened and dimpled. "We came here to celebrate, and celebrate we shall."

He rifled around in another pocket and came out with an elegant stainless-steel flask that was encased in smooth cedar, his initials carved into the exterior. It had been a gift from his wife Mary last year on their anniversary. For a time, he wasn't sure that they would even have another anniversary. They had strayed so far from what had brought them together, each growing, and each growing apart. Verity had listened to him grieve for a dying marriage and had given him advice and encouragement along the way. Eventually, he and Mary had fallen back in love with each other, even taking special pleasure in being giddy. They were old enough now to not care what other people thought. As long as they loved each other, they could overcome everything else.

He twisted off the lid and offered it to Verity. She took the flask and sipped it before handing it back to him. Geoff, for his part, took a generous pull.

"I would appreciate it if you would keep these for me," Verity said as she handed the papers back to Geoff.

"Oh no you don't. Those belong to you." He slid them back. "You worked too hard to have me take those away. Keep them; they're yours."

"Fine," she conceded. "Thank you again."

"You're welcome." He patted her knee in a fatherly fashion. "I should let you go for the night."

"I'm sure Mary would be glad to have you home soon anyway."

"Yes, I suppose you're right." He smiled.

"Good." She rose to her feet and held out her hands to help him stand. They embraced again. She whispered in his ear, "I can't thank you enough."

"It was a pleasure."

Lightning flashed in the distance, reflecting in a rare clean spot on the mirrors hanging opposite the giant windows. Geoff gave Verity one quick final embrace, holding her too close for too long for it to be just a congenial friendship. Eventually, he released her and navigated through the house and out into the wild, untamed land around it. He sipped from the flask again. He screwed on the cap and pocketed it before climbing back into his car and steering down dirt roads until he was on pavement again.

As he drove into the busy traffic, he pulled out a handkerchief from his trouser pocket and wiped his forehead. He was perspiring more than usual. His stomach tightened slightly, and he wondered if he would need a toilet soon. Brushing the thought away, he remembered that he'd been particularly stressed at work lately, trying to figure out who at the firm was going to make a play against him. He had his suspicions but couldn't work out how it was going to be done. There were only two ways to gain power in an architectural firm. One was having the most prestigious clients, and the other, well, the other was waiting for one of the board members to die and then making a run to be the replacement.

Geoff came to a stop at a red light. While he waited for the light to cycle through, he checked the time on his watch. He would be home later than he'd planned, but Mary would forgive him. His stomach constricted again. He might be in for a rough evening. Regardless of his round figure, he had a fairly robust constitution and couldn't imagine what he ate that was giving him trouble. If his opponent was waiting for one of the board members to die, then it would be a long game they were playing. Although the board members were far from young, they were still quite away from kicking the bucket. The subtle inconsistencies he had been noticing were accumulating quickly, and he didn't think a long game was in the picture.

Geoff was startled when a fit of coughing escaped him. He wiped his mouth ungracefully with the sleeve of his suit jacket and was surprised to see it covered in frothy saliva. What in heaven's sake was going on? He looked up as the light turned green and blinked away his blurry vision. He stepped on the gas pedal as his gut retched. There was nothing for it now other than to hurry home. He would have to have the car professionally cleaned, but he felt momentarily better. His stomach rolled, and he heaved as another cramp in his abdomen bent him nearly in half.

When his throat closed, his eyes grew wide with fright. Panic took over. He grabbed at the tie around his neck and struggled to release it, but he couldn't think, couldn't concentrate, and couldn't breathe. He lurched in his seatbelt to breathe through his constricted throat. The steering wheel twisted, and the car curved awkwardly on the road, nearly missing a nearby car, but not missing the steel pole of the next traffic signal.

Some drivers slowed down for a time, but for a few minutes, none stopped, other than a black pickup that pulled up behind Geoff's car. The driver's door was bent in half and open at an unlikely angle. Geoff's face was covered in sweat and blood, his body contorted in the wreckage of the car. His body convulsed as he watched the door of the black truck open and a figure stepped out onto the road.

Geoff's world became eerily quiet. The rushing sound of nearby traffic had been dulled by the shock of the accident, and it was impossible to concentrate on anything but his pain and fear. Footsteps crunched on the broken glass, which was scattered like spring flower petals on the asphalt. The figure crouched down to take his measure of Geoff and the carnage around him. Geoff couldn't move his body enough to get a look at the figure's face. Through the haze of blood and sweat burning his eyes and clouding his vision, he could only remain where he was, helpless and dying.

Geoff tried to speak to the figure but only managed a disgusting gurgle. The stranger reached in and fumbled around the pockets of his jacket until he finally pulled away with Geoff's flask in his hand. He was dying, and this stranger was robbing him of something sentimental? There was no sense to that until, in another fit of choking and wave of nausea, Geoff arrived at a sickening conclusion. The figure stood up, ignoring Geoff's strangled attempt to beg for help, and took the flask with him, while Geoff heard something being tossed into the backseat just as the footsteps faded. His last fleeting thoughts were of primal fear and helplessness.

CHAPTER TWO

Mary Otto sat in her car for a long time. The sun beat down on the black car, making it uncomfortable to stay, but the alternative was worse. Her heart hammered against the inside of her ribcage as her hands shook. Anxiety was not a good look on her. She was used to being strong and independent, but ever since the call informing her that her husband was dead, she couldn't seem to pull herself together. All she wanted to do was cry, but she knew herself well enough that if she allowed herself to cry right now, she would never be able to stop. She looked down at the ragged piece of paper in her hands. It had been twisted and crinkled as her hands worried about it. Mary tried to smooth the little note out against the center of her steering wheel, but it was useless.

Mary was a practical woman and knew she wouldn't find any answers by wallowing here. She gathered her courage to enter the Fort Collins Police Department. Like everything else in the city pretending to be more modern than it was, the police department housed itself in an expansive modern building with long sweeping curves of glass and brick. The state flag waved proudly, flanking the entrance with the national flag like two sentinels standing guard. The bright blue skies overhead mocked the shadow wrapping around her.

Getting a call from the police was about as enticing as receiving a letter from the IRS, but no one ever expected to get a call from a stranger telling them that their loved one was dead. There was no reception desk, only a long counter reminiscent of a row of bank tellers. Was that what the police department was now? A bank teller with justice as currency? That wasn't exactly right. If there was any justice in the world, Geoff would still be alive.

An officer standing behind the acrylic partitions greeted her.

"Ma'am?" He was a burly man with broad shoulders and a military-style cut.

"I am supposed to be meeting a"—she looked down at the wrinkled paper in her hands—"Detective Parson."

The officer thumped away at the keyboard in front of him, but Mary could swear that one of his eyebrows raised slightly at the mention of the detective's name. It was probably nothing. She was probably just being overly sensitive.

"Detective Parson will meet you outside interview room number three."

"Lovely," she muttered.

"It's on the second floor. Take the stairs," he emphasized with a large stubby finger. "It's down the long, curved corridor. Parson is finishing up with something else and will be a few minutes."

"Thank you," she replied politely, although she didn't feel like being polite to anyone. She felt like screaming, but she followed his directions and made her way to the second floor.

The corridor outside the interview rooms curved and faced the streetside. One wall was bland, with plain doors at regular intervals marked with simple placards affixed to them, denoting which interview room they were. Between them, large landscape photography prints hung in a corporate attempt to dress up the place. The other side of the corridor displayed floor-to-ceiling windows.

Three simple chairs rested along the wall outside of each interview room. She dropped slowly into one of them and stared at the passing traffic. Her hands worked at the paper still in her hands like she was worrying a tissue. She tried to calm herself by smoothing out her black skirt. Mary was old school. She relied on her impeccable manners, just opinion, and shrewd business sense. She was usually implacable, but the death of her husband left her usual stalwartness shaken.

Mary tried her best not to think about Geoff, so she simply stared out the window. The muscles in her face were strained at the effort of trying not to indulge in the grief that constantly threatened to overwhelm her. Familiar footsteps brought her back to the present, and she turned to see her closest friend walking toward her.

Anita Belker was half her age, the perfect modern housewife, and an optimist. While she acted as the exact counterpoint, she and Mary got along splendidly. Seeing Anita's youthful face was more than she could have asked for. Mary rose and let herself be swallowed up by Anita's tight embrace.

"Mary!" Anita proclaimed in her soft, feminine voice.

"You are a sight for sore eyes." Mary sighed into her friend's golden hair.

"What happened?"

"Geoff is gone."

"No!" Anita said, astonished. Mary understood the shock. She'd had the same initial response. All she could do was nod. "What happened?" Words wouldn't be enough, and she feared losing her grip on her emotions if she tried to say anything else. Anita seemed to recognize Mary's struggle. "How can I help?"

"You've already done enough." Mary allowed herself a weak smile to let her friend know how grateful she was. "Just being here for, for whatever this is, is enough."

The two friends sat down next to each other and let silence fill the space between them. They had been friends since Anita's husband had joined the firm. Mary and Geoff had thrown one of their usual dinner parties, and the two women had connected immediately. Their friendship blossomed over the last few years, and now they were close enough that there was no longer any uncomfortable silence between them. They simply sat there, holding each other's hands, and waited.

Mary was thankful for Anita's silence. There was nothing her friend could say that would ease her pain, her grief, but the opportunity of companionship with no burden or expectation of conversation was a blessing. Mary's sense of time had crumbled at the first horrible words on the phone when she was told that Geoff had died, so she had no real sense of time or the passing of time, but eventually, the silence was broken. Perhaps it was more apt that the silence had been punctuated by the unmistakable sound of a woman's heels as they clacked against the tiled floor. Mary and Anita turned their heads in unison and found themselves staring at something completely incongruous.

As though straight out of a classic noir film, a woman made her way along the corridor towards where the two friends were sitting. The woman wore an emerald dress that cut to just below her knees and hugged the hourglass curves of her body. She was neither tall nor slender, but vintage style came off her in waves, and the wide-brimmed black hat she wore accentuated the look perfectly.

"I'll tell you later," Mary said.

"Alright," Anita replied, rather disbelievingly. "If you're sure." Mary's only response was to pat her on the arm congenially.

Other than Mary, Anita, and the other woman, the long corridor was empty. The three of them sat in silence, staring at the traffic out the windows in front of them. Mary hardly noticed the other woman's presence. She didn't fidget or fuss as most young people did. Even Anita shifted every now and again, but the other woman did not.

It wasn't very long before another set of footsteps announced the presence of someone making their way toward them. The three women all turned together like some contemporary comedy. Coming towards them was a woman who carried her work with her in every step she took. There was no mistaking the arrival of Detective Parson. She was a petite woman with salt and pepper hair tied into a simple ponytail at the base of her neck. Mary wasn't sure if the woman had ever worn a stitch of makeup. Her steps were heavy, but they didn't drag.

"Ladies," she said by way of greeting. "Mary Otto?"

"Detective Parson?" Mary asked.

"That's me," she answered Mary brusquely and then turned to the other woman. "Miss Georgeson?" The other woman nodded. "Good. I'll be with you next. Mrs. Otto, please come with me."

Mary rose, gave her friend's hand a tight squeeze before clutching her purse as though it were a life preserver, then followed the detective through the door to interview room three.

The room was small and sparse. Four chairs flanked the table in the center of the room, two on either side. A large mirror on one wall gave Mary the creeps, which probably meant it was a two-way mirror. Although the room was brightly painted, clean, and well lit, this room was meant for questioning. Mary wondered if this was how the police treated all widows.

"Please have a seat, Mrs. Otto," the detective said. Mary obliged, trying her best to look calm, but she felt as though she were on display. Detective Parson sat down across the table from her and laid a folder that had been tucked under her arm on the table in front of her. She didn't open it. Instead, she rifled around in her trouser pocket and pulled out a notepad and pen. "Thank you for taking the time to come in and speak with me today. I can't imagine how you must be feeling, but I have some questions I need to get answered regarding your husband's death."

"He died in a horrible car crash. What more do you need to know?" Mary said bitterly. The detective eyed her peculiarly, and Mary's skin crawled. The notion that there could be something more to his accident settled at the back of her mouth. The hint of bile threatened everything.

"We believe that your husband's accident was a side effect of his real cause of death."

"The accident isn't what killed him?"

"No. Unfortunately, the tox screen showed a lethal amount of arsenic in his bloodstream. How he—"

Mary leaned forward sharply and interrupted her. "I'm sorry, but did you just tell me that Geoff died of arsenic poisoning?"

"Yes."

"That's absurd." Mary's hands shook. "That sort of bullshit doesn't happen outside of a Christie novel or *Murder, She Wrote*."

"In this case, Mrs. Otto, it also appears to have caused the death of your husband," Parson said bluntly. She wasn't being unkind; there was no sympathetic way to explain murder to surviving family members. Especially when those people were also prime suspects.

"Did you know that most murders are perpetrated by someone the victim knew?"

"No. I didn't know that. What does that—wait just a minute! Are you trying to tell me I am a suspect in my own husband's murder?" Mary's voice broke. Her heart skipped a beat at the mere thought of Geoff being murdered. This was worse than just an accident. Accidents happened, but murder, murder was infinitely worse. Her shaking hands covered her mouth as though they could protect her from the truth. Detective Parson didn't flinch or shift in her chair, merely watching Mary's reaction to the news and making a note of it.

"Anger and jealousy, Mrs. Otto, money and sex, these are the main ingredients in almost every murder ever committed."

"I am not angry at Geoff. Our marriage was fine," Mary said and then added thoughtfully, "It was great actually."

"Are you sure about that?"

"Of course I am. Why would I lie about something like that?"

"People lie all the time," Parson said plainly.

"Well, I don't," Mary fired back.

The detective nodded and opened the folder sitting in front of her. There were prints of photos, but Mary couldn't make them out from her place. Detective Parson pushed the stack of printed photos with one finger across the table. Mary instinctively knew that she would not like what she saw, but she wasn't the sort of woman who flinched from the truth.

She pulled the photos closer and turned them around so that she could examine them the right way up. The first photo was grainy and out of focus, but there was no mistaking the robust figure of her husband. He was getting in his car, and barely discernible in the background was some kind of wilderness or garden. "Where was this taken?"

"We don't know," Parson said. "I was hoping you could tell me."

"Geoff is not an outdoorsman—was not," she corrected herself with a shake of her head. It was going to take her a while to adjust to that. "I can't imagine where he would be." Wherever he was, it was night. She flipped the photo to the back of the stack and recoiled slightly at the image on the next photo. Geoff was standing intimately close with a woman, a woman who was not Mary. The woman in the photo looked suspiciously like the woman sitting just outside this very room. "Who is she?" Mary demanded.

"You don't recognize her?"

"Of course I recognize her. She's sitting right outside." Mary couldn't look away from the condemning photo. "I've no idea who or what she is to my Geoff."

"You've never met her?"

"No. I don't think I could forget a woman like her."

"She does leave an impression, doesn't she?" Parson admitted. Mary flipped through the next few photos, which showed her husband in even more compromised positions. A hand rested on the woman's waist, a kiss planted against the neck. She was silently grateful that nothing more scandalous was shown. Her nerves frayed, and she set the photos back on the table.

"Who is she?"

"Verity Georgeson. She's a client of your husband's."

"Verity? I think Geoff has mentioned her before."

"Anything else you can recall?" Parson asked. Mary shook her head, but her mind skimmed through memories.

"I think he might have been working on a restoration with her."

"A restoration?"

"Yes. Geoff is—was—an architect. Usually, his clients asked him to design something new, but he enjoyed projects that let him save a piece of architecture." Mary smiled at a memory of her and Geoff driving through the older neighborhoods in town and daydreaming about reviving the natural beauty of the past. "He took great pleasure in resurrecting something from the past even though he didn't get the chance often."

"Because of the business."

"Yes, the firm was popular, and business has been good, especially with the exponential growth of the city lately." Mary's face pinched at the thought of this woman causing problems. "Could she have had something to do with Geoff's death?"

"We don't know."

"Where did you find these?" Mary asked, her finger stabbing the photos angrily for emphasis.

"We found them in the back seat of his car."

"He had them with him?"

"We think he was being blackmailed."

A sour expression curdled on Mary's face. She looked back at the photos. They'd had their rough patches, but they made it through. They were better than ever. How could this have happened? Detective Parson reached forward and retrieved the photos, putting them back in the folder, out of sight. Mary flinched at the thought of Geoff's hands on the Georgeson woman.

"What do you want from me?"

"Can you think of anyone who would want to blackmail him?"

"Other than her, you mean?"

"Of course," the detective replied impatiently. Mary thought about it and couldn't come up with anything. They had money, but she wouldn't call herself rich. They had a nice house and nice cars, but what they had wouldn't be enviable enough to cause someone to go to this length. Another thought struck her.

"What does his murder have to do with blackmail?

"How do you mean?"

"I mean, why go to all the lengths to blackmail someone and then kill them? How is he going to pay off a blackmailer if he's dead?" Mary asked. She didn't expect an answer; it was rhetorical. A knock sounded on the door, and then it opened. A uniformed police officer poked his head inside.

"I've got that report you asked for, Parson."

"Thank you," she replied and then turned back to Mary. "I'll be right back." The detective left the room for a moment, but Mary hardly noticed. She was lost in her thoughts. The shock of Geoff's death had been hard enough to manage, but now her anger bubbled up. How could he have been such an idiot to do something like this? After everything they had gone through, everything they had survived? Her jaw clenched, and her knuckles blanched, curling into tight fists.

She decided she didn't believe any of it. This was not her husband's doing. Blackmail was more like it. She didn't know who would have envied his life so much to go to all this trouble, but if this detective woman would not do the right thing, then it would be up to her.

Mary looked toward the door, and in a moment of rashness, she flipped open the folder, thumbed through the images, and pulled one of them out. She quickly folded the photo and shoved it into her handbag before closing the folder again. She hoped everything looked like it did before the detective had left the little room. Mary settled herself back into her chair as the door opened and Detective Parson reentered the room.

"All right, Mrs. Otto. That's all I need from you today," Parson said, holding the door open for her. Mary rose, and when she faced the detective, Parson added, "Do me a favor and stay in town until we get this all sorted."

"I have a funeral to arrange, Detective. I'm not going anywhere," Mary said coldly. The detective gave her a curt nod. She made to leave and could see Anita sitting anxiously outside the room when a thought occurred to her. "Detective, there is one thing you can do for me."

CHAPTER THREE

The elevator ride down to the sub-basement was discon-certing. Mary and Anita stood huddled together behind the uniformed officer as they rode in silence. The doors opened, and the fragrance of antiseptic permeating the air took Mary aback. The corridor beyond was utilitarian. Fluorescent light kept the space brightly lit and accentuated the white walls, white floors, and white ceiling.

"Are you sure you want to do this, Mary?" Anita whispered into her ear. The uncertainty in her friend's voice echoed her feelings. No, she wasn't sure she wanted to do this at all, but she needed it. She needed some sort of closure. She had gone to bed last night happy, if not slightly irritated with Geoff for not calling to tell her he'd be coming home late. Now she was miserable, and Geoff would never come home.

"This way, ladies," the officer instructed as he stepped out of the elevator and led them down the sterile corridor. Their footsteps echoed gently in the vast empty space. About halfway down the corridor, the officer stopped at an industrial metal door. Mary looked at the letters stenciled on the door,

CORONER, and her skin crawled. She steeled herself against the horrors lurking just beyond. The officer pushed down on the metal lever and pushed the door open so brusquely that both Mary and Anita jumped. Mary feared that the coroner would be right in the middle of his work and she'd be forced to see something truly horrific. Upon seeing a large office decorated in filing cabinets, a large desk, and a few chairs, she let herself relax, if only a little. The office was larger than she might have expected, but just along the nearest wall was a set of double doors. She realized this room was large enough to move gurneys through.

Mary and Anita huddled behind the officer just as the double doors burst open, making the two women jump. The officer raised an amused eyebrow. Strolling through the doors as they swung open was an awkwardly tall, gangly man dressed in a white lab coat, jeans with the cuffs folded up, and leather sandals. He was drying his hands with some paper towels. Mary felt her face wrinkle in disapproval but checked herself. Who was she to judge this man's work attire?

"Doc," the officer addressed him. "This is Mary Otto. She's here to see her husband. Mrs. Otto, this is Ackers. He's the one working on your husband"—the doctor frowned—"husband's case." Mary and Anita both raised quizzical brows at the slip of tongue.

"Who's lead on the case?"

"Parson."

The doctor grunted slightly with a nod. "Far be it for me to argue. Come with me."

Mary turned to Anita. "I'll be fine. You just wait here for me."

"Are you kidding? I'm not letting you do this on your own," Anita declared. "I'm coming with you. No arguing."

Mary smiled weakly at her friend. She was grateful to have the younger woman in her life. The women followed the tall man through the double doors. Mary couldn't help wondering if he needed to get all his pants altered due to his extraordinary height. Once through the double doors, Mary and Anita froze. There was no mistaking the room they had entered. The large room appeared like a hospital. Along two walls were broad counter spaces, refrigerators with transparent doors in which vials of blood and other substances were stored, and a lightbox for reading X-rays. The other two walls were lined with large square doors from floor to ceiling. They were the sort seen in procedural dramas, the sort that held bodies, dead bodies. Mary immediately hated this room.

The center of the room was spacious, with two empty metal tables spaced apart. Mary shivered at the thought of Geoff lying on one of those tables, being picked apart by someone who cared nothing for him. This had been a bad idea and she wanted to turn and tuck tail, but she was here. She had Anita with her and needed to see him regardless. They watched Ackers as he crossed the room to the farthest bank in a few long strides. Checking the label on the door second from the bottom, he nodded and opened it. Mary was frozen. She didn't want to see, but she needed to. Anita gently placed a hand between Mary's shoulder blades, causing Mary to practically jump out of her skin.

"It's okay," she said in her soft feminine voice. "I'm here. I'm not going anywhere." Anita's youthful face was furrowed, her concern etched in every feature. Mary marveled briefly at how strange it was to be so intimate with someone nearly half her age. Anita was still in her early thirties, but she was open and kind and the exact opposite of all the people Mary had surrounded herself with. It was a difficult job being the wife of a prominent business owner in town. There was an image to uphold and relationships to nurture, but her friendship with Anita belonged to her alone, and right now, she was eternally grateful for that.

Mary nodded once, determinedly, and crossed the room to stand just beside the open door of the storage unit. It was dark within, but she could still clearly see the institutional white fabric covering the figure lying on the metallic slab. Ackers reached in and gripped the edge of the slab and pulled it out. It hung in the air between them. The mountainous figure, unmoving beneath the clean fabric, was all that was left of her husband. She couldn't meet the coroner's gaze, but she could feel his gaze on her. He was waiting for some sign from her that she was ready. It was unfair of her to waste his time on something she probably shouldn't be doing, and it was childish to stand here frightened. Mary clenched her fists tight, pressing her nails into the palms of her hands, finding some comfort in the pain as they bit into her skin. The sharp pain brought her to the present. It was time. She sighed and nodded curtly.

With more gentleness than she expected, he bent down and gripped the cloth with both hands, folding it down just beneath the cadaver's chin. Lying before her was her husband, ashen and lifeless. She had always heard that when someone passed, they often looked as though they were sleeping, but that was a lie. She had slept next to this man for decades and there was no way to mistake death for sleep. His face was slack and gray, lips colorless, his wrinkles accentuated by deep shadows. This was her husband, there was no denying that, but it also wasn't him. Geoff was buoyant and jolly, shrewd and sharp. This, this was nothing like him.

Mary wanted to close her eyes to block out the visage of the shell of her husband. She didn't, though. She owed him this, to see him. As she looked more closely, she noticed a crusty substance around his lips, and her head tilted unconsciously at it. A large gash in his forehead curved around towards his right temple. The wound was clean and open, which caught her off guard. The body was an amazing thing and often began the healing process quickly, but nothing hinted at any healing. This wound was open when he died and never had a chance to start that miraculous healing process. She sighed.

Geoff's stubbled chin was proof of his late night at work, but the steely hairs contrasted against his inhuman pallor. Against the unnaturally white skin and stubble, deep purple lines raked into the flesh. Mary's face cinched into a scowl.

"What are these?" she asked as she pointed to them.

"Scratches," Ackers replied. "He scratched himself."

"Are you sure?"

"Very."

"How do you know?"

The coroner reached across Geoff's body and rolled the fabric back just enough to reveal one of Geoff's arms. Ackers lifted the arm towards Mary's face. Geoff's fingers were curled in a way that unnerved her, but Ackers paid her frayed nerves no mind.

"I scraped out tissue samples from under his nails. They are a match for him."

"Why would he do that?" Mary asked aloud, but the question wasn't meant for anyone else in the room. She was certain of the answer before she even asked the question.

"Arsenic is nasty stuff," Ackers said as he returned the hand to Geoff's side and covered him up again. "Enough?" he asked. She nodded. The coroner pulled the fabric up and over Geoff's face, making him once again a faceless body, and returned her husband to his dark drawer.

Anita came to stand next to her. "Mary?" she prodded gently. Mary just stood there, rooted to the spot.

"Ladies," the officer called to them.

"Mary?" Anita's voice was tinged with worry. "Mary, are you all right?"

"Yes, yes, I'm fine," she finally answered, but in truth, she wasn't fine. All of this was wrong. Geoff shouldn't be dead. She shouldn't be standing here in a morgue. This sort of thing didn't happen in real life.

"Yes," she said again, turning to her friend. "I'll be fine."

"I think we should get out of this place."

"I can't agree more." She patted her young friend's hand before she turned back to the coroner. "Thank you for letting me see him." Ackers dipped his head slightly at the acknowledgment. "Let's go, Anita."

"Gladly."

Mary and Anita follow the officer out of the chilling autopsy room, through the coroner's office, and back down the corridor to the elevator. The trip back up to the main floor was quiet, but Mary felt as though the officer's eyes were glued to her. Every time she looked at him, though, his gaze was turned away. She was unnerved. It was a new feeling to her, the sense of being watched. There were many times in her life that she'd known she was being watched, but that was a consequence of living a social life in the spotlight of the city. Geoff was part of a prestigious business, and as such, they were often involved in social events, dinners, fundraisers, grand openings. This was different. This was something darker.

A shiver ran up her spine as the elevator doors opened. She stepped out of the elevator and back into the lobby bustling with people going about their business. It was like she'd been in purgatory and now she was stepping back into the world of the living.

The officer led the women to the bank of glass doors at the entrance. "We'll call you if we think of any more questions."

"I understand," Mary answered. The two friends walked out of the police department and back into the sun. Mary faltered just outside the doors. The sun shone brightly, birds chirped nearby, and a squirrel investigated a nearby tree. The juxtaposition of death and life, of Geoff's death and her life. She collided into it and couldn't move.

"Mary?" Anita called out, but Mary wasn't listening. Death hung on her as though it were an invisible shawl draped over her shoulders. It was heavy, immovable, and cold. The sun shone but offered no heat. Something was wrong. This was all wrong. She needed to get away, to run away from the haunting things inside that building.

Her feet moved. Faster and faster, she dashed across the parking lot, looking for sanctuary, for safety. She felt exposed out in the open.

"Mary?!" Anita called out from somewhere behind her.

She moved faster. Faster. The sunlight chased her across the parking lot until she ran right into her car. Mary was panting and shaking as she fumbled for her keys. Where were her keys?

Why couldn't she find her keys? Why couldn't she pull herself together?

"Mary, wait!" Anita called. "Mary."

Finally catching up with her friend, Anita panted while Mary shook. "I've really got to up my cardio if I'm going to keep up with you." She clutched at the pain in her side. "You're a gazelle, Mary. I never knew you had it in you."

"What?"

"I said, you're a—oh, never mind."

"I'm such a fool!"

"You are not a fool," Anita soothed. "You're just hurt."

Mary turned to face her friend. "Anita, you are wonderful, but perhaps you're a fool too."

"Gee, thanks, Mary."

"Geoff was, was not what he seemed," Mary said. She slumped back against her car and buried her face in her hands.

"Oh Mary, I'm so sorry for all of this. This is all too much." She reached out and pulled her friend's hands away from her face. If she was expecting to see her face covered in tears, she hid her surprise well. Mary wasn't grieving, not yet. Her fury left no room for grief.

"Look at me," Anita said, and Mary complied. "Come on. Let's get out of here."

"Where?"

"You need a distraction, to clear your head," Anita announced as she grabbed her friend's handbag and walked away from the car."

"Where are you going?" Mary called out after her.

"We need a bit of a palette cleanser after all that," Anita said over her shoulder. The words were almost carried away by the breeze that threatened to feel pleasant. Mary broke into a jog to catch up to her friend.

"What on earth are you talking about, Anita? Anita!"

But it was no use. Anita simply sped to her car, opened the door, started the engine, and waited patiently for Mary. Mary, for her part, stood there like an idiot. A pillar of black salt, in her classic skirt and matching blazer. She looked around the parking lot, sure that this horrible display of childishness was being watched. She sighed, then surrendered. It was only a moment, but by the time she slid into the passenger seat of Anita's car, a wall buried deep within her had begun to crumble. Her eyes stung more than they had before. Mary wasn't ready to break down, to give in yet. She turned to face her friend, who surprisingly wore a gentle smile on her young face. "What are you up to?"

"Nothing untoward," Anita answered in a voice an octave higher than usual. Mary felt the mockery of herself.

"Really?" she asked as a smile threatened to breach her dour defenses.

"You need a drink." Anita started the car. "Actually, I need a drink, and if I need a drink, then I'm definitely sure you need a drink." And with that, Mary knew she had lost a minor skirmish. She was in the hands of her best friend. All she had to do was surrender to her and trust that she knew best.

Mary leaned back into the tan leather seat and closed her eyes. The car rolled into motion, the sun permeating the windows. The light cast shadows behind her eyelids, rich ambers, and crimson shapes moved, shifted. For the first time since she had received the worst call of her life, she felt the warmth of the sun. The pain was still there, but maybe if she put her trust in her friend, some of the ice that had wrapped itself around her heart would melt away.

"You're absolutely right," Mary said in a dreamy, tired voice. "We need a drink." Mary Otto gave in to the weariness she had been carrying around with her all day and drifted off into a dreamless sleep.

Chapter Four

Domenic's was a warm, moody gastropub, and when Mary and Anita stepped into the front room with the bar lining one wall, back-lit shelves showcasing more top-shelf booze than not, a little of the tension the women had been carrying slipped off them. Small tables filled the other side of the narrow room. The cobalt and amber glow from the pendant lights barely illuminated each table. Mary and Anita followed the familiar hostess to the table in the far corner. Geoff would bring Mary here regularly enough that a framed black-and-white photo of them hung on the wall behind the table. The two women sat down and the hostess handed them lunch menus.

"Mrs. Otto," the hostess began, "everyone here is so sorry for what happened."

"Thank you," Mary said. She didn't know what else to say. Which was a terrifying prospect, considering she was going to have to address comments like this for the foreseeable future. The hostess left them alone with their menus and frayed nerves.

"Is this going to be okay?" Anita asked. "I know you two came here often, and I . . ."

"This is perfect, Anita." Mary smiled sadly. "It feels good to remember the good times Geoff and I had, and this"—she looked around at the moody little restaurant—"this is just the right way to remember."

The friends sat in companionable silence, each woman alone with her thoughts while staring at the menu. By the time the waiter came to take their order, they had agreed on sharing a bottle of wine and a simple charcuterie plate. Mary knew she should probably eat something, but her stomach was raw from stress and the haunting sight of her husband lying on a cold metal slab. She wondered if she would ever forget that image. When the wine arrived and she took that first warming sip, she concluded that she wouldn't. That image would be seared into her memory forever. It was up to her to come to terms with the mess he had made so that she could put this all behind her.

Anita didn't look to be faring any better than her. Her friend's hand shook slightly as she brought the glass of wine to her peachy lips.

"Anita?"

"Hmm?"

"Are you all right?"

"You know, does this all feel a little strange to you?"

"Very." Mary laughed. It wasn't a humorous sort of laugh, but the kind one belts out when they're sore from the abuse of a cruel universe.

"I was just thinking." Anita leaned forward to whisper across the table. "I don't mean to push the issue, but how often are people murdered in Fort Collins? I mean, it just seems so bizarre." She took a shuddering breath and then another deep drink from her glass of wine. They had discussed some of what the detective had told Mary, but there was more to it all. She didn't realize until just that moment that she would not make it through this mess without having someone she could confide in. Mary frowned. The ugly truths Detective Parson had laid bare had hit Mary in a tender spot. Her trust in Geoff had been shattered. She needed to trust someone.

"It's not just you," Mary said. Her mind was spinning with possibilities as the waiter returned to deliver their food. Both women leaned back in their chairs, the air between the friends heavy with mystery and something else. They waited patiently for the waiter to leave, but as soon as Mary was sure that he was out of earshot, she leaned forward and stabbed a piece of prosciutto with her fork. "There's more to it all than just Geoff being murdered."

"What do you mean? Isn't murder bad enough?" Anita asked.

Mary snorted sarcastically between bites. Anita was starting to get a little manic, and Mary tried not to laugh at the absurd situation they found themselves in.

"That detective woman—"

"Parson," Anita said indelicately with a mouth full of food.

"Come again?"

"Parson. Karen Parson."

"How did—"

"I heard some of the officers talking," Anita answered sheepishly. Mary raised an eyebrow. "I was snooping, okay! I'm sorry, but I take my job as your friend very seriously, and I was just trying to learn anything I could."

She flopped back into her chair and expelled an exasperated breath. Mary looked at her friend and couldn't contain the laugh that escaped. The deep soft chuckling from Mary caught Anita off guard, and she pouted like a petulant child.

"Well, did you learn anything?"

"Oh, for crying out loud, I'm sorry." Anita threw her arms in the air.

"Anita, dear. I just found out that my husband was poisoned and it's very likely because he was cheating on me. I think your eavesdropping is the least of our troubles. Besides, who am I to judge?"

"Geoff was cheating on you?!"

"It would seem so."

"I don't believe it," Anita said as she leaned in close. "Geoff loved you, Mary. He would never do anything to hurt you, especially not that." She poured herself and Mary another glass of wine.

"Unfortunately, there seems to be more than enough proof," Mary admitted. She stared down into her glass and felt herself nearly getting caught by the undertow of grief, anger, and betrayal.

She sighed. Mary needed to let herself trust someone. She wouldn't make it through this mess otherwise. Setting her glass down, she rifled through her purse to dig out the copy of the photo she unceremoniously shoved into her purse. She wasn't technically supposed to have it, but she would eventually have gotten access to it when Geoff's case closed, assuming the police could even solve it. The photocopy crinkled loudly in the quiet pub, and Mary looked up to make sure she hadn't attracted any unwanted attention. Anita's gaze followed.

The door to Domenic's opened again, and another patron entered. It was a man in his late thirties wearing a neat gray suit with the jacket open. His sky-blue shirt was unbuttoned at the collar, and a newspaper boy hat crowned his blonde hair. He had a cherub face, and his light blue eyes caught the light.

"Ladies," he said in passing.

Mary shivered. She had never met the man before, but something about him set her teeth on edge.

"Hello," Anita returned in almost a whisper. The man, for his part, bowed his head and continued without stopping or missing a step. The two friends watched as the hostess took him beyond the main area and through a doorway that led to a set of private dining rooms. Mary could hardly see him as he was seated at a table.

"Do you know him?" Mary asked Anita.

"No. I thought you did."

"I've never seen him before."

"He gives me the creeps."

"Glad I'm not the only one," Mary said before she took a sip of wine. She watched the man from over the rim of her glass. He didn't look her way. He merely took off his jacket and draped it over one of the empty chairs around the table.

"Can I get you two another bottle of wine?" the waiter interrupted. Both ladies had been so engrossed in watching the newcomer that they jumped slightly.

"We probably shouldn't," Anita announced sadly. "Must be responsible and all that."

The door to the restaurant opened again, and Mary nearly choked on her wine as she watched Verity Georgeson stroll through the door. Anita's mouth fell open at the sight of the boldly vintage woman. The hostess was instantly smitten with her, but Mary's blood curdled.

"Mary?" Anita whispered.

"I know" was all Mary could manage as they watched her get ushered through the restaurant. "On a second thought," Mary added, "we'll have that wine after all."

The waiter, oblivious to anything other than his job, glided off to retrieve more wine. The woman, the other woman, now that Mary thought about it, gave them a polite nod as she walked past their table but nothing more. Anita sat there with her hand halfway to her mouth, about to take a bite of food, watching the woman go by.

Mary had to admit the woman was classy. Few could pull off a vintage look and still come across as supremely modern. Nothing about her made Mary cringe or shiver. It was utterly unlike the feeling that the other man gave her. Despite seeing the evidence, she just couldn't picture her with Geoff. He was round, and she was fit; he was warm and boisterous, and this woman seemed supremely cool.

Mary and Anita watched as the hostess led the Georgeson woman to the same table as the creepy man. She took her hat off and set it on the seat next to her, along with her handbag.

"It is just not fair," Anita whispered. It was just what Mary needed to bring her back to her senses.

"Don't go getting jealous now."

"Ugh. Some women have it all."

"And some women are prime suspects in my husband's murder," Mary asserted.

"What? Her?" Anita hissed skeptically. Mary nodded. "How do you know? Wait, don't tell me. Is that why she was there today too?"

"Let's just say Detective Parson showed me the light." Mary turned to check on the odd couple sitting in the private room. She didn't know what to think about those two meeting right after her visit to the police station. Confident they weren't looking, she fished out the crumpled photocopy from her bag and smoothed it out on the black table linen before pushing it towards her friend.

"Oh . . . my . . . god!" Anita said, breathy and overcome. "What in the hell was he thinking?"

"I'm sure he wasn't." Venom-laced sarcasm was the best tone she could achieve under these circumstances. When the waiter returned, Anita covered the photo with her napkin until he departed again. Mary took another sip of wine.

"It's bad enough I have to deal with Geoff's death, but now I have to come to terms with this bullshit." She stabbed her finger on the wrinkled photograph.

"I don't get it, Mary. You and Geoff were great. I never saw this coming."

"That makes two of us," Mary said sourly. Anita bent her face over the photo, and Mary took comfort in the look of shock growing more by the second. "There has to be something more to it."

"How so?"

"I mean, this is just so out of character for him. What if there's more to it than just this?" Anita waved around the photo for emphasis. "Maybe he was working on a deal for some project."

"What sort of project?"

"I don't know, Mary. I'm sorry. I guess I'm not being much help." Anita handed the photocopy back to Mary, who folded it with more care this time before returning it to her purse. "I just can't imagine what would have made him think that was okay."

"It's not your fault. If there was someone to blame, I suppose it would be me."

"Now, how do you figure that?"

"I must have done something to push him away."

"No. Just, no. This is not your fault," Anita declared. Mary sighed and shook her head. "There just has to be something, some reason for it all."

"Like what?" Mary asked. Anita's face crumpled with concentration, and Mary found it endearing.

"Maybe she was the instigator. I mean, the photo only shows them standing closely."

"Very closely."

"Yes, yes, but were there any other photos of them kissing, or . . ." Anita let the rest of the sentence go unsaid. Mary didn't want to ruin what little hope her friend was clinging to, but there was no point in hiding the truth.

"There was more."

"Oh."

"I didn't want to risk taking more than this one photo," Mary said.

Contemplative silence settled between the two friends. Although there was no use in arguing the facts, maybe something lay behind Anita's words. Sure, her husband had cheated on her, but Anita could be right. Maybe there was a reason for it. Mary couldn't imagine any worthy explanation, but just maybe there was something more.

"I don't recognize the place," she said absently.

"In the photo?" Anita asked.

Mary nodded. "Wherever it is, it's a mess."

"It's wild," Anita agreed. Stuff was scattered all over the place, and it looked like it was falling apart. Mary craned around to stare at the Georgeson woman and her companion. Her heart jolted when she saw that they were both boldly staring at her. Instead of turning away, she returned their gaze. She was now sure there was something more to all of this, and for the sake of the memory of her marriage, she was going to figure it out. She gave the odd companions a curt nod and then turned back to her friend.

"Those two give me the creeps," Anita said.

"I am going to figure out what they had to do with Geoff's death."

"How do you know they were involved?"

"A feeling."

"What if your feelings are wrong?" Anita asked.

"There's only one way to find out."

"What are you going to do?"

"I'm going to start by heading over to Geoff's office. I have a feeling he might have been working on a secret project."

"What makes you think that?" Anita asked, then shook her head with a smile threatening to grow on her face. "Never mind, it's just a feeling."

"Are you with me?"

"Yes," Anita said, "and no. Just call me tonight and let me know if you've found anything out. I have to get home before Richard, or he'll have a fit." Anita raised her hand to let the waiter know they were ready for the bill.

"You know, Anita, I love you dearly, but that husband of yours is a real piece of work sometimes," Mary said disapprovingly. Then she shook her head at that nonsense. "Never mind. My husband was apparently an ass, so who am I to judge?"

The two friends settled up and checked the table one last time to make sure they hadn't forgotten anything. As they made their way through the narrow room, Mary stopped at the hostess station.

"Excuse me?" Mary asked quietly.

"Yes?"

"Can you tell me who that gentleman is, the one sitting in the back room?"

"Oh, yes." The hostess's face lit up. "That's Mr. Blackwood. He's a regular."

"Do you happen to know what he does for a living?"

"Oh, sure. He's a collector."

"What sort of collector?"

"He's got some kind of antique shop with rare items and things like that."

"Thank you," Mary said, and with that, the two women left the little restaurant. Mary's grief had taken a back seat to her anger and curiosity. She wasn't going to let another woman taint her memories of him. Her memories were the only things she had left of him to hold on to.

Chapter Five

Mary didn't speak as Anita drove her back to her car. Her mind was spinning out a list of questions she desperately needed answers to. What had pushed Geoff into the arms of that Georgeson woman? Who wanted Geoff dead? And why? Other questions nagged at the back of her mind too, questions she couldn't put into words yet. She'd had too much wine at lunch and the buzz filling her head had put a chink in her armor, but the drive back to her car gave her time to sober up and find some clarity again.

Mary and Anita parted ways with a promise to talk to each other later that evening. Mary was forever grateful for her dear friend, but she was also glad to have some time to think. By the time she was back in her car, she'd formed a rudimentary plan of action.

Her mind wandered through the weeds of this mystery until she stopped her car and found herself at her husband's firm. It was as good a place as any to search for clues about her husband's extracurricular affairs. Before locking her car, she checked for the photo in her purse. She couldn't lose this tiny, tangible bit of proof that she wasn't crazy, that there was indeed something more going on than a random affair. She hoped she was right. Mary couldn't stand the thought that Geoff had cheated on her for the mere sake of satisfying some desire she couldn't fulfill for him. Those thoughts were too dangerous, and she shoved them to the back of her mind before heading in.

Once inside the prestigious architectural firm, she found her footing. She had spent much time here with Geoff, especially in the early days. Although it had gone through several remodels throughout its half-century of existence, it still reminded her of when she and Geoff were young. They had endured the struggles of entrepreneurship and youth together, and she didn't want to lose those memories of the past simply because the present had tainted them. She straightened her spine, standing tall and proud, and pushed through the double glass doors into the reception area of the firm.

The offices were arranged along the exterior of the large space. In the reception area, a young woman took calls, ran errands, and brewed a steady supply of coffee. The wood-paneled walls between offices offered some privacy, but the front-facing wall of each was entirely glass. That meant that any passerby could see most of what was going on in the other offices. The dark woods and carpeting teamed up with glass, and steel gave the space an indelible masculine quality.

"Mrs. Otto!" exclaimed the receptionist.

"Janice, good afternoon."

"We weren't expecting you," she fumbled, "not, not with everything going on." Although Janice was young, she was capable. Mary had liked her. She was a no-nonsense type of girl who dressed professionally but realized that she worked for men. She held a certain balance between business attire and the preferences of the good ol' boy expectations. She walked that line well, but watching her fumble like this set Mary on edge.

"I've never needed to call ahead before, Janice."

"Oh no, of course not. Can I help you with something?"

"I'm just here to visit Geoff's office," Mary said.

"His door is locked," Janice said, a little quieter.

Mary stopped. "Why would Geoff's office be locked?"

"I don't know, Mrs. Otto," Janice said in a hushed tone. "I usually check all the offices first thing in the morning for old coffee cups. You know how they are, but I couldn't get into Mr. Otto's office."

Mary couldn't remember the last time his office was locked. "It's all right, Janice. I'm quite sure I still have a key somewhere in my purse."

Mary dug around in her purse. Her hands shook slightly as she rummaged around, keenly aware of the young woman's eyes on her. She dug up her spare set of keys to the office from the very bottom of her handbag, but in the process, she managed to drop her purse. It collided against the ground with a soft thump, and Janice was quick to come around the desk to help her. Before Mary could take inventory of the mess she made, she watched in horror as the young woman unfolded the photocopy Mary had stashed in her purse. Mary watched Janice's eyes grow wide in shock.

"I, I-I'm so sorry, Mrs. Otto, I didn't mean to pry. I was just checking that it wasn't something from my desk mixed in with . . ."

Mary sighed. "It's not your fault."

Mary snatched the picture from her and stuffed it unceremoniously back into her handbag. Mary made to stand up again, but the receptionist grabbed her wrist.

"Ms. Georgeson is one of your husband's clients," she whispered. "I never would have suspected that, though."

"Neither did I."

"No, you don't understand." The young woman frowned and checked behind her suspiciously before bringing her face close to Mary's. "It's not that. It's that I've, well, I'm pretty sure that she and Mr. Belker have something going on."

Mary's head twitched to face the receptionist. "Are you trying to tell me she was involved with both men?"

Janice nodded her head emphatically. "Except, I didn't know about her and Mr. Otto. They always kept things very professional, but . . ."

"But what, girl?"

"Well, it's just that Mr. Belker is . . ." The young woman seemed to fight for the right words. "Well, he's a bit more hands-on, if you get my point."

"I see. He's an ass. Is that what you're saying?" Mary asked. The receptionist gave her a sheepish look. "I understand. Thank you for letting me know." Mary stood, and the receptionist joined her.

"I just don't want you to think something horrible about Mr. Otto."

"It's too late for that."

"He is the best boss. He's never tried anything like that with me," Janice said quietly. Now that the two women had stood up, they were both in the eyeline of everyone else in the office. Mary looked around and withered at the sight of all the eyes on her and the receptionist.

"It's all right, Janice. I understand. Well, actually I don't understand, but I mean to. I just need a moment in Geoff's office."

"Yes, ma'am," Janice replied, but the young woman still looked troubled.

Mary patted Janice gently on the arm before stepping over to the door of Geoff's office. Her spare key had worked, which was good. She didn't think she could take the embarrassment of not being able to get into his office. She closed the door behind her and stood there for a moment, taking in the room. Behind her, the glass wall showcased every moment to the rest of the office, but she studied the still-life to her husband's legacy. Opposite her was a large plate-glass window with a great view of the downtown area. This building was only three stories tall, but downtown Fort Collins had no metropolitan high-rises. Between was the large mid-century desk, Geoff's first major purchase. The curved lines and graphic inlay always made her think it was straight out of an Agatha Christie novel. It had a low hutch full of broad thin drawers to store plans, and photos of his career highlights covered the walls.

Her shoulders slumped. Everything looked as it should. She almost wished it was a mess, just like everything else in her life right now. As she strolled around the office, her fingertips ran along the smooth wood surfaces. She examined the pictures on the wall and could recall every one of those memories. Most of the photos were taken by her. She had always supported him, and as such, he made her a part of each of his victories. When she came around to the working side of the desk and sat down in Geoff's leather office chair, she found herself confronted by a photo of the two of them. She remembered the moment but never knew he had printed it out, let alone sitting on his desk.

She remembered their last anniversary. Geoff had taken her out to dinner, they'd had champagne, and they were blissfully happy. She picked up the framed photo of the two of them. Their heads were bent together, ridiculous smiles plastered across their faces, and for one blissful moment, she had forgotten all the pain inside her. She hadn't realized she was crying until a tear fell off her chin and splashed onto her hand. She wiped her face dry with an angry motion and set about to the business she had really come here for.

Mary pulled out each of the drawers, looking for anything that would give her a hint of what Geoff might have been working on. It wasn't until she reached down and opened the lower right drawer that she found anything unusual. She'd been expecting to find it full of hanging files but instead came across a collection of whiskey and some low-ball glasses, and a single file folder. She looked up, expecting all the eyes in the office to be on her, but was surprised to see no one staring at her.

Nonetheless, when she reached into the drawer and retrieved the file, she kept it low and opened it on her lap. The desk obscured enough of the view that she could look at the contents without being observed. She didn't know why, but she was suddenly frightened of what she might discover. There was nothing for it, though, and she opened the file, expecting to see something horrible. Instead, she wasn't quite sure of what she was staring at.

The folder sat open in her lap, exposing a collection of photographs. She picked up the topmost photo, her brow creasing as confusion set in. It looked like some derelict, abandoned house in an overgrown patch of weeds. A thought tingled at the back of her mind. She fished the abused photo from the depths of her handbag, pressing it out as flat as possible on her lap. Mary couldn't help but look at the image of her husband's hands around another woman's waist. The woman, Verity Georgeson, had her hands on his tie. She was an astonishing woman; Mary couldn't disagree. She brushed away the prickles of jealousy along her skin and looked deeper. It was the surroundings in the photo she was curious about. Wherever the two of them were was just as dilapidated as the photos in the file. Although the environment was dark, she could just make out some of the architecture. Mary ran a manicured fingernail gently along the lines of the windows. They were the same. There was no doubt in her mind that these photos were taken at the same place, but where was it? She couldn't recall ever seeing a property like it. Maybe that was her first clue. She needed to find this place.

Mary continued to compare the photos, her eyes darting away from the intimate couple, when something caught her attention. In trying to avoid staring at her husband's hands on another woman, she noticed something else. A glare in the photo, no, not a glare. It was a flash! She pulled the photo closer to her face, oblivious to her surroundings as she inspected it more closely. The light from the camera must have been caught in the reflection. She didn't know what it meant, but she clung greedily to this nugget as another piece of tangible evidence that she wasn't crazy. And then she saw it, a figure in the photo. She had been so distracted by her sense of betrayal that she stupidly ignored the fact that, to have this photo, someone had to have been there. Someone had been watching them. Someone knew about them enough to follow them to this secret rendezvous and capture this picture. What else did that person know? Who were they?

Mary placed the photo on the desk. She had forgotten herself, carried away in the moment of discovery. Smoothing out the photo more fervently, she continued to look for clues. The figure, nearly completely washed out by the darkness and desolation of the surroundings, was impossible to discern clearly, but one thing was certain. Whoever the stalker was, they were a man. The shape of the figure, the broadness of their shoulders, it all lent itself to the shape of a man. Who else would care enough to catch the couple in the act of betrayal? What other man would care enough to do this?

Mary's face brightened. A woman like Verity Georgeson was bound to have at least one man in her life. Perhaps more than one man existed in Verity Georgeson's life if she was to believe Janice. He was probably the one angry enough to do something like this. She leaned back in Geoff's leather office chair, satisfied as a cat with her new morsel of truth. Her eyes closed, the wave of accomplishment washing over her. Mary knew just what she needed to do next. She had to learn everything she could about Verity Georgeson because the things lurking in that woman's life had something to do with why her husband had to die.

The sense of purpose felt good. Mary knew that this new passion wouldn't alleviate her grief about Geoff's death. She would have to deal with the reality of her husband being dead, but for now, she had something to work her teeth on. She opened her eyes, excited to once again see the world as it should be, and instead found herself staring at Richard Belker, who happened to be intently watching her in return.

Mary vehemently did not like him. He was misogynistic, macho, egotistical, and controlling. The glass walls separating them might as well have been ice for the look he was giving her. Her senses bristled, and her skin prickled. Mary's fingers twitched, and the photo beneath them crinkled slightly. Her brows knitted together as she peered down at the image. She looked back over to where Richard was and nearly jumped at the realization that he was still staring angrily at her.

Mary sucked in a breath sharply at a thought that floated to the surface of her mind. What if Richard was the man in the figure? What could he have had against Geoff? What if he couldn't have cared less about the mess Geoff was in? What if he was more interested in the woman, in Verity Georgeson? She didn't like to think about that because of the insinuation that he might have been unfaithful to Anita. It wouldn't have shocked Mary, but she was protective of her young friend. Janice wasn't one to lie, if Mary was being honest with herself. The last thing she wanted was to see her friend hurting like she was.

Richard broke their gaze first by grabbing his briefcase and leaving the office brusquely. As soon as she was free of his gaze, her nerves settled a little, but something had changed. She realized that Geoff's office didn't feel familiar to her at all. The bitter aftertaste of his betrayal, his death, and the secrets he kept from her had ruined everything. His presence lurked everywhere here, and the shame too. It was time to leave.

CHAPTER SIX

Anita's hands were buried in the dark, rich soil of her garden. She loved tending her garden. She enjoyed the satisfaction of the slow burn reward the most. The rest of her life was curated for one purpose: to drive the image and goals of her husband, Richard. She recognized what her marriage looked like to outsiders. Men saw what Richard had and envied him. He had a modern home to accentuate his acquisitions, prestige, and his docile wife. Women saw something different. They saw a gilded cage. She had everything and nothing, but she couldn't help whom she loved. They were comfortable with each other, and Anita knew that comfort and stability were worth more than passion.

Her fingers dug into the soil around her peonies, breaking up the chunks of clay and soil, turning the area from a dry grayish brown to nearly black. The freshly turned soil was dark and moist, begging to be put to use. She sat back on her haunches and admired her hard work. Anita had already pruned the spent blossoms, giving the plants freedom to put their energy into making new ones. The soil was tilled, the plants and blossoms were fresh and green, and she was satisfied.

Her oversized straw hat kept most of the direct sun off her face, but she would need to reapply her sunscreen on her forearms if she didn't head inside soon. Her arms were freckled from her rewarding work in the sun. Working in the garden was more than simply a hobby; it gave her mind room to run. While her hands worked, her mind would run free, thinking and mulling over the events of her day.

She was worried about her friend. Surviving the death of a loved one was difficult enough, but for it to happen under such horrible circumstances was worse. It was strange to think that Mary was now a widow. Anita would be the first to admit that her mind worked in stereotypes based on old television shows like *Murder, She Wrote* and Agatha Christie's Poirot. The word "widow" depressed her, and she hoped Mary would overcome any negative tropes she knew people would assume.

Despite the heat of the day, the hairs on the back of Anita's neck stood up, and a chill sprinted the length of her spine. She shook it off and turned back to head inside. One of her favorite rewards for working in her garden was a little sit-down with a cup of tea and a good book. She saw Richard leaning against the doorframe, one hand stroking his tie in a lazy, unconscious motion.

"Richard!" she said, startled.

"Ani." His voice was rich and sensual. He never rambled or chattered. His patience was the quality that she found most attractive about him. Richard Belker was ambitious and assertive, but he never rushed anything, whether he planned to work his way up to the top of the firm or was making love to her.

"What are you doing home?" she asked, a hand on her chest to soothe her startled nerves.

"I have a meeting later today, just came up." Richard stepped out of the doorway and out into Anita's garden. He looked so out of place, his sharp gray suit and dark hair contrasting against the wild environment. He was a modern man who belonged to a modern world.

As he made his way along the little stone path to where she'd been working, her heartbeat quickened. A breeze flitted through the garden, setting the purple tips of the Russian sages waving in ripples across the garden. The heavy fragrance of the nearby lilacs made her lightheaded, or perhaps it was just her lust for her husband doing that. He approached her, sliding his hands around the thin linen fabric of her dress. The hairs on her arms rose to attention, and her body sang. He bent his head, and his warm lips brushed against the skin of her neck. "There are some papers I need from my studio for the meeting."

"I could've brought them to you," she announced in a breathy voice as his lips moved to just behind her ear.

"But then I wouldn't have been able to see you like this." She wanted nothing more than to wrap her arms around him and let her fingers rake through his thick hair, but she knew him better than that. She wouldn't do anything to mess up his suit, especially if he was expected back at the office. When their eyes met again, he was examining her.

"What?" Anita asked.

"I saw Mary today."

"Really?"

"I thought you were with her."

"I was," Anita answered, watching him pull away from her and turn back towards the house. Their moment was gone. She sighed. "I met her at the police station. What a nightmare."

"I suppose there are always loose ends to tie up, even for accidents."

"That's just it, Richard. It wasn't an accident." She ran a few steps to catch up to him. His legs were long and his stride matched, but he stopped dead in his tracks and turned around to face her.

"What do you mean that it wasn't an accident?" Richard's bright blue eyes pierced through her.

"Oh, Richard, it's just terrible. The police think Geoff was murdered."

"Murdered?" he asked slowly. Anita nodded. "That changes everything."

Anita thought, for the briefest of moments, that he might have actually smiled at the notion of Geoff being murdered. She brushed the thought away. It was just too horrible. When he turned back toward the house again and went inside, Anita ran after him, stripping her hands free from her dirty gardening gloves and following him through their modern house decorated in creamy whites, glass, and steel. A set of pocket doors off the living room led to his private studio, where he worked on projects for his clients when he wasn't at the office. It was his domain. Like the garden belonged to Anita, here was where he asserted his privacy. He slid the doors open and went inside the masculine office. Anita stood in the doorway, not daring to enter.

"How does Geoff being murdered change anything," she asked, "other than making his death that much more horrible for Mary?"

He was bent over a drawer and thumbing through the files, searching for something in particular, but he looked up from his search and at his wife.

"Geoff's death has already caused ripples at the firm. The old boys have been in meetings all morning to decide what to do." He returned to his search. "Otto was a senior partner. His death has left a power vacuum." He pulled out a glossy black folder from his desk, checked it briefly to ensure that it had what he needed, and then closed it again. He made his way back to his wife. "This could be my moment, Ani. This could be my chance to get in as a junior partner." He kissed her forehead before he stepped past her.

For a moment, she glimpsed the folder Richard had in his hand. She hadn't noticed it at first, but when it caught the light just right, she saw a logo imprinted on it in matte black. It looked like a bumblebee. It seemed familiar, but she was too distracted to concentrate on it. He was in motion again, and she followed in his wake.

"Don't you think it's a bit early to be thinking of a promotion? I mean, they haven't even buried him yet."

"It'll be fine. This is perfect. Don't you see? I thought I was going to have to work for years before I got this chance, and now, to have it show up practically gift-wrapped, I would be an idiot not to take advantage of it." He continued on his way through the house, Anita close on his heels. "Anyway, Ani, my meeting is probably going to run pretty late," he said as he picked his briefcase up off the kitchen table, "so it's probably best not to wait up for me."

"That late?"

He stopped and turned around. Richard was much taller than Anita, but she didn't mind. She was a bit old-fashioned and preferred needing to be on her tiptoes to reach his lips. He seemed to sense her worry and reached out, cupping her face with his free hand. His eyes roamed her familiar face and focused on her lips for a moment before he placed a soft kiss on them. "Don't worry," he said, "you'll give yourself wrinkles."

Her whole face scrunched at that, but by the time she had found words to come back at him, he was already out of the house and getting into his car. Anita stood there in the doorway as he waved goodbye from his car, which was already pulling out of the driveway. She stood there for a moment, even after he was out of sight down the road, but her mind was spinning with ideas. She turned around and went back into the house with no real intention, so she found her way back out into the garden.

Anita sat down at the patio table and worried at the gloves still in her hands. There was something more to that folder Richard had come home for, of that she was sure about. Richard's apparent joy at Geoff's demise bothered her. It wasn't right to be so glad that someone was dead. Her hand drifted to where he had cupped her face. She couldn't help smiling at the memory of his warm and familiar touch, but she was still worried. What if his happiness had been related to Geoff being dead? Was that even possible? She didn't want to think about it, but the thought just wouldn't go away. Before she could talk herself out of it, Anita jumped up to her feet, returned inside the house, and went straight to Richard's studio.

With only a moment's hesitation, she entered the sacred space. She knew he would never have allowed her in there under normal circumstances, but her overactive imagination had her thinking that Richard had something to do with Geoff's death. As she maneuvered through the office, she was careful not to leave a trail of evidence. She sat down at his desk and went through the drawer he'd been looking through first, but since he took what he needed, nothing remained for her to find.

In fact, she didn't come across anything of any particular note until she opened the middle drawer. There, sitting innocently amongst all the obsessively ordered items of the desk, was a single business card. She hesitated briefly before reaching out for it. The unique card was black, but if she tilted it this way and that to catch the light, she saw a logo of a bumblebee in glossy embossing in the center. Anita turned the card over and saw that it, too, was black. She almost thought it was blank, but with a tilt of the card, she saw a name. Just one name was printed on the back of the card. Verity Georgeson. Her blood turned to ice.

This was the same woman who had been having some sort of affair with Mary's husband. The police had even brought her in for questioning regarding Geoff's death. Anita couldn't imagine a woman going to such lengths to get rid of a man, but what if Verity Georgeson was after something else, something more? Her fingers shook as her mind spun elaborate webs of deceit. She eventually let her mind come to the most horrible of conclusions, and her hand drifted to cover her mouth from the shock of it. Why did Richard have this woman's card in his desk? How did he know her? Anita hoped her husband wasn't mixed up in all of this, but she couldn't dismiss his strange behavior today. She didn't know what to do, but she had to do something.

She closed the drawer to Richard's desk and left the room. As she slid the pocket doors closed and sealed herself off from

Richard's private studio, she went directly into the kitchen to brew herself a cup of hot coffee. This was more than a simple tea and scone sort of problem. She needed to be fully caffeinated if she was going to come up with a plan to save her husband from the treachery of Verity Georgeson.

All right, so she might have gotten herself a little overexcited, but what else was a decent woman supposed to think after finding the business card of a potential murderer in her husband's desk? Of course, she could take the less sensible path and assume they had business dealings together. No, she was a sensible woman. She was all or nothing.

So there she sat at her kitchen table, twisting the ominous black business card between her fingers as she thought. Several cups of coffee later, she realized she didn't have enough information to work with; even after a thorough Google search, she knew very little. Verity Georgeson had a website that was simple and beautiful and just as mysterious as the business card. It simply said she was some sort of couture project management curator. What did that mean anyway? The only way someone could contact her was through a simple form that let them enter the type of project they had, what they needed, and the timeline that they needed it completed by. A very detailed explanation of the contracting process made Anita's eyes cross in an attempt to read it. The internet showcased a few photos of her, mostly at grand openings or local fundraisers, but nothing personal and nothing older than five years. It was as if Verity didn't exist until five years ago. How could that be?

She flopped back in her chair, resigned to the fact this Verity woman was simply a ghost. How could someone be so hard to find anything about in today's age? She couldn't imagine how anyone could keep secrets with everyone's business being blasted over social media. She downed the last dregs of a very cold cup of coffee and decided she needed to tell Mary what she'd found. She changed back from her gardening clothes into something more presentable, swished around some mouthwash to get rid of her coffee breath, and grabbed her car keys on the way out to see her best friend. Mary was the most sensible person she knew. Even with all the grief and stress of everything she was going through, Mary would know what to do. With Verity Georgeson's business card shoved into her back pocket, she hoped Mary could help her find something more, or at the very least, help her connect the dots so that she could understand what her husband had to do with her.

CHAPTER SEVEN

Detective Karen Parson sat at her desk with Geoff Otto's case file open in front of her. Her office wasn't what one would call glamorous. It was barely more than a utility closet. Her desk was one of those large metal utilitarian desks, void of any style. A wide filing cabinet rested along one wall, and stacks of old case files in boxes were lined along the other. The room had no windows, but she had a small plant on the corner of her desk. The fluorescent lights were more than enough for the happy little splash of green that brightened the sterile room. Other than the plant and a few framed awards for excellence, the cramped office lacked personal touch, which was just the way she preferred it. She would only call a few people in the force her friends; everyone else was intimidated by her or just an ass, and she didn't want them having any more insight into her private life than was necessary.

She sat at her desk, staring at the case file. Otto's widow was right. People were murdered every day, but it was rare that poisoning popped up as the cause of death. These days, most people had too much rage and intolerance to wait for poisoning. The cases that crossed her desk were usually blunt force trauma, gunshot wounds, and vehicular homicide. This case differed.

Poisoning required patience and knowledge of the victim. The perpetrator had to get close to someone to do the job right. Someone in Geoff Otto's life didn't like him, and as always, Parson's first instinct was to look at the wife. Not only were most murders committed by someone intimately close to the victim but also was poisoning personal. The spouse almost always committed the crime, and in this case, she would agree with the old saying that poison was a woman's weapon. A thought nagged at Parson, that this case would get messy before she figured it out. Her work had been cut out for her.

A knock sounded on the door.

"Yup," she called out without taking her eyes off the file. The door opened, and she bolted her posture upright when her eyes connected with the captain in the doorway.

"Got a minute?" Alex Garcia was short, muscular, and bald. He'd recently started shaving his head smooth after struggling with hair loss for a few years. His dark skin advertised his Hispanic heritage.

"Sure," she said, waving a hand at the empty chair on the other side of her desk. He took a seat and leaned back, crossing an ankle over his knee. The captain wasn't a large man, but his intelligence and experience always gave him the impression of being larger than life. "What's up, Cap?"

"Your new case," he said. Parson studied his brown face and saw something there that she didn't see often: worry. She looked down at the open file and then back at Garcia.

"Something about it catch your attention?" She only knew a trace of the hurdles he had to overcome to become captain. Fort Collins was a progressive town, but racism lurked everywhere, even here. No matter what bullshit he endured, he never wavered on his principles. The deep furrows crossing his forehead exaggerated as he decided whether to tell Parson what was on his mind.

"You know how every cop has that *one* case they can't get out of their head?"

She nodded. Garcia leaned forward and tapped the file on her desk. "Be careful with this one," he added.

"Why? What do you know about it? Better yet, how'd you even know about this case?"

"I have the system alert me when specific names are pulled into active cases."

Parson wasn't satisfied with that answer. She knew he was being vague on purpose.

"Which name?"

"I don't want to taint your opinion before you get all the facts."

"Which name?" she asked again. Garcia remained silent for a long time before he finally answered.

"The Georgeson woman."

Of all the people involved in Geoff Otto's death so far, Parson had to admit Verity Georgeson wasn't at the top of her suspects list. Despite the evidence found at the scene of Otto's death explicitly drawing attention to Verity Georgeson, nothing else had risen to the surface. Parson was more inclined to think a jealous lover or an angry wife caused his death. Her instincts told her that Verity Georgeson was just a casualty in the larger scheme to off Otto, but Garcia had been around longer than she had. She'd be foolish to discount Garcia's input.

"You've had dealings with her before?"

"Once you pull up her aliases, you're bound to find out," he said before placing a tattered file on her desk.

Parson pulled the worn file towards her. It was several inches thick and held together with tape and binder clips. She gave her captain a curious look.

"She's changed her name since then," Garcia said, "but no matter how different she seems now, she's still the same person."

Parson opened the file, and on the very first page was a copy of a booking sheet. A photo was paperclipped to it, which took Parson aback. The woman in the photo was unmistakably Verity Georgeson, but she appeared so different. Her long hair was piled into a messy bun atop her head, and her clean complexion was free of makeup but marred with dark circles under her eyes and the yellow and brown rings of old bruises. She couldn't connect this haggard, beaten-down woman with the woman she'd interviewed earlier today. It was a sad statistic, but most women in abusive relationships rarely left their abusive partners, especially if there were children involved. More often than not, those women died from some complication of the abuse.

"What the hell happened to her?" Parson asked.

Garcia shook his head as though he were shaking an old memory loose. "I was brought in the case after the cause of death was determined. The 911 call had come in the day before. We still have the recording in storage, but her husband had suffered some sort of fit and collapsed in the kitchen. By the time the ambulance showed up, the guy was dead." He frowned.

Parson couldn't help but pick up on the grain of similarity between the deaths of these two very different men.

"What sort of fit?"

"Turns out it was arsenic."

"That can't be a coincidence," she said.

"I didn't think it was an accident either, but I couldn't get any evidence to pin it on her."

"What did you do?"

Garcia leaned forward, dropping his elbows on the desk and meeting Parson's eyes. "I did everything but hound that woman. I tried every way I could think of to make her break. No matter what, that woman never flinched."

"No one is that good."

"She is," Garcia admitted. Parson didn't believe it. He was the best damn detective she knew and was having a hard time believing that he couldn't break her into slipping. She flipped through a few pages of Garcia's old file, and something caught her attention.

"There was a kid involved?"

"Yeah, their daughter."

"And you couldn't leverage the kid against her?"

"Kids shouldn't have to deal with this shit." Garcia exclaimed. "I did everything I could to keep that kid clear of being collateral damage. I'll give her that much credit. That woman is completely devoted to her kid, trust me."

"Is that something that only a parent could understand?"

"I know it sounds cliche, but it's the truth," Garcia said. She'd met plenty of deadbeat parents throughout her career, and a few decent parents too, but since she wasn't a mother, she didn't have a frame of reference to put to it. She thought about it for a moment.

"Was there any other evidence you had to work with?"

"No, that's just it. I knew in my bones that she had killed her husband, but other than the fact that he regularly beat her, I had nothing."

"And you think this"—she tapped the Otto file—"could be her again?"

"I don't know what to think. What I do know is that you're going to have to watch yourself with her," Garcia said. Parson couldn't help but catch a hint of defeat in his voice. She hated seeing him like this, but she also knew he would never leave himself this vulnerable in front of anyone else here. She nodded her head as though agreeing with herself about the next course of action.

"All right, Cap." It was all she needed to say, so he stood up to leave.

"I've got a meeting I have to get to, but my door will be open if you feel like hashing through some of this together."

"If I need you, I'll stop by, promise," she replied. He turned to leave the small office but hesitated at the door.

"You're a good detective, Parson. Don't let her get under your skin." He departed her office, leaving behind more questions than she had before.

CHAPTER EIGHT

Verity Georgeson loved coming home. Every time she crossed the threshold of the little Victorian house with the red brick and black-painted decorative trim, her muscles relaxed because she was safe to be herself once again. She had been smitten with the house the first time she saw it, but that had been before this life.

Before she'd become who she was today, she would walk past the place every day on her mid-day walk. The covered porch with its slate tiled roof and arched brick pillars were something she had dreamed about even as a little girl. She had grown up poor, and to have something that other people could envy was still novel to her. Now it was hers.

Verity unlocked the black lacquered front door with the stained-glass bee and hive motif and stepped into her sanctuary. Her heels clacked on the restored hardwood flooring. She closed the door, momentarily mesmerized by the amber and gold patterns of light cast throughout the foyer as the setting sun shone through the stained glass. Dorian, her black cat, greeted her with his customary parade of figure eights around her feet.

A content smile grew on her fair face. She didn't have the large doe-like features that were so popular these days, and never would she call herself beautiful. Her features were more dangerous than beautiful. Verity had clear skin with a few freckles dotting the tops of her cheeks. Her jawline was strong and decidedly unfeminine, and her bold eyebrows, which had only recently come into fashion, nearly cast shadows over the only feature about herself that she liked: her eyes.

Verity's eyes were dark green, like a forest of pine trees, encircled by a thick ring of steel gray, and showed no mercy. They were her burden of truth. She was a terrible liar and was always surprised when someone believed a fib she told. Her mouth was on the thin side, but more than one man had commented on her smile, so she had learned to use it. Her mouth had become one of her greatest weapons. Her slightly parted lips were a tool she used to get what she wanted. When all that was teamed up with the knowledge of knowing when to speak and when to hold her tongue, she started to get all the things she desired.

She would be the first to admit that today was exhausting. The trip to the police station was only the beginning. Detective Parson might not have been the friendliest of personalities, but Verity understood what it was like to work in a field dominated by men. Everything a woman did, from her successes to her failures, was judged through a misogynistic lens. If she failed, it was because she was too emotional. If she succeeded, it was because she was a bitch. Every woman either learned to play this game so that they could succeed or refused to play, which would result in dying in obscurity. It all depended on what a woman wanted.

Verity wanted everything, everything she was told she couldn't or wouldn't have. So, she suffered the questioning and judging of Detective Parson. She suffered the jealous glares of the other women; they didn't know her anyway. By the time the detective had had enough of her and she was free to go, she was exhausted, but there were still tasks to complete before she could relax even if just a little.

She set her handbag on the antique table inside the door, took the large envelope she'd had tucked beneath her arm, and set it down before taking a look at herself in the mirror above the little table. Her auburn hair was perfectly coiffed beneath her hat, which cast a shadow across her face. She pulled the pins from her hat and carefully hung the hat on a nearby rack. The shadows on her face still hung below her eyes. They emphasized the strong structure of her face and gave her a sickly quality to her appearance. It was all worth it. She was so close to getting what she'd been working towards.

She picked up the yellow envelope again and headed upstairs to her bedroom. Her hand slid gently up the banister, the warmth of the wood beneath her fingers a gentle reminder she was home. Her bedroom was at the front of the house overlooking the street. Decorated in deep blues and greens, it always reminded her of the ocean. An antique armoire served as her closet. No original closets remained in the house due to its age, but that was okay with her. She didn't own many clothes, but the clothes she did own were of fine quality and worth the expense she'd put out towards them. Her bed was centered against the wall opposite the picture windows looking down onto the street and was the only modern piece of furniture in the room with a tufted leather headboard that mimicked the style of an old wingback chair.

She sat down on her bed and slipped her feet out of her shoes. Dorian jumped effortlessly on the bed and settled next to her. He was just as peculiar as she was. There were two individuals in her life she couldn't live without, and Dorian was one of them.

"Hello, Dorian," she said, carefully peeling off her French silk stockings and laying them on the bed beside her. "How was your day, good sir?" Dorian's only response was to rub his head against her and purr. "That sounds like a lovely day. I'm sorry to say that mine was a bit tedious, but nothing I hadn't been expecting."

She placed a kiss on the top of his head right between his ears, one of which had a triangular cut taken out of it. He was an ally cat who had adopted her, rather than the other way around, when she'd bought this place. He had simply shown up and never left. She was perfectly fine with this arrangement, as they were both peculiar souls well suited to each other.

Verity picked up the large envelope she'd brought home with her and sighed at its secret contents before getting up and crossing the room to the only piece of furniture in the house that had any sentimental value to her. It was a vintage secretary desk with a fold-down writing surface and a narrow cupboard attached on either side. It belonged to her father. After his passing, her mother had offered her the desk, and she gratefully took it. Verity and her father had been close. Sometimes she wondered if they were the same person. The only thing she'd had done to the desk was have the finish restored. The rich mahogany tones that only got deeper when the sunlight hit it always made her smile. She used it as a vanity, a special place she came to twice a day to apply her costume and to remove it, but she had more pressing things to take care of at the moment.

Above the old secretary desk was a stormy landscape of a brooding Victorian manor resting like a monolith at the end of a dirt lane, probably off the English coast somewhere. The artist was someone obscure and the portrait itself had practically no monetary value, but it suited her and camouflaged the wall safe she'd installed herself to keep its existence a secret. Verity reached out and ran her finger along the edge of the frame that matched the desk in style and stain. A floorboard creaked behind her.

"What took you so long?" A man's voice from behind her startled her. The only thing that soothed her nerves was the familiarity of it. It wasn't deep or high, but a voice made for laughing. She almost gave away one of her secrets, and although she shared many things with him, her safe was not one of them. She calmed herself quickly before turning around and smiling despite herself.

"Impatient much?" she said, her smile turning up, lopsided on one corner. Verity set the envelope down on the desk and walked over to him. "Patience is a virtue, you know."

"I never said I was virtuous." His hands slid around her waist and pulled her in close. He kissed her deeply, and she kissed him back. Several moments passed before they came up for air, by which time the ambient temperature in the room had risen several degrees. The two of them were passionate, letting their hands work on familiar curves, his tongue tracing along the line of her jaw until he could kiss her neck, all the while his hands following the curves of her body. They were familiar with each other. They had explored every patch of flesh, every birthmark, and freckle throughout the nights they'd spent with each other.

"I didn't mean to keep you waiting, Henry." She was out of breath and eager for more pleasure, but there was still one more appointment scheduled for the day.

"It was very inconsiderate of you," he said, but his soft laughter sent a tingle throughout her body. If she didn't reign this moment in, they were going to get carried away, and she would be late for her next appointment. She needed everything to continue according to plan, so she wrapped his ruddy face in her hands and, with one singular kiss on his lips, declared they were done for the moment.

"I'm sorry, Henry." She turned around and gazed at him from over her shoulder. "I didn't mean to come home late. I had to stop by my attorney's office to pick up some paper-work." Henry's sky-blue eyes flickered to the envelope sitting on her desk, but he brought them back to her. "Could you get the zipper for me, please?"

He was happy to oblige her. Henry was a blue-collared man. He worked for a living, and his ruddy complexion was proof of the time he spent outdoors. His close-cut blonde hair con-trasted against his permanently tanned face and forearms. He was slender but muscular, with a body like a swimmer. She loved running her hands along his broad shoulders and firm body, but now was not the time. They were a bit of an odd couple, Verity with her vintage clothes and fair skin and Henry with his T-shirt and jeans, but one thing was never in doubt: Henry was completely and utterly devoted to her.

"Is there anything you need me to take care of while you're out?" he asked while his fingers slid beneath the fabric of her dress, allowing it to fall to the floor. His hands found what they wanted, and it took all her concentration to resist the temptation. She stepped out of the dress puddled on the floor and gave him a mischievous wink.

"Thank you, but no," she said. He admitted defeat with a sigh and flopped down onto the bed. Dorian had been curled in a tight little ball and, at the disruption to his nap, opened a single eye and glared at Henry.

"I'm meeting Blackwood in a little while, and I need to have my wits about me. He's a shrewd one. I'd hate for all this to fall apart because I was careless."

"I don't like him."

"I don't particularly like him either, but I need him." Verity opened the armoire and pulled out a silk blouse and some tweed trousers. "For now, at least." She bent in half at an alluring angle as she stepped into the trousers. Turning to face Henry, she buttoned her blouse and tucked it in artfully. She pulled out a different set of shoes from the armoire, which she closed once she had dressed.

Verity went to the bed and straddled her lover, who tightened expectantly beneath her. "This part you can't help me with. I have to do this on my own." He didn't like it, she knew this, but he never tried to tell her what she could or couldn't do. She treasured this about him. Henry wrapped his hands around her waist, curling them back until he could run his fingers along her spine and pull her close. The lovers kissed deeply before she pulled away again. "I have no plans for tomorrow. You could come over and help me waste an entire day."

"Fine," he complied, "but I'm going to make you work for it." Verity let out a fit of laughter, which had him laughing along. She held out her hands to help him up off the bed, and they held hands all the way downstairs as she let him out. He gave her one last kiss and made it count. "Be careful around him."

"I will." She couldn't help but feel her affection for him grow. He worried so much about her. "I promise." She waited until he'd driven away before she shut and locked the door. Dorian purred against her leg, and she looked down at the black cat and scowled. "Traitor," she said. "How could you let him be in the house and not let me know?" Verity turned and made her way back up to her bedroom. "We've got to work on our communication."

As soon as Verity returned to the sanctuary of her bedroom, she approached the desk and the painting. This time, confident that she was alone, she pulled the painting aside with the piano hinge she'd installed along the side. She wasn't an un-handy woman. Until now, she had worked hard for everything in her life. Her childhood was troubled, and she had to learn every lesson the hard way. She was so close to finally having everything she'd wanted, though. After completing a few tasks, she could sit back and be patient. The rest of the puzzle would put itself back together.

Behind the painting was her safe. She's splurged on something that was strong, excessively safe, and could survive a fire and water event, should something truly terrible happen. She keyed in her passcode, pulled a small key from the center drawer of the desk, and used it to unlock the safe the rest of the way. A person would need both the key and her passcode to get into the safe. Once the heavy door opened, she took up the envelope and slid it in along the side of a few other belongings like her journal, a significant amount of cash, the deed to her house, and the item she had come for.

Tucked in among all the other items was a small wooden jewelry box made of burled wood. She wrapped her slender hands around the box and pulled it out into the light. It was a beautiful relic of the Art Deco era. The varnish had begun to yellow, giving it an orange tint. The lid of the box was intricately carved in the sweeping flourish of the age. She opened the box, removing its contents and placing them carefully in the safe until she needed them again. Satisfied that she had what she needed to barter with Blackwood, Verity locked the safe, deposited a kiss on Dorian's head, and left the house.

CHAPTER NINE

The Armstrong Hotel dated back to the twenties and liked to reinvent itself every few years. The current décor was mid-century modern and full of rustic oranges and creamy whites. The ground floor of the Armstrong held the reception desk, the porter's offices, and, of course, a bar. Christopher Blackwood sat at the bar, stroking his tie and waiting. In his hand, a glass of bourbon mixed with the water from the melting ice. It wasn't the moodiest bar he'd ever been to, but it wasn't one of the overly popular places in town and allowed him to have more discreet client meetings. He and Verity agreed to change the locale of their meetings after they realized the widow frequented the same place. It would not do to linger in that circle more than was necessary, although he was fairly certain that Verity had everything to do with Geoff Otto's early demise. He knew better than to ask his customers for any details like that. It was bad for business.

The door behind him opened, announced by a soft musical tone that reminded him of his grandmother's doorbell. He watched the reflection in the mirror lining the back of the bar and was glad to see Verity coming through. She was a classy dresser and secretly wished everyone put as much effort into their appearance as she did. He silently ordered another round of drinks by holding up two fingers to the bartender. As soon as Verity sidled up to the bar, taking the seat next to him, a drink was waiting for her.

"Thank you, Mr. Blackwood."

"I keep telling you, please just call me Christopher."

"I'm a stickler for boundaries, Mr. Blackwood."

"Fair enough. Did you bring it?"

"I did." Verity produced the item in question. "Are you always so eager to rush right into business?" She took another sip of bourbon, turned to face him, and crossed her legs one over the other, all in one smooth motion. She was a slick one.

The two of them sat at the meticulously polished bar, staring at each other. The space was a little too bright for his taste. The bar, installed along one side of the lobby, was open and well lit. Spherical pendant lights dangled above them. Christopher looked Verity over and felt the tension between them. Most of the people he worked with were shady, not an exaggeration, but they acted as though they were some high-stakes criminal who the police were actively searching for. Most were the usual casual criminal with a low IQ and high regard for their cleverness. They were easy to bully, and it was never too diffi-cult to push them into the decisions that he needed them to make. Cleaning up the mess afterward was usually simple and something he could hire out. However, working with Verity Georgeson differed. She was independent and self-assured. He could not bully her around, and although it made business negotiations take longer than normal, he found it refreshing to work with someone on his level, or as close to his level as he was ever likely to get.

"I've been waiting a long time to track it down, Verity," he said, testing her name on his lips. She raised an exquisite eyebrow at him. "Ms. Georgeson?" He wondered if she knew he was aware of the history behind the name she'd chosen for herself and decided that she must. She was at least as creative as he was. In a way, they were kindred spirits. "I suppose I can wait a little longer."

"Good." She took a sip of her drink and gave him an approving nod. "I would hate for you to be disappointed after all this time."

He was glad to see she enjoyed what he'd ordered for them. She had excellent taste. "Besides, today is just a cursory examination. It won't be transferred into your possession until I'm done with it."

"And how long will that be?"

"Not long now." She gave him a curious look, almost like a cat. "I assure you, by the time I'm done with it, you'll have more than enough provenance to accompany it than you know what to do with."

"I do like a good story."

Behind the bar, the youngish bartender had stayed clear of them except to pour them another round of drinks. Christopher became momentarily distracted as the bartender diligently cleaned the surface of the bar with tight circular motions, causing his backside to shimmy in a rather alluring way. *Business first*, he reminded himself. *Pleasure later.*

"I wouldn't expect any less from you," she said. "There are very few people alive who know of the existence of the box, let alone the story to go with it."

"I like unique things. One of kind is even better."

"This will satisfy that in spades." She set her glass down and swiveled on her stool to get a look at him. "I'm hoping we will work together on future projects."

"Do you have more unique items in your possession?" He would be surprised, but there was no harm in checking.

"I have more than a few items that would pique your curiosity, but we should see this arrangement through first."

"Agreed," Christopher said. She was smart, shrewd, and sexy, for a woman, that is. There was more to her, but that was definitely for another time. He tossed back the last of his drink and then turned to give her his full attention. She gave him a smile, and he wasn't quite sure he understood the meaning behind it. Was it acquiescence or tolerance? Who could tell? Verity, for her part, had taken whatever snapshot of him she needed and decided that now was the time to continue.

She strained herself and pulled the leather tote she'd brought with her into her lap. From the depths of the bag, she withdrew a black velvet cloth and laid it out carefully on the bar top in front of Christopher. He was intrigued. His clients were usually too brutish to properly care for the items he acquired, but this woman was deliciously different. Maybe he should have considered doing business with her again, and then maybe not. He was uncomfortable with loose ends. Christopher's fingers twitched eagerly as she reached into the bag again and, this time, emerged with what he had been longing to see.

Held between Verity's manicured hands was a small wooden jewelry box. She placed the little box on the velvet cloth in front of him and sat back. With a single nod, she permitted him to examine the box. He rubbed his fingers together with expectation before he finally reached out and ran them along the surface of the box. It certainly appeared to originate from the twenties, handcrafted and carved in the beautiful sweeping, elongated curves of the period.

"It's very nouveau," he commented.

"Very."

"Other than the slight yellowing of the varnish, it looks practically new." He made to open the box but hesitated.

"You may," she answered his silent question. He lifted the lid to the jewelry box and found it was attached by the most delicate piano hinge he'd seen in a while. The interior of the box was laid out in a few compartments and lined in red velvet, real velvet. His heart sank when he saw nothing in the box. He knew the history and had expected to find a little treasure trove of personal belongings of the original owner.

"It's empty."

"And when our arrangements are complete, it won't be."

"There is more?"

"Much."

"Tell me," he demanded as he threw a hand up to signal the pretty bartender for another round.

"There are several significant pieces of jewelry, a few letters of some local historical significance, and then there is this." She swiped at the screen on her phone and turned it towards him so that he could see the photo she'd just pulled up.

"Is that what I think it is?"

"Yes."

Christopher thought he noted a sultry drop in her voice. This must have fascinated her as much as it did him.

"You're intrigued."

"Of course I am." She put her phone away again. "I wouldn't be who I am today if it wasn't for her."

"You do know her story, right?" Christopher asked.

"I know some of it, but I was hoping you would indulge me."

She understood her business partner. Christopher acknowledged her shrewdness and his inability to refrain from telling a good story, but there was something else about her. She was cunning. He looked at her, really looked at her. She was pretty to look at, but Christopher was sure that what made her attractive to other men wasn't simply her looks. It was her eyes.

Verity Georgeson's green eyes gave her away. They revealed her intelligence, her compassion, even her dislike. They held honesty there and spoke to the sort of person she was. Despite all the things she washed away from her past and the trail of pain she'd been leaving in her wake, she would be the first person to be honest about it. Well, maybe not completely honest, but she would be truthful in her own ways, towards her own desires.

The two of them had met several times already since they were first introduced together at a local art gallery. Something about her appearance today was putting him off, and he couldn't quite put a finger on it. He leaned forward, closer to her, squinting his eyes slightly as though looking at one of those hidden image posters. Maybe if he unfocused his eyes, he would see it.

"Are you feeling all right today?" he asked.

She offered him a mischievous smile before breaking his gaze and taking another sip of bourbon. "I am not feeling myself today, but it is merely a necessary consequence of authenticity."

Christopher leaned back abruptly and gave her a thoroughly confused look. He didn't like puzzles unless they were of his own making. She laughed at him. It was soft and genuine. The corners of her eyes crinkled, and she tilted her head back. It was in that honest moment that the light in the room caught just the right angle and he realized why she didn't look well. Pale purple shadows rimmed her eyes, adding a depth to her fair face he hadn't noticed before. Now, he saw the brilliance of her plans. She was an artist, willing to poison herself to cast blame elsewhere.

"You are a naughty woman, aren't you?"

"I know what I want, and I'm willing to do whatever is necessary to succeed."

"Your predecessor was the same way, I think."

"Only a few women back then were like her."

"She was a business owner, a landowner, exceptionally wealthy, and above all," he said thoughtfully, "unapologetically single."

"Some of the letters"—she nodded towards the little jewelry box still sitting on the bar top in front of him—"hint at her uncomfortable position with the local patriarchy. So, I would have to agree with you."

The two of them raised their glasses before taking another sip and sitting in silence. Verity didn't move a muscle. She often sat still but not in the way most people would stop moving. The crazy social media-infused standards of modern society meant that most people never stopped moving. Verity Georgeson, on the other hand, remained still. Christopher had never seen her rush, and although she wasn't overly slow, every movement of hers lacked urgency.

Christopher enjoyed his downtime. That was why he lived in the next town over. It was small and quiet, without the bustle of the city. But to keep living life at his acquired standard of living, he needed to venture into the city for meetings like the one he found himself in now. He had extravagant tastes, and he would never be able to fulfill those quirky needs of his without venturing out.

Staring at the little jewelry box and feeling Verity's stillness next to him, he believed she would accomplish her goal, but he wasn't sure he was patient enough.

"How long?" he asked.

Verity tipped her head to look at him, and he marveled at the smoothness of the maneuver. She had seen this question coming.

"Soon."

"I don't suppose—" he started, aiming to niggle a more precise answer from her, but she interrupted him with a smile.

"Two weeks at the latest, but I'm certain you'll have everything in less time than that." She sat upright and reached across the bar top to reclaim the little box. Christopher watched as she carefully folded the velvet cloth up and over the sides, completely wrapping it and hiding it from his sight. She placed it back in her leather tote with care.

Standing up, she tossed a few twenties onto the bar and, after hoisting her leather tote onto a shoulder, turned to face him. "I understand your impatience, Mr. Blackwood, but I assure you that your patience will be rewarded."

"I don't like to be disappointed, Ms. Georgeson."

"That sounded suspiciously like a threat," she implied in a soothing voice.

"Not a threat, my dear. I just want you to know what you've gotten yourself into."

Christopher leveled his blue eyes at her. As Verity met his gaze, he could see some sort of calculation going on in her mind. When her red lips curled up into a slow luscious smile, it took all his nerve to not openly shiver. He prided himself on secrets; he collected them, along with his trinkets and their stories. Looking at Verity and that wicked smile of hers, he realized she had secrets of her own and was not afraid to use them to get what she wanted. She leaned in close, kissing him on each cheek in the French manner, and whispered in his ear.

"I've been to your little shop, Mr. Blackwood. I know what you pander." His spine stiffened imperceptibly. "If you are truly interested in getting top dollar for our little arrangement, then I suggest you let my little endeavor play out to its end."

Christopher realized she was not only intelligent and clever, but also dangerous. He would have to watch himself with her. He gave her a conciliatory nod, then watched her walk away, tapping out a message on her phone.

"She doesn't seem your type." The bartender's voice startled him. Christopher wondered how long he had sat there thinking about what to do about Verity. He turned to face the bartender and smiled.

"She's not," Christopher said. The bartender folded his chiseled arms under him as he leaned on the bar top.

"What is your type, then?"

"I'll answer that question if you have a drink with me."

"I'm not really supposed to drink on the job," the bartender started, "but you look like you might be a pink champagne sort of gentleman."

Christopher winced. The bartender was wrong and not wrong.

"Bit too Nelly for my taste," Blackwood countered, and the bartender's muscular shoulders drooped. "But I'll order another round of bourbon if you let me keep watching you wipe down this immaculate bar."

The bartender smiled as he reached for the bottle of bourbon he'd been filling Christopher's glass with. He gave Christopher a playful wink. Both men looked around the brightly lit bar and lobby and laughed. The bartender filled Christopher's glass and then poured himself one.

"What's your name?"

"Jason. Yours?"

"It's a pleasure to meet you, Jason. Christopher, Christopher Blackwood." They clinked glasses, and each knocked back a sip of bourbon.

"So, Christopher Blackwood, you were going to tell me what sort of woman you prefer."

"I was? I don't recall agreeing to that," Christopher said with a sly smile.

Jason just shook his head. "You're such a tease."

"Now that I will agree with."

Chapter Ten

Henry didn't miss the irony as he sat at one of the patio tables at Henry's, a local restaurant with a decent burger and substantial array of local draft beers, but it was half a block down from the Armstrong and he had a clear view of anyone going in or out. He'd already finished his meal and was leaning back in his chair, digesting while drinking his beer. He checked the time on his watch and realized Verity would probably be finishing up with her meeting soon.

Old Town Fort Collins always bustled. It was the idealized hub of the town, which made it easy for him to sit openly, hiding in plain sight. The sun was bright, and he could feel the heat burrowing into the back of his neck. He took another deep swallow from his glass of beer and, when he set the tall glass back down again, noticed Verity's familiar silhouette emerging from the vintage hotel just down the block from where he was sitting.

Her auburn hair caught the sunlight, and even at this distance, he wanted to touch all the curves of her body. She wasn't particularly tall or short, but she was fit and voluptuous. Henry knew Verity since before she had started wearing her disguise, since before she was Verity, and although her curated image and demeanor were exceptionally attractive, his favorite moments were when she put the disguise away and was just herself.

His phone vibrated in his back pocket. He took it out and read the message from Verity. *Need some time to myself. Heading out to the old house.* Henry smiled. He didn't blame her. Although he wasn't a fan of the old house, he knew what she saw in it. He also wasn't upset to have some extra time to take care of this bit of business.

Henry looked up and watched as she waited for a gap in the constant traffic before she ran leisurely across the street to where she'd parked her car. He took one last drink, finishing off the beer and setting the empty glass on his tip so that it wouldn't blow away, and made his way down the block to the Armstrong Hotel. He had long athletic legs and crossed the distance quickly despite his efforts not to rush, but after he watched her car pull away, he went inside.

The Armstrong Hotel always felt a little pretentious to him, but he was a simple man with simple needs. He didn't care for the kitschy designs or the openness of the space. The open space he liked was the outdoors. He could easily lose himself in a decent hike or spend the entire day fishing. Although Verity was comfortable in the busy world, he knew what she was like in the privacy of her own home. She liked things simple too, which was why they both couldn't wait for all this secrecy to be done with. He was impatient to get her all to himself.

The girl at the reception desk, probably eighteen, gave him a funny look. It was one he recognized as attraction, but there was no experience in the girl's face. She was a pretty thing, but she wouldn't know what to do with herself. He ignored her and instead made for the brightly lit bar with a single patron sitting there having some conversation with the bartender. As he crossed the lobby towards them, he caught the bartender's attention. Henry had been afraid that Blackwood wouldn't linger after Verity had left, but he was glad to see the man still sitting there. He had some business to attend to with the slimy rat.

Blackwood dropped some cash onto the bar and stood up to leave, but Henry reached out and clamped his hand firmly on Blackwood's shoulder. He was very satisfied when the man startled.

"Sit down," Henry ordered. Blackwood obliged with a curious expression on his moon-shaped face. Henry hadn't met the man in person, but he'd already decided that he didn't like him. Between the dealings Verity described to him and the gory details of what the man collected, he was sure that the world would not be worse off if he just disappeared.

"Of course," Blackwood said, sitting back down on his stool at the bar and looking over to the bartender. "I think we're going to need another round." The gym-chiseled man behind the counter turned to Henry.

"What'll you have?" the bartender asked.

"Got any WeldWerks?" Henry asked. The bartender nodded and turned to pour the brew.

"Well," Blackwood started, "you've got my attention. What can I do for you?"

"I don't negotiate empty-handed."

"I see. So, we're about to start negotiations for something," Blackwood said with an eager smile. "Lovely."

Blackwood's agitation at being startled ebbed away quickly. Henry saw the man settle into the moment. His eyes were attentive, his demeanor relaxed. He hated weaselly people like him. They were always looking out for themselves, never caring about others. They were all pariahs. Henry's eyebrows knitted together, and he had to fight back a sneer of disgust. He needed to do his part to protect Verity. Nothing good was going to come out of her working with an asshole like him.

The bartender deposited a beer in front of Henry and offered a fresh glass of bourbon on the rocks to Blackwood, then lingered nearby, wiping the already spotless bar top. Henry caught the bartender's eye and shot him a look that could curdle blood. The bartender took the hint and disappeared down to the far end of the bar near the register, out of earshot.

Henry drank his beer in silence. Blackwood swirled his glass and stared into the amber liquid but said nothing. He waited patiently as the heavy silence dragged on. It wasn't the same as when he could enjoy the quiet with Verity. This silence was full of anxiety and tension, and something else, something Henry wouldn't admit to anybody: fear. He hated that he was afraid. The hint of bile lingered at the back of his mouth, tainting everything, every experience and moment.

"Well, handsome," Blackwood said with a questioning tone, "I do have other engagements today. Are we going to negotiate, or are you just trying to intimidate me?"

Henry met the man's eyes. For just a minute, he thought he saw fear sparkling in those wicked blue eyes. That was what he was going for, after all, but the fear he thought he saw seemed to evaporate right before his eyes. His heart hammered against his fear. Blackwood wasn't afraid of him, and that worried

Henry. What was it going to take to get him to leave Verity alone?

"You're not a very patient man, are you?"

"I am very patient when it comes to things I want"—Blackwood took a sip of his bourbon —"and not patient at all for things that irritate me."

"You could save us both the trouble then and turn Verity down on whatever deal she's made with you," Henry suggested before reacquainting himself with his beer. Blackwood smiled. It was a knowing smile, unnerving him.

"You don't even know what kind of arrangement the lovely Ms. Georgeson and I have, do you?"

"It doesn't matter." Henry leaned in close. "I might not be able to touch you now, but when Verity is done with you"—he let that implication hang in the air for a moment—"well, let's just say I will enjoy myself."

"Oh, how crass of you." Blackwood shivered in a mock cringe. "I enjoy working with her. She's lovely and cultured and enjoys the elegant dance of negotiation nearly as much as I do."

"You're going to leave her alone anyway. She doesn't need a creep like you to get what she wants."

"Of course not. She's got you to do her dirty work." Blackwood laughed as Henry panicked. *What did Blackwood know? How could he know anything?*

"Just keep your hands off her." Henry's voice grew cold and menacing. Blackwood eyed him again, this time cocking his head to one side like a condescending cat. Henry didn't like cats. He tolerated Verity's cat, but only because he wanted to be near Verity herself. The cat was a non-negotiable part of their relationship.

He'd been hoping that Blackwood wasn't nearly this stupid. He hadn't expected it to take this much effort to get his point across. Instead of being intimidated, Blackwood chuckled. *What the hell was wrong with this guy?*

"You're so sweet, Henry," Blackwood said through his amusement. Henry's blood chilled. He never introduced himself to the man. How the hell did he know Henry's name? He couldn't imagine Verity being so careless as to talk about him. "You seem to be under the misconception that I'm going to make a move on your woman."

"How do you know my name?"

"It's always good to know the key players in any negotiation."

"You didn't answer my question."

"Look, handsome, you have nothing to fear. I've got no romantic interest in Ms. Georgeson at all," Blackwood said, still amused. "She isn't my type."

"Really?"

"Honest." Blackwood threw up his arms in defeat. "I'm only interested in procuring a very significant item from her." An amused smile lingered on his lips.

"Well, then, what is your type?" Henry said irritably as he stared into his beer morosely. This wasn't going at all as he planned.

"Oh, you know, muscular, dark-haired, a little five o'clock shadow even." Blackwood's voice softened. Henry whipped his head around to stare at him and caught him with some sort of dreamy expression on his face.

"What are you talking about?" Henry asked.

Blackwood simply tilted his head and looked sideways longingly. "You really are a bit slow, aren't you? I wonder what she sees in you. I don't actually. I know exactly what she sees in you."

"Enough already."

"She's simply not my type." Henry was about to lose his temper. The moon-faced man leaned in close to Henry, who wanted to punch him in his stupid face. "You, on the other hand, are just delicious. I could eat you right up." Henry leaned back in disgust; that was not what he was expecting. Blackwood laughed at him. "Homophobic, much? I would watch that; it's unbecoming. I would hate for you to drive the lovely Ms. Georgeson away all because you were so closed-minded."

"I've got nothing to worry about there," Henry said defensively.

"Of course not. Otherwise, you wouldn't have come in here uninvited to pass off your best attempt to intimidate me. But listen here, sweetheart. I am at the top of the food chain and don't appreciate having some terrified child trying to wheedle his way into ruining my business dealings. So, I suggest you step out of the way and let Ms. Georgeson and I do what we do best. While we're at it, why don't we talk about how to properly threaten someone? You see, the first thing you need is something to hold against them. What is it you think you have against me?"

Blackwood leveled his unearthly pale blue eyes at him. Henry was caught in a trap. He never imagined that someone with such a youthful face and irritating manner could be quite this frightening.

"That's right, you don't have anything. You're just sitting there, betting on the fact that you're stronger than I am. No matter how delectably handsome you are, I will always be your superior in intelligence and shrewdness. I may not look it, Henry, but I'm a dangerous man. You may think that's something exceptionally arrogant to say, but I say it to warn you. I am not someone you want to fuck with."

Blackwood held Henry's gaze for a moment and then turned towards where the bartender had been lingering. "Jason, dear, would you please get this gentleman another beer? I think he's going to need it."

The bartender wiped his hands on the apron around his waist and went to work.

"You're an asshole."

"I can be, but only to those people who get in the way of my business. Other than that, I'm a perfect gentleman."

The bartender placed another bottle of beer in front of Henry. Henry met the eyes of the bartender and was shocked to see pity. He wasn't the sort of man who ever wanted pity. Angry and frustrated, he realized he was completely out of his depth. He couldn't believe that Verity had gotten herself tangled up with the guy. Blackwood was right; he was dangerous. Something was going to have to be done to rectify this problem.

Blackwood stood up and paid the tab, which included Henry's beers. He placed his soft, buttery smooth hand atop Henry's. Henry resisted the urge to pull his hand away. Blackwood leaned in close and spoke softly in his ear. "You are far too handsome to be so homophobic, especially when I happen to know that your very own Ms. Georgeson's tendencies aren't so straight and narrow." Henry didn't like where those assumptions led. "Regardless of all that, I happen to know just enough about you to be cautious."

"You know nothing about me." Henry hissed.

"Naivety is not a good look on you. Would you like me to explain to Verity all those lovely juicy details behind the unexpected death of her husband? Or, better yet, I could go to the police and give them the evidence they're looking for in Geoff Otto's death? I think they would find what I have to be very interesting."

Henry's head whipped around to face Blackwood. The two men faced off, each one leveling invisible threats in the heavy silence between them. Henry had suddenly learned that Blackwood knew enough about him to ruin his life indefinitely. What was to stop him from doing just that?

"What do you want?"

"Ah, you do have a modicum of self-preservation after all." Blackwood smiled and pulled his gaze away from Henry's lips to meet his glare. "I want you to stay out of my affairs. If I find out you have hindered my business arrangements with Ms. Georgeson, then I will do everything in my power to ruin you. It will be significantly demoralizing for you and exceptionally pleasurable for me."

Henry shifted uncomfortably on his stool. Blackwood smiled as he watched his prey squirm, and Henry realized that he'd been snared in a trap he should've seen coming from miles away. "I realize this must be an unsettling situation for you to find yourself in," Blackwood started. "It's the product of sitting at the grown-ups table, but I need you to give me a sign that you've understood what I've told you."

Blackwood, disarmingly youthful, candid, and lethally dangerous, aimed an emotionless glare at Henry. Henry was trapped, which was bad enough, but he realized Verity was trapped as well. There was no way out of a deal with Blackwood. He didn't know what to do, other than the only thing he could think of at the moment. Henry looked Blackwood in the eye and nodded. He'd been captured like a wild animal, and the only way out was to sacrifice everything. He wasn't prepared to do that yet. Blackwood patted him on the shoulder, a consolation prize of sorts, and then left.

Henry sat there at the bar, a cold beer in front of him, but his stomach had gone sour. The bartender watched him from a distance, but Henry didn't notice him. He thought of Verity again. Her life was on the line if anything went wrong with her plans. He knew that Verity wouldn't be able to get herself out of this mess; he was going to have to do it for her. How could he break a contract with that jerk without making Verity suffer through the fallout?

The glass of beer in front of him perspired, and he reached out for it. His hands shook. He curled them into fists until he felt the sting of his nails break the skin on his palms. Physical pain could be therapeutic sometimes. He concentrated on the pain, the pain and the beer, until he was calm enough again to leave. But there was no hope. Henry's thoughts had become lost in rage. Henry's thoughts had grown murderous.

Chapter Eleven

Richard stood in Verity's solarium. He hadn't realized the door was just one of those old spring-type doors, and it slammed shut behind him, making him jump. He looked around, glad that he was alone and that no one saw how undignified that was. He hoped the slam of the door didn't garner any unwanted attention. Luckily, modern society had created a breed of humans that were mostly antisocial.

Back when this house was originally built, neighbors were often best friends and would not only know each other's business in exquisite detail but also could be counted on to be alert to any misgivings on behalf of each other. Now, people hated social interaction unless it was through faceless, fake social media.

The room was bright despite the emerald green paint on the walls and trim. A simple black and white checkerboard pattern decorated the floors, a ceiling fan spun lazily overhead to circulate the air, and three of the walls were just framed in screens. He looked around at the space and felt too close to nature. There was a bistro set with black-and-white-striped cushions and a silver tea set. He picked up the empty kettle, flipped it over, and was surprised to see that it was actual silver, not some cheap silver-plated knockoff. The tea set alone was probably worth several hundred dollars, too old-fashioned for his taste.

Potted plants were everywhere. Greenery hung from the ceiling, potted plants tucked in various plant stands, and ivy crawled up the painted walls. It wasn't as rustic as an actual garden, but it was still more outdoorsy than he preferred. He crossed the warm sunroom towards the interior door to the house. It was original to the house, he assumed, a paneled door with a cut-glass knob. He turned it and found that it was locked. *At least she had some sense,* he thought.

With a little bit of work using one of the credit cards in his wallet, he managed to get the door open. He stepped into Verity's home and closed the door behind him. Richard stood in her kitchen, which was surprisingly more modern than he would've thought. He didn't know what he was going to find, but he knew Verity was a conniving woman. He needed to know what she had over Otto. Otto's death was just the thing he needed to push his way into a junior partnership at the firm. Otto had introduced him to Verity. He had said she was the reason why he and Mary were doing so well as of late.

The markets had taken a turn for the worse over the last year, and his financial goals weren't being met. Richard had talked with this broker and his financial adviser, all of whom had encouraged him to just wait through the worst of it. He was a patient man, but he didn't like losing ground on something he had been working so hard on. Unlike all the other senior partners, Otto was calm about the market shifts. Richard had invited the rotund man out for drinks to try to twist the secret out of him, but when Otto finally revealed that his secret was working with a private project manager, Richard had thought he was joking. Otto insisted that he'd met an unusually intelligent woman who had the keenest business sense he'd ever known, a woman named Verity Georgeson. Geoff had given him her business card.

Since then, Richard had visited this place many times while he worked with her. Otto had been right. Verity had a good sense not of where the market shifts were going to be, but of more predictable avenues to save and grow money. She even helped him create a more tangible plan to work his way up the ladder at the firm. A plan that was turning out to be surprisingly accurate. She had planned for nearly every eventuality, including the death of a senior partner.

But he was unnerved by Mary Otto's presence at the office. He hadn't seen her there often, usually only at functions where the full regatta of the firm was needed for show and tell. The politics of architecture always involved some pageantry. Mary Otto had been the perfect wife for that. She was smart, not aggressive or competitive. In fact, it was Mary Otto's visit to the office that spurred his idea to come and pay Verity a visit.

Richard passed through the kitchen and entered the hallway beyond. Regardless of his frequent visits to this place, he'd never made much farther than the living room. The purple wallpaper and hardwood floors lent a Gothic feeling to the vintage house. A few doors in the hallway led to a guest bathroom that he ignored and what he assumed to be an old butler's pantry. There were dried goods on the shelves, paper products bought in bulk in the floor cabinets, and a washer and dryer, along with plenty of counter space. Richard didn't think he would find anything important here, but he made a diligent search anyway.

Although everything that Verity encouraged him to do was technically legal, there was always some subversion to it. Mostly, she explained, because if the people he considered his enemies knew what he was doing, they might plan to cut him off. He thought it was legitimate advice. If the senior partners knew the aggressiveness of his plans to join them, then they might change the bylaws of the firm to prevent him from getting his junior partnership. He couldn't have that. There was nothing here, so he moved on.

Beyond the hallway was the living room. He was familiar with this place. Verity would have him sit in one of the chairs, and she would sit opposite him. His body reacted without his permission as he thought of her tight skirt, high heels, and deep-cut blouses. She would sit there with her pad of paper and her pen, staring at him seductively. On occasion, she let him get his hands on her, but she never divulged anything more than her body to him.

He checked the drawers in the bar, the magazines and books on the coffee table and end tables, but nothing. He stomped around the living room, looking behind paintings, pulling furniture away from the walls, and lifting the rug. There were no secrets there. He worked his way meticulously around the room, ending up at the foyer by the front door, where he saw a mirror hanging on the wall and a small table with a drawer. He tried to step up to the little table but got tangled up with her cat when it launched itself at him from under the table, hissing and spitting.

"Dammit." He howled. "Stupid cat!" Richard swore before getting himself under control and taking more than one nervous look around the house. He had tried to not make too much noise during his search, but the cat had startled him. He hated cats. This one didn't help matters by being black. He kicked at the black cat. Richard didn't think of himself as superstitious, but there was no sense in tempting fate. *Who the hell would keep a black cat as a pet anyway?*

The cat had run down the hallway and he secretly hoped it choked on its next meal. He soothed his nerves, mirroring his mental gymnastics by smoothing his tie. Richard stepped up to the little entry table, and his reflection in the mirror caught his eye. He admired what he saw in the reflection. He'd worked hard at everything he put his mind to, whether it was his career, his women, or his appearance. First impressions were everything, and that included one's appearance. He despised slobs like Otto.

The drawer opened smoothly. It wasn't a large drawer, but a few things were in there. He noticed a notebook, a pencil, and some mail, along with what was probably a spare set of keys, and a few other odds and ends. He pocketed the keys. No one would notice a spare set of keys going missing. One only noticed shit like that when they needed them the most. The small collection of mail was the usual stuff, a mailer for a local politician making a run for the mayorship and a few bills, but the one sitting on top of the pile caught his eye.

It was nothing unusual, just a magazine subscription to some country living type glossy covered magazine. That wasn't what was unusual. What caught his eye was the name on it. It was addressed to Louise Jones. He flipped through the rest of the pile of mail, and it was all addressed to the same woman. Who was Louise Jones? He took the magazine subscription, folded it up, and tucked it into his back pocket. He swiped away at the other contents of the drawer, looking for anything else that didn't fit, and found something almost right away.

Richard reached down into the contents of the drawer and pulled out a photograph of two women. He couldn't believe his eyes. One of the women was younger, much younger, but it was the other one who caught his eye. She was the spitting image of Verity Georgeson, well, very nearly. The older woman in the photo had ashy brown hair cut bluntly at her chin and she was wearing jeans and a T-shirt, but other than that, the face was the same. Richard was certain that the woman in this photo was Verity, but not like he'd ever seen her. He couldn't imagine Verity without her sultry auburn hair, and he definitely couldn't imagine her wearing jeans and a T-shirt. She was standing in a full embrace with the other younger woman. Their smiling faces beamed out of the picture, and Richard noticed some unique similarities. The shape of their mouths was similar, the way their cheeks rounded as they smiled; he even thought the curve and shape of their eyebrows were the same. They could be sisters, but Verity had never mentioned having a sister. They'd spent many long nights working together; something like that should have slipped out. He also thought, *Why would she keep a photo like this stuffed into a drawer instead of in a frame sitting on the mantle?*

Richard examined the photo again. He wondered if rather than a sister, the other woman could be her daughter. Their age difference made more sense that way. Verity was an attractive woman, but she wasn't young. He flipped the photo over, and there, at the bottom in blue ink, it read, *Lou and Jenna.* His face curled into a devious smile.

"Gotcha," he said under his breath. A car door slammed outside, and he jumped. He didn't know how much time he'd spent in the house, but it was time he got himself clear. He went to the front window and pulled the lacey curtains open just enough to look out at the street outside. A woman parked across the street was walking up the path to the house on the opposite side of the street. Other than a black truck parked down the block and a run-down VW beetle parked nearby, the street was empty. It was still early enough that those working weren't yet on their way home, but he would be stupid to press his luck. He tucked the photo inside the breast of his suit jacket and took his time looking through the space to make sure he didn't leave any traces behind. Then he worked his way back the way he'd come.

The house itself had been cool, and he hadn't realized it until he stepped out into the solarium. He wasn't prepared for the humidity in this little space. It was then that he comprehended the house had been retrofitted with some sort of air conditioning. That decision probably took away some of the value of the hundred-year-old house, but he couldn't blame her. Colorado was an arid state, getting hotter each year. Some things were more than luxuries; they were necessities.

He reached in and locked the door to the house before pulling it shut behind him. The sun was just starting to set, and although the sky was still blue, the sun had fallen behind the tree line of the neighborhood. It cast long shadows throughout the backyard. He looked back at the screen door he was holding on to as it closed. It was just an old spring-type door, and he didn't want it to slam shut again. When he turned and took his first step into the backyard, he felt cold metal against his throat.

Chapter Twelve

Verity stepped back into her home feeling refreshed. Spending time at the old house always restored her. Most people would not be able to find rest in a house that was crumbling around them, a place where nature was trying to reclaim it back to the land.

She shut the front door behind her and dropped her tote onto the small foyer table, leaning back against the door, taking a moment to breathe. There was something about the smell of plant rot and old varnish that appealed to her, that called her home. Verity hadn't planned on going back there today and was irritated with herself for not having her garden boots with her. She hoped her shoes could be saved. She should just leave a pair in her car. When she was finally free to start fixing the old house, that would be the first thing she planned on fixing. She was going to clear a proper path to the front door. With that old argument with herself settled, she dug the antique jewelry box out from her tote and headed upstairs.

It had been exhausting dealing with the police, Blackwood, and Henry. They were all so needy and greedy. She just wanted to spend the rest of her days restoring the old house, planting a decent garden, and reading books. She was so close. Being smart with her money and shrewd in her business negotiations had already earned her enough to restore the old house, but now she was working on her retirement fund. A few well-planned business deals later, she would have everything she needed. Then she could disappear. She'd disappeared once before; she could do it again.

Back in her bedroom, she went straight for her wall safe. Walking around with her only means of completing her latest project made her nervous. Verity reached into the safe and pulled out the linen drawstring bag she had stored the box's contents in while she took it to Blackwood for inspection. She returned the letters, some beautiful vintage jewelry, and an antique pharmacist's vial carefully to the box. Putting everything back in the safe, she spun the dial to ensure it was locked.

When she was sure that everything was as it should be, she returned the painting to its original position, hiding her safe from prying eyes before collapsing on the plush bed. She stared at her ceiling, which was painted in a gold celestial pattern. She'd done that herself. Verity loved being creative, and she loved everything celestial. She plucked her feet out of her shoes and closed her eyes. Of all the aspects she had worked on throughout this crazy plan of hers, the only thing she was really worried about was Blackwood. She had known of him by reputation before she'd insinuated herself into his life. He was dangerous. His tastes ran towards the morbid side, and she'd seen a few items in his little shop of horrors that she couldn't unsee. But she needed him. He had the budget and the desire for what she had to sell.

Verity tried to set her worries aside for the time being. What she needed right now was to slip into her silk night set and brew herself a cup of tea. Tea made everything better. There was nothing better than slipping into silk, sipping tea, and petting her cat. She sat up. *Where was that cat?* She hadn't realized anything was wrong because she'd been so exhausted when she came home, but Dorian had never greeted her. He always greeted her at the door. *Where was he?* What mischief was he making? Something tingled at the back of her mind. Something wasn't right. Fear whispered to her. She tried to ignore it.

Her green eyes moved over every surface of the room, searching for any hint about what her brain was tingling about, but nothing seemed out of the ordinary. She sat very still, listening. A single woman living on her own was very good at picking up stray noises. Most women were. It was all part of growing up in a world that wanted to kill her, subvert her, or simply just be mean to her. It was hard being a woman.

Verity couldn't hear anything in the house but the usual sound of soft rushing air coming from the floor vent as the air conditioner did its best to keep the hundred-year-old house cool. Her laptop hummed quietly on her desk, but nothing else stirred. She got up and padded across the room to the hallway. Her bare feet made no noise against the coolness of the floor. It helped that she knew where every squeaky floorboard was.

Verity checked each room upstairs. The master bedroom, the bathroom, even the little reading nook that looked out over the backyard, but nothing seemed out of place. The sun had set and the old neighborhood didn't have much in the way of street lights, so everything was thrown into darkness. She stood at the top of the stairs, one hand on the newel post, her manicured toes curled over the edge of the first step down. There was no reason she should be feeling so paranoid, but she'd yet to see that damn cat of hers.

She listened harder. From her place at the top of the stairs, she could see most of the living room and all of the foyer. The house was empty, she was sure of it, but she was far enough into her plans that now would be the perfect time for something to go spectacularly wrong. Verity was frightened, and she hated being frightened. It would remind her of her old self, the woman who feared everything.

It had been over five years now since she'd been given a second chance. With one exception, she'd rid herself of everything from her old life. Her name, her address, and her personality differed from the past. She changed everything about herself, but fear was patient. This fear bubbling up was a reminder that no matter what she did, she couldn't change who she truly was.

Verity took a deep breath and then slowly descended the stairs. She side-stepped the third riser down since it was a notoriously squeaky step. She craned her neck around. As she descended to get a look at the entire space, the familiar shadows of night crept up the walls. Although she couldn't see anything out of the ordinary, something was different down here, and she knew exactly what it was.

The space had a different smell to it than usual. A hint of cologne lingered. Whether she was so tired when she came home or simply distracted, she didn't notice it before. Now she couldn't get the scent out of her nose. She had smelt it before, and she worried as she silently stepped off the stairs and into the living room and foyer. Her eyes roamed the space for anything out of place, or even a glimpse at that black shadow, her cat. She tip-toed over to a small closet, and she was about to open the door when something caught her attention, something just at the corner of her eye. She stopped in her tracks.

Icy shivers ran down the length of her spine as she saw that the little drawer of her entry table was ever so slightly open. That was not her doing. Verity was rather neurotic about leaving drawers slightly open. She bent over the drawer, and after taking a quick look around to make sure she was still alone, slid the drawer open slowly. *Nothing was really important in there,* she first thought, but as soon as she saw the pile of mail cast in shadowy blues and grays, she knew she was in danger. She didn't need to look far to know she had been compromised.

She closed the drawer, returned to the coat closet, and deftly reached in to grab her baseball bat. No, she didn't play baseball. She despised most sports. She hated to sweat, and the only vigorous activity she enjoyed doing was best done behind closed doors with an attractive partner. She used the bat for the same reason most single women did: for defense. She hoisted the aluminum bat over her right shoulder and pressed on with the search of her house.

Now that she knew a man had been in her home while she was out and that it wasn't Henry, her guard increased twofold. The only man she allowed in her home was Henry, and she didn't even like him being left alone in her house. She enjoyed his company, but she had secrets, even from him, and needed to keep them that way.

Verity made her way through her house, meticulously checking each room on the bottom floor, and eventually made her way through to the kitchen. The light was off, but a startling yowl made her jump out of her skin. "Dorian!" she hissed as the cat yowled again. "Don't do that!" she chastised him, even though she still couldn't see him hiding in the shadows.

The solarium just beyond the kitchen was separated by the back door, which was ajar. That was decidedly not the way she'd left it. Verity heard Dorian hissing and spit from out there. He rarely went outside, and she wondered what he was doing out there, not to mention why the door to her little conservatory was open.

Verity stepped out into her solarium. Because of the windows and plants, the little room was hot and humid. The ceiling fan was spinning in lazy circles, but it didn't do much more than stir the air. She loved her little conservatory. She wanted to sit out here with her tea and book and let the rest of the evening just slip away, but she wasn't going to relax until she made sure no one was lurking. With one hand firmly on the baseball bat, she reached out and gripped the handle to the back door. She put her face to the screen, but only darkness lurked outside.

When she stepped out into the night, she put her hand on the door to make sure it closed silently. It was a loud door that slammed, and she'd purposefully left it that way. It reminded her of her childhood home. That slamming was the sound of her father coming home from work to give her giant bear hugs. She stood frozen, like an animal wary of her prey, listening. The night air was full of bird calls, children playing, and crickets, the suffocating heat already dissipating.

Verity stepped down into the grass, which was cool against her feet despite the heat of the day. *Shit, I should have brought a flashlight,* she thought. Verity stood in the dark with her back to her house and gave her eyes a few minutes to adjust to the dim light. Then she heard it. A sound so soft she almost missed it. If she hadn't been standing still, she might have made just enough noise while walking around to obscure it.

What was it? She couldn't place the sound. She'd never heard it before. It was irregular and inhuman. Verity craned her neck to one side in a movement reminiscent of Dorian, her cat. It was coming from the left. The cobbled path and iron gate over that way led to the front yard. She was exceptionally concerned at the thought that someone had come into her house, for who knows what, in broad daylight. What if they'd had intentions worse than just ferreting out her secrets? What if someone already wanted to harm her? She couldn't have that. Not when she was so close.

She followed the sound, the cool grass keeping her alert until her feet stepped in something wet and warm. Her blood ran cold. She didn't want to look, but she had to. Her eyes turned toward it, the rest of her body following reluctantly, fear making each movement painfully slow.

There, tucked into the shadows of the house where she wouldn't have looked, next to the recycling bins, was a lumpy form she somehow automatically knew was a person. She stumbled back a step involuntarily, the bat falling out of her hands. Her shaking hands covered her mouth to stifle a scream, and it took her a second to gain enough confidence to step in close. She knelt and found herself staring into Richard Belker's eyes. The sound she'd heard was the wet gurgling coming from the wound in his throat. All the blood had drained from his face, and his usually sharp eyes were wide in fright.

"What happened?" she asked. It was a stupid thing to ask. He wasn't going to be speaking any time soon. His hands reached out almost blindly. He grabbed her arms with his slippery, blood-covered hands. He still had some strength, and

Verity found herself pulled in nearly on top of him. She tried to push herself away, but he kept his hold on her. Every move he made caused blood to leak out of him. He pulled her in close, and his lips pressed against her ear. He managed to rasp out a single word before he dissolved into a fit of choking. Or was it gagging? Maybe it was both. One word. That was all he managed.

"Henry!"

"What?" She pulled back instinctively. "Henry did this to you?" Verity asked. He struggled and shook, but she could swear that he nodded. "It's okay, Richard. He's not here. It's just me." She tried to soothe Richard, to let him know that help was on the way. "I just need to go in and get my phone, okay? I need to call for some help."

"Don't," Richard struggled to speak, "don't leave—" Verity crouched there over him, pulled in again by his failing strength. The damp earth soaked through the fabric of her trousers. Richard's grip was failing, so she finally managed to free her hands and grip his throat where blood was escaping. Her other hand cupped his once handsome face. She put aside all the times he laid his hands on her body without her consent, and she merely remained there, keeping him company.

"I won't go." Her voice was soft. She had no emergency training, but her instincts were screaming at her. There was no way a person could lose this much blood and still survive. "I'm here, Richard."

The night air, usually crisp and smelling of freshly cut grass, was now filled with the tangy scent of blood.

CHAPTER THIRTEEN

The old neighborhood sparkled as the light from a dozen emergency vehicles strobed and reflected off every surface. Detective Karen Parson pulled up and parked nearly half a block away. A few of the officers on the scene were doing their best to keep the bystanders at a distance while a few more were working on taping off the property. She'd heard enough when the call came in to know that it was a grizzly one. The city had its share of death, like any other, but domestic violence and alcohol were the leading causes. A slit throat and bleeding out was out of the norm.

She approached the house and showed her badge to the officer guarding the perimeter. He held up the ubiquitous yellow tape for her as she ducked under it. Once through the throng of onlookers and within the perimeter, Parson could get a better feel for what was going on. Even though it was no quieter here, there was an order to it. Every crime had order and reason. It was her job to decipher it. An officer greeted her at the door.

"Detective, I'm glad to see you."

"Bad?"

"Pretty messy," he said, bobbing his head. "Some of my units are still a little green, then they saw that mess and got a bit greener."

"I see." She hated it when people tried to make jokes. She understood that murder scenes weren't fun and everyone had their coping mechanisms, but joking was a method that could bite an officer in the ass if they were unlucky enough to be standing close to a reporter.

"The homeowner is over there with the EMTs," he said, delivering his report to her. Parson was diligently notating everything he said in her notebook. "Georgeson," he added as he checked his notes. "Verity Georgeson."

At this, Parson's head snapped up. "Was she injured?"

"Nah, just shock. It's not every day you find a guy bleeding out in your backyard."

"Anything else?"

"Not much, just an overprotective boyfriend trying to get up in all our faces."

Parson didn't doubt it. "Let me guess, a guy by the name of Henry."

"You know him?"

"Not yet, but he's been on my radar about a different case."

"Have fun with that one."

"Thanks." Her voice was laced with sarcasm.

"You wanna see the crime scene first or get statements?

"I'll check out the scene first."

He handed her a pair of medical-grade shoe covers, and she stood around for a moment looking like a depressed flamingo as she slipped them over her work boots.

"Head straight to the back."

Detective Karen Parson walked through the eclectic home, past the clusters of uniformed officers, out onto the back patio, and into the backyard. She'd been to every kind of crime scene at every level of society. She had thought this house was mildly nice, but it was too dark and moody for her tastes, which were simple in the extreme. A couple of floodlights had been set up on the lawn with tripods, and they cast the space in an unforgiving light. The backyard was simpler than she'd been expecting after seeing the rest of the place. She'd talked to Verity Georgeson before, and with her retro outfits, secretive demeanor, and moody style, she'd been expecting something more. Karen couldn't put her finger on it, but just more. Instead, the lawn was simple, green, and closed off to prying eyes with a privacy fence. There was a ramshackle shed at the back, with paint peeling off and boarded-up windows. She jotted that down along with a note to check it out. For someone who acted so meticulously with the rest of her life, it seemed odd to have something around that looked so shabby.

She gave her attention to the matter at hand, or to the corpse at hand. He was a tall man, folded into a sitting position against the house. His skin had an ashy, ghostly appearance. She wondered what his shade of skin had been. Once the blood stopped being pumped through the body, it couldn't quite keep its color. Karen crouched down and examined the body. The wound on his neck was surprisingly small. She wondered how long he'd been propped up here bleeding out.

"Has the M.E. seen this yet?" she asked the officer hovering behind her.

"Not yet," he replied. That meant she couldn't touch anything. Other than any life-saving steps deployed, he would have to remain untouched until the medical examiner could take a proper look. So, she used her eyes to gather the evidence. The wound was small but precise. That meant it was probably intentional, which didn't bode well for him. Someone probably meant for him to die slowly. The blood on his neck was smeared, and Parson thought she could see the vague shape of a handprint.

"Did the EMTs do anything when they arrived?"

"Nothing more than to pronounce him and calm the homeowner down. Apparently, she was about to lose it."

Karen looked up at the officer from where she was crouching and pointed to the smeared handprint with her pen. "Oh, that, the homeowner tried to put pressure on the bleeding, but there wasn't much point in that."

Well, that's something. Her intuition was screaming at her that something was missing; she just couldn't put her finger on it. She scanned the area where the body was propped. The exterior of the house was clean for the most part, so he probably hadn't been stabbed here. Neck wounds, even small ones, tended to leave a big mess. The plush grass around him had been crushed though, and she thought she could see some indents about the size of two kneecaps as if someone were kneeling down to save him. Blood surrounded him everywhere else, though. The victim's suit was drenched in it, and even though she wanted to go rifling around in his pockets, there was no way she could do that without wearing his blood. She'd have to wait for the ME for that.

The floodlights washed much of the color away from the scene, but as her eyes roamed the scene in a familiar pattern, something caught her attention. Lying by the yard bins was a baseball bat, an aluminum one. Considering the woman who lived here, she thought it seemed out of place.

"I need a photo of this."

The officer flagged down one of the other officers with the camera. She patiently waited as someone laid an evidence marker down and took some shots both close up and with the body in view. When they finished, she pulled a latex glove from her pocket and used it to pick it up. The bat was clean, not a speck of blood on it. Parson was going to have to ask the Georgeson woman about it.

She needed to get the Georgeson woman's side of what happened. One of her officers told her about the side path to the front yard, so she followed it through an iron gate, constantly scanning the ground with her penlight. It hadn't rained in months, so there was no hope of having any convenient boot prints. There was also the fact that most of the path was paved in flagstone, with just some little tufts of grass growing between them. Nothing looked trampled. Whatever happened here, the perp had not come through the side gate. She tucked that thought away. She knew better than to make assumptions before she had all the facts.

Karen Parson emerged from the path and out into the front yard. The scene was still buzzing with officers, and a crowd was starting to gather around the taped-off perimeter. The ambulance was parked directly in front of the house, and Verity Georgeson was sitting in the back, wrapped in one of the wool blankets. Henry was wrapped around her as though he were a rescue blanket as well.

Karen could tell as she approached the couple that Verity Georgeson was shattered. Her eyes were bloodshot and a little glassy. Shock. Karen had seen it so many times. Henry looked like he would snarl at and bite anyone who approached her. *This should be fun*, she thought.

"Ms. Georgeson," Parson announced as she approached the couple. Henry's head whipped around, but Verity turned her head towards the detective slowly. She was exhausted, emotionally and physically, and Parson could see it in her movements.

"Detective Parson?" Verity asked.

"Sorry to have to ask you some questions, but I'll be quick."

"Whatever you need," Verity offered. Parson noticed her words were slower, and she didn't seem quite as sharp as she'd been last time she'd questioned the woman. She opened her little notebook again and clicked her pen.

"Can you take me through what happened?" Parson asked.

Verity seemed to shake the cobwebs out of her head and regain some composure. "I, uh, I had just come home. I had been at a business meeting and was tired, so I just went upstairs to my room to change."

"Did you notice anything unusual?" Parson interjected.

"No," Verity said, "not at first."

"What do you mean, not at first?"

"Well, it was Dorian, really. He—"

"Who's Dorian?"

"Her cat. Dorian is the cat," Henry sneered. Not a fan of cats, she guessed.

A couple of med techs led a gurney along the path to the backyard. Parson watched as Verity's eyes followed them, growing wide. It was hard to fake horror like that. Parson had a feeling, and her feelings were usually right, but she was starting to think Verity was just as much a victim as the dead man in her garden.

"Dorian always greets me at the door, you see. I was just too tired when I came home to notice he hadn't actually greeted me at the door. It wasn't until I was upstairs that I noticed he wasn't around."

Henry tightened his grip on the woman. Parson was having some serious reservations about Henry Williams. She'd seen enough overbearing control freak boyfriends come and go in her line of work, and she wanted to slap Verity to get her away from him.

"Ok, what did you do after you noticed the cat was missing?"

"I went downstairs to look for him. He's usually not a fussy cat, but he sort of adopted me and I worry about him."

"Did you go straight outside to look for the cat?"

"Oh no, he doesn't go outside. I went back down to the foyer. He sometimes takes naps under the little table there."

"And was the cat there?"

"No. He wasn't, but . . ."

"But?" Parson pushed.

"But I noticed that the drawer in the desk was open just a little bit."

"Is that out of character for you to leave it open like that?" Parson asked, to which Henry snorted.

"Yes," Verity added softly. Parson watched her wide and frightened eyes look up into Henry's face. "Henry, her picture was missing."

"What!" he exclaimed.

"What picture, Ms. Georgeson?"

"I kept a picture, a photograph, in that drawer."

"What's the significance of the photo?"

"It was a picture of Verity and her daughter," Henry answered.

"You have a daughter?" Parson asked, feigning surprise. She hadn't gotten back the background check on Verity, but Garcia's warning clamored in her memory.

"I do," she replied. Parson knew there was more to it than that, but she'd save that for when she could speak with the woman privately. "It was when I noticed the photo missing that I got worried about someone being in the house."

"That's when you went outside?"

"Yes. It was so horrible. I almost didn't see him. It was dark, and I just, I just heard him." Parson watched the woman visibly shudder. The human body could make some terrible noises when life was slipping away. Parson spent her time around criminals and grievers, but she'd been present to witness more than a few deaths. She couldn't blame the woman for her reaction.

Parson caught a momentary break in the growing crowd behind them and couldn't help but notice the arrival of Mary Otto and Anita Belker. She wished they hadn't come here. This wasn't the way she needed to find out about her husband. Parson needed to divert her before she saw something she couldn't forget.

"One more thing," Parson said. Verity looked at her, slightly wild and completely spent. *Well, shit*, she thought. Verity and Henry had seen Mary and Anita. The detective watched as they all made eye contact with each other. The tension and mistrust were thick as cold honey with these folks. "Do you own a baseball bat?"

No answer.

"Ms. Georgeson?"

"What? Yes, I'm sorry. What did you ask?"

"Do you own a baseball bat?" The detective watched them all tentatively. Mary was shooting daggers at Verity, which wasn't unexpected. Parson had realized quickly that she'd absconded with one photo of her husband when interviewed last, so she was stinging from the betrayal. This wouldn't go well. It was hard enough to just grieve, but dealing with an affair on top of that would make things ugly. Verity looked honestly horrified by a potential confrontation from the other two women. Parson couldn't blame her.

"No," Henry said. His expression was different, and she couldn't quite pin it down.

"Yes," Verity corrected. He looked at her, utterly perplexed. "It was a gift." But Henry didn't seem pacified with that answer. Parson thought he recognized the "we'll-talk-about-it-later" look and hoped the man was smart enough to give the woman some space. Coming from the path along the side of the house was the articulated sound of a gurney bearing weight. The EMTs were finally moving the body. Shit, she needed to get Anita Belker out of here before she saw it.

"All right, that'll be all for now. An officer will take you down to the station to get your formal statement. Until then, you two can just rest for a minute, but you'll need to move from here." Parson had eyes only for Anita Belker, but Henry was having his own confrontation. As the gurney passed by them, Verity retreated. Henry pulled her in close again and wrapped his arms around her to protect her from the sight.

As Detective Parson approached the perimeter of the scene, she made eye contact with Anita, who seemed worried. Parson was pretty sure she was just a caring woman and worried for her friend. She didn't yet realize she had her own troubles to worry over now. Karen raised a hand in the air to signal the nearest officer and then pointed.

"Let those two in," she said. The officer complied, and both women ducked beneath the taped barrier reluctantly. The gurney was being wheeled towards the ambulance behind Parson and she watched as the two women stared at it, but she didn't realize anything was wrong until Mary Otto reached out to stop Anita. Parson didn't know what happened, but the look of shock on their faces was the first hint. Parson turned around and saw one of the EMTs tucking an arm back under the cloth that kept Richard Belker's gruesome body out of sight of all the bystanders. Shit.

Chapter Fourteen

Anita's face was splotchy, her eyes bright red and puffy, and she was walking around like a deer caught in headlights. There's just no way to grieve pretty. Mary had her gently by the elbow as they followed a police officer once again through the network of hallways and reception desks at the police station. She'd completely lost track of time, but it was still dark outside. Was that a good thing or a bad thing? She didn't know.

Eventually, they found themselves back in the same curving corridor that they'd visited after Geoff's accident. Anita and Mary shared a look and a deep sigh. *Here we go again*. They followed the officer down the corridor with the long curving wall of glass. Traffic drove by, decorating the view with red and yellow lights, and then they were deposited outside the same interview room as before.

There, sitting in one of the chairs was Verity. The eclectic woman looked nothing like she had the last time Anita had seen her. Then, she had been composed, elegant even. Her outfit was proper, and her expressions were perfectly sublime and polite even if she had been having a sordid affair with Geoff. Anita had to admit that she'd found the woman beautiful. She hated being jealous. There was no point in it. Anita couldn't be like Verity, but maybe it was like shopping. She could love something and still not buy it.

Anita and Mary sat side by side in the two empty chairs, but they clung together like a child and a mother. Anita watched Verity from a sideways glance. She couldn't help but notice the tremor in the woman's hands. She wondered if the woman was just as shattered as she was. Anita couldn't help but notice that although Verity's hands seemed mostly clean, her classically manicured nails still had blood tucked into the edges. Her blouse and trousers were covered in blood too, which was drying to a dark ugly brown color. It was all Richard's blood. *How had this happened?* Anita and Mary were widows now, within the same week.

None of them spoke. What could one say at a time like this? Mary gave Anita a comforting squeeze, her face full of concern. The creases at her eyes and around her mouth had deepened. Anita wondered if the frown on her face was going to be permanent. That would be awful. Mary was glaring hatefully at Verity, and Anita was glad it wasn't she who had displeased Mary so much. She could be frightening when protective.

Anita looked back at Verity. Her hands were still shaking, and her face was slack. She was staring at something on the floor. Anita looked, but nothing was there. Their attention was drawn by steps echoing slightly from down the corridor. When Anita looked up, she was staring into the hardened face of Detective Karen Parson.

"Ladies," Detective Parson said, announcing herself. All three ladies pulled their heads up to look at the detective. Mary barely managed to compose her anger. Anita, who was overwhelmed and exhausted, leaned into her friend for support. And Verity, in shock and lost to the present, stared blankly.

"Mrs. Belker, I know it's been a long night, but there are more questions I need to ask." Anita turned to face Mary, who gave her a stern nod and a gentle push. She followed the detective into the interview room and looked back only once. Her friend and the other woman sitting there together with only an empty seat between them to keep the peace didn't seem like enough. The detective closed the door behind them, and Anita was cut off from her friend, the only thing keeping her sane right now.

Anita peered around the small room and realized in horror that she'd somehow found herself in a cliched procedural drama. Here she was in the interrogation room, about to face down the hardened detective. This could only go downhill from here. Detective Parson gestured for her to take a seat and then sat herself down across the table. At least there wasn't a single shoddy electric light dangling overhead. The room was modern and minimalist, and the ceiling had clean fluorescent lights that lit the room up too much. The mirror on one wall gave her the shivers. She didn't like the idea of being watched by someone she couldn't see.

"First off," the detective started, "I'm sorry for your loss."

"Thank you," Anita whispered.

"I'm sorry about all the questions, but if we're going to figure out what happened to your husband, it needs to be done." Anita could only nod her head at that. The detective opened the folder she'd brought with her, filled with typed papers and a few other items, but nothing she recognized. "I've read your statement. There's not a lot here."

"Okay."

"I've gotta ask, What were you doing there?"

"What do you mean?"

"I mean, what were you and Mary Otto doing at Verity Georgeson's place?" the detective asked.

Anita remained still, her lips parted and her eyes wide. "Um, well, Mary wanted to talk to her."

"You mean, Mary wanted to confront her husband's mistress in the middle of a homicide investigation?"

Well, yes actually, but it sounds ridiculous when you say it like that, she thought.

"That's what I thought," the detective said as if reading her mind before she scribbled down some notes. "Look, I'm not gonna sugarcoat this for you. It looks damning as hell that you and Mary show up to the crime scene, especially with all the drama going on between those two already."

Anita had to agree. She's not wrong. "I've got evidence that Mrs. Otto's husband was murdered, that he was having an affair, and then"—the detective leaned in close—"your husband turns up dead at the mistress's house."

The silence was uncomfortable.

"I don't know what to say, Detective."

"What if I told you that I think your husband had broken into Verity's house looking for something?"

"What?"

"That's right. Something was stolen from her home."

"What on earth could he have wanted?"

"I'm not sure. I know he found something that rattled that woman." The detective pointed a finger towards the general area where Mary and Verity were presumably still sitting, waiting. "And honestly, in my personal opinion, that woman isn't easily rattled."

"The first time I saw her I couldn't imagine anything rattling her, but now . . ."

"Having a man die in your hands will mess a person up."

"Are you telling me she killed Richard?"

"No, she tried to save his life."

"What?"

"That surprises you?"

"Well, yeah, I mean." Anita struggled to find the words. "I guess it shouldn't. I don't know her other than—"

"Other than as a secret mistress to your friend's husband," the detective finished for her.

"Yeah, that."

"Do you think anything was going on between the Georgeson woman and your husband?" Detective Parson asked.

Of course she had to ask that. Anita hesitated. She wanted to say no, but she couldn't. The twitch of the detective's eyebrows indicated she noticed her hesitation. She reached into her back pocket and fished out the business card she'd found in Richard's desk and handed it to the detective.

"I found this in his desk the other day." Her fingers fiddled with her wedding band unconsciously. "If you'd have asked me that question a week ago, I would have said no way, but now, I don't know what to think."

The detective examined the business card, tilted it this way and that, nodding her head subtly. Anita knew she was checking it in the light to see the subtle logo printed on the black card. The detective flipped through some of her notes before looking intently at Anita. She squirmed under the scrutinizing gaze of a woman so unlike herself. She thought the detective was trying to make up her mind about something, and when she had come to whatever conclusion it was, she turned her intense eyes to Anita.

Detective Parson pulled out a small photograph and laid it in front of Anita. Two women, so similar in their features that they had to be related, smiled out at her. "Do you recognize this woman?" Parson pointed to the younger of the two women. Anita stared at the young woman in the photo, but no matter how hard she stared at it, she couldn't recall ever seeing the young woman before. She didn't look at all familiar. She shook her head slowly.

"No, I'm—" And then she saw it, "wait! Is that Verity Georgeson?" She snatched the photo off the table before the detective had a chance to take it back. It wasn't the younger woman who had caught her attention. She'd never seen the younger woman before in her life, but the other woman was a different story. The face was the same. The hair differed, along with the makeup and the clothes, but the woman was the same. She flipped the photo over. "Louise and Jenna?"

"Yes," the detective said with a sigh. "It would seem she has a daughter."

"You didn't know?"

"There's a lot about that woman we don't know," Parson said in an attempt to steer the conversation.

"Where did you find this?"

"It was on your husband's person."

A heavy silence filled the sterile space as the strange circumstances around all of this sunk in. Anita lifted her gaze from the photo.

"And you're sure she didn't hurt Richard?"

"I'm not certain of anything right now, but I don't think she killed your husband."

"Why? Why don't you think she did it?"

"Well, other than her general state of shock, she's also right-handed."

"What's that got to do with anything?" Anita asked a little more harshly than she meant to. The detective's unkempt eyebrows crept up.

"Your husband was stabbed in the neck at an angle that suggests a left-handed individual performed the attack."

"Could she have faked that to protect herself?"

"Your husband was also a tall man. It would have taken more than just pretending to be left-handed for her to get the job done."

Anita was skeptical. What were the chances of that Verity woman being involved with both Geoff and Richard, and then both men turning up dead? She didn't like thinking that her husband might have been cheating on her but admitted that she'd already come to that conclusion on her own. It stung to think about Richard dying in the arms of that woman. He should have died in her arms. He wasn't the gentlest of people, but he was hers. What was she going to do without him? She wanted to get out of here and be with Mary. Mary would know what to do.

"Can I see him?"

"Not yet. The medical examiner needs to finish first, but I'll let you know when you can."

Anita nodded her head absently until she realized what the detective was talking about. Her eyes grew large as saucers when she realized that it was an autopsy. The detective meant that she could see him after he'd been cut up.

"Do you have a place to stay?"

"I'll just go home."

"I don't think you should be alone tonight."

"I'll be fine."

"Your husband has just been murdered, and I can't say yet whether you might be a target."

"Someone's going to come after me too?"

"I don't know, so I'd feel better if you could stay with a friend for a day or two."

"I'm sure I can stay with Mary."

"Even better." Detective Parson packed up her notes. "I'm sure this goes without saying, but stay in town until we get this sorted, all right?"

"I'm not going anywhere until I see someone pays for killing my husband," Anita said. The detective looked a little taken aback, and to be honest, Anita surprised herself with her words. She might have wanted to shrink back in, but there was no one left at home to protect her from the rest of the world. She was going to have to relearn how to be on her own again. She was a widow now, and she refused to wilt away and be forgotten.

"Here," Detective Parson said, handing a business card to Anita, "if you think of anything that could be useful to the investigation, or if anything happens, please call me."

"Thank you, Detective Parson." Anita took the card with shaking hands.

"Don't be surprised if you see a patrol car outside the house. I'm going to have someone keep an eye on you for a day or two."

Anita didn't have any words left and simply nodded as the detective opened the door to the interview room and guided

Anita out. Mary sprang up from her chair, startling the already shattered Ms. Georgeson, and strode to Anita's side.

"May I take her home now?" Mary asked in a surprising motherly tone, which didn't suggest she was actually asking anything but rather making a statement.

Anita peered over Mary's shoulder where she could see Verity Georgeson staring right at her. The woman looked haunted. Anita wondered if being present for Richard's death had linked the two women together forever. She realized that before all of this was said and done, she would have to talk to the woman. Verity Georgeson was the last person to see her husband alive, and Anita needed to know everything about Richard's last moment. She hadn't been there, and she could already taste the sourness of guilt and regret crawling up her throat.

Chapter Fifteen

Mary took hold of Anita again and guided her along as they followed an officer back towards the reception area. Anita looked back over her shoulder to see Verity rise and follow Detective Parson, but she turned to look as well, their eyes meeting. Anita felt sorry for herself, but there was something miserable about the woman. No one should come home to find a man bleeding to death. No matter how much she wanted to hate the woman as Mary did, she just couldn't find her way to that. Verity was pitiable. Anita had envied that life of hers. She was jealous of Verity making her own way, dictating her own rules, but look at her now. Here she was being questioned by the police and no one was here for her. At least Anita had Mary to take comfort in.

The officer they'd been following deposited them at the lobby with another reminder to stay in town until everything was resolved. The reception counter was mostly empty. Outside the front windows of the station, the parking lot was beginning to glow slightly with the impending dawn. The sun was coming up. What had started as a simple curiosity with her and

Mary wanting to confront Verity about her relationship with Geoff turned into something much grislier.

The two friends stood there together. Their lives once mundane and quiet were filled with mystery and horror. They were both widows now, and Anita didn't know what to do with that. It was one thing to be Mary's age and to have a lifetime of memories, but for Anita and Richard, they had just started out. The rest of her time with Richard had been stolen away from her. Her stomach twisted into a tight knot, and her face burned. Unfamiliar emotions bubbled to the surface, and it frightened her. She looked to her best friend for guidance, but only found her feelings reflected back at her like a mirror. Mary Otto's face was hard and full of rage.

"Mary?" she asked, her voice a timid whisper.

"I know," her friend said. "It hurts."

"What are we supposed to do?"

"I don't know, but what I do know is that I'm not about to just sit around and wait for the police to come to the same conclusion I already have. Besides, other people could be in danger"

"What's that supposed to mean?"

"I mean," Mary leaned in close, "it all has to do with that Verity woman, all of it." Mary's voice was laced with anger and frustration. Anita knew exactly how she was feeling, she just didn't necessarily agree with her conclusion.

"I don't think it's her fault."

"Don't be naïve." Mary practically snorted. It was the most indelicate thing she'd ever seen her friend do. "Everything is connected to that woman."

"Just because everything keeps happening when she's nearby doesn't make it her fault," Anita rebutted. Mary gave her a look that would've made her want to wither and die if she didn't understand just how she was feeling. Anita wanted answers and justice as badly as Mary did, but she was starting to think that Verity was just stuck in the same mire as they were.

"The only thing common between Geoff's death and Richard's death is that woman's involvement," Mary said as she looked away, or perhaps she was looking for something in particular. Anita was too distracted by her own emotions to pay too much attention. Her mind was spinning with ideas.

"That's not exactly true," Anita offered distractedly.

Mary whipped her head around to scowl at her friend. "What are you saying?"

"Well, there's also the fact they both worked at the same place."

"Where Verity was a client," Mary tossed back. Anita had to admit that Mary had a point. Anita turned, looking over her shoulder trying to see Verity through the corridors and walls between. It was then that Anita saw a familiar face. Emerging from one of the nearby corridors was the man she'd seen with Verity at her house, along with a couple of uniformed officers. He'd been holding her, Anita remembered. How could she have forgotten something like that? Verity wasn't alone after all.

"Mary," Anita whispered. Mary turned back to Anita. They both gawked as the officers released the ruggedly handsome man. He glared at the officer's backs as they walked away.

"He doesn't look so happy."

"You're right about that, dear," Mary said, a curious tone slipping through her words. Anita's brow furrowed.

"What are you thinking?"

"I'm thinking you may be right after all."

"I am?" Anita asked, more confused than ever.

"Yes," Mary answered distractedly. "Maybe you're right that Verity Georgeson could just be another victim, like us. Well, to a certain degree, that is. I'm not going to victimize the little witch for having an affair with my husband."

"What are you talking about?" Anita asked.

Mary turned to her and drew her in close. "I mean, what if this has everything to do with Verity, but it's not her doing?" Anita turned to look back at the man and nearly jumped when she found his scowl piercing right through her. In all honesty, she was already raw from the ordeal; why would he harbor such strong feelings toward her?

"What a horrible man," Mary said. Anita was disturbed by the man's intense glare, but she couldn't quite agree to label him horrible.

"Mary, I don't think—"

"That horrible man from the restaurant is here."

"Wait, what?"

"Look," Mary said with a knowing tilt to her head. Anita turned and saw the man from Domenic's, the one who Verity Georgeson had met with after they had all been questioned about Geoff's death. It hadn't been her that the man was glaring at; rather, these two men were glaring at each other. Anita couldn't imagine what animosity was brewing between them, but she didn't like being stuck between them either. "Come on, let's get out of here," Mary said. "I'm starting to take a dislike to this place."

Anita understood the feeling. They had spent more time here in the last few days than she'd ever thought she would in her entire life. Mary hoisted her purse higher on her shoulder, straightened her back, and walked towards the exit leading to the parking lot with Anita at her side, arms wrapped protectively around herself. They passed the man from the restaurant, who tipped his hat as they walked by.

"Ladies," he said in passing. Mary ignored him, but Anita gave him a nervous smile before Mary gently pulled her along. They pushed their way out the glass doors and emerged outside. The cool morning air brushing against Anita's face was a blessing. She hadn't realized how frightened she'd been until she breathed in the crisp morning air. An antiseptic quality to the air lingered inside the police station, but now that she filled her senses with the cool, clean air, she felt relieved to be free of it.

"Something about that man frightens me," Mary confessed. Anita turned to her best friend and saw that her lined face was tilted up slightly, a little prayer to the oncoming dawn. The sun had not yet crested the horizon but had already begun chasing away the darkness. Out here, Anita could almost forget the nightmare from last night. She could forget she was a widow.

But Richard was gone. Richard had been murdered. Someone had been crazy enough to think that whatever problem they were tangled up in, Richard's death was the solution.

"He doesn't seem to feel all warm and fuzzy towards the police. That's for certain," Anita said.

"That boyish thing he has going on is hiding something sinister. I can feel it," Mary whispered.

Anita frowned. She hadn't thought he looked boyish at all. She could see why a woman would be attracted to him. He was strong and stoic, and Anita recalled how he wrapped himself around Verity last night. "He's the devil, that one."

"Mary, who are you talking about?" she asked. "Because I don't think we're thinking of the same person." The doors to the station opened to the handsome man they'd seen earlier. He rubbed at his wrists distractedly before he noticed the two of them standing there. Anita wondered if they had considered him as a suspect. Had they handcuffed him? They must not have thought it was he, though, if they were letting him just walk out the door. Mary watched him too.

"Anita, you stay here. I'll be right back," Mary said. Anita remembered the other man, the one who had been meeting Verity at Domenic's. They'd only encountered him twice, but he was never anything more than polite to them.

"Wait, Mary, where are you going?" Anita called out, but her friend had already disappeared back inside the station.

Anita hugged herself, with nothing for her to do but think about what had just happened. Her husband had been murdered. Someone had hated him enough to stab him in the neck. She shivered at the thought. *Poor Richard*, she thought, *I should have been there for you*. She couldn't have saved him, but it would have been something to at least be there for him. Why had he been there in the first place? She couldn't imagine what he would've needed that she couldn't have gotten for him. Anita hated all these secrets. Did she know her husband at all?

She'd been so lost in her thoughts that she hadn't noticed Mary's return until she spoke.

"He's up to something. I'm sure of it."

Anita snapped back into focus, though she felt lost trying to keep up with Mary's train of thought. "What on earth could he be up to? And why does that have anything to do with us?"

The handsome man met her gaze for a moment, and Anita was startled by the amount of emotion on his face. Had living with Richard numbed her to the fact that there were men in the world who could feel anything more than desire or greed? Richard could be kind, but he typically acted this way to get something he wanted. This man was worried; Anita could see that plainly. He must have cared for Verity very much. Anita withered uncomfortably, sharing this man's pain, and broke their gaze. When she looked back, he was holding his phone to his ear, walking away from them in the opposite direction.

"He's connected to the Georgeson woman, and for some reason, there's no lost love between him and that one," Mary said, giving a curt nod toward Verity's man. Anita had to agree with her on that, but she was too tired to think very hard about it.

"Mary?"

"Hm?"

"Can I stay at your place for a few days?" Anita asked through a yawn that nearly unhinged her jaw. Mary turned to look at her and, after a moment's consideration, gave her a sad smile.

"Of course, Anita. I'm so sorry. I've been going crazy with this tangled-up mess around Geoff, and I haven't thought of you dealing with Richard."

"Oh no, Mary, you've been wonderful. I can't imagine going through any of this without you."

"Look at us. What a mess."

"I am exhausted. I just want to curl up in the bottom of the shower and cry my eyes out. But . . . I'm just afraid."

"Afraid that if you start, you won't be able to stop," Mary added. It wasn't a question, Anita realized. Her fear was being thrown back at her. Mary had been pushing like this for days, ever since Geoff had died.

"Mary, have you not cried?" Anita asked.

Mary shook her head, but her expression remained stoic and unrelenting. In that moment, Anita resolved to help her friend. Maybe they could help each other. "We've spent enough time dealing with this." Anita waved a maniacal hand at the building behind them. An errant officer gave her a curious look as he walked past them. "We're going home. We're going to get drunk, we're going to cry, and then we're going to become the best damn modern incarnations of Jessica Fletcher the world has ever seen. I don't care what we must do to solve Geoff's murder and lock up the bastard who killed Richard, but we're going to do it. Together."

She bobbed her head emphatically and was momentarily terrified when Mary Otto burst out laughing.

"What?" Anita asked, but Mary simply tucked her arm through Anita's and smiled at her. It was a warm and genuine smile. She hadn't seen that expression on Mary's face in what seemed like ages.

"What would I do without you, my friend?"

"Well, you'd probably wallow around in misery and have no one to drink with."

Chapter Sixteen

Christopher Blackwood entered the Fort Collins Police station quietly. He was a quiet man, except when conducting business, of course. Some people lumbered through life, wearing the baggage of their lives like a winter shroud. Christopher wasn't like that. Sure, he had his fair share of trauma tucked away in his past, but rather than let it burden him, he allowed it to shape him into a stronger man. He carried himself through this world with confidence and charisma.

His navy three-piece suit, silver tie, and pocket watch made him the most fashion-forward person in the building. While he took pains to ensure that his attire evoked class and business acumen, it was only when he was home, alone with his collection, his cabinet of curiosities, that he truly felt himself. Even though he considered himself a fan of classic fashion, it didn't mean that he was oblivious to other things. His intelligence was just as sharp as his wardrobe, and the moment he stepped into the utilitarian building, he felt the tension. It didn't take long for him to spot the angsty Henry Williams being led around by a few uniformed officers.

Christopher clicked his tongue in dismay at the ridiculous situation that man had found himself in. He was far too cavalier with his emotions. Christopher recognized Henry was dangerous, but not for the same reasons he was dangerous. Henry was dangerous because of his blind devotion to the woman he loved. But Christopher had been cultivating his little empire for many years now, and he understood where true power came from. His power came not from muscles or being a bully but from knowledge. It was not all about accumulating knowledge. That was only part of the equation. One must know how to use that information to their benefit and their enemy's detriment. That was what Christopher had perfected over time. He saw how people had used knowledge and secrets against him in the past and refused to ever be used like that again. His alcoholic homophobic father taught him that lesson.

Now, he collected secrets. He kept them until he found a use for them. He'd also learned that only a few truly kind people existed in the world. Everyone wanted something. Everyone needed something. And everyone was usually needy and greedy enough to forgo kindness if it meant that they could be safe. Safety was an illusion, though. Someday, he would face off against an opponent who would be clever enough to end his little empire, but for now, he was the king and he feared no one.

Christopher lingered by the entry for a few minutes while he watched bemusedly as Henry was released from custody. He was a delicious-looking man and Christopher would love to do very naughty things with him, but he knew the other man wasn't flexible when it came to his sexuality. It hadn't surprised Christopher that the local constabulary would consider him a suspect. He had all the right anger, and of course, he was more than capable of completing the gruesome task of butchering Richard Belker.

But Belker had earned what he got. He'd been pretty on the surface, with his perfectly sculpted body and his perfect little life with his perfect little wife. But Christopher collected secrets, along with other unique trinkets, and Richard Belker had a few. Christopher thought the recently deceased Mr. Belker was lucky that none of his secrets had managed to get pregnant. That would have ruined his perfectly precious life really fast, or maybe not. His wife wasn't made of the same stuff as Verity Georgeson, or Mary Otto, for that matter.

Henry shook off his uniformed escort and was giving him the most wicked look. It would have taken more than that to scare him off a profitable arrangement.

"Who are you?" Mary Otto was suddenly standing there in front of him, demanding a response.

Speaking of the devil, he thought wryly.

"I'll ask you again, Who are you?" She stiffened her spine. It was almost petulant. He offered her his hand.

"Christopher Blackwood, at your service."

"And just what sort of services do you offer?" Her eyes squinted with mistrust.

"I have a quaint little curio shop one town over. You might like it."

"What is it you sell, Mr. Blackwood?"

"Oh, a little of this, a little of that. I curate rare items with unique provenance for my clients."

"And what sort of answer is that?" She scoffed.

He reached into his inside breast pocket, pulled out a business card, and handed it to her. "My address is there. Why don't you stop by to see my collection?"

"Is that why you've been lingering around us lately?"

"Oh, you mean you and your little friend, Mrs. Belker? Poor thing. My business is my own, but I'm acquainted with the lovely Miss Verity Georgeson. It is quite a mess with all the goings-on lately."

"You need to stay away from us."

"Gladly, dear, but if you ever change your mind, I'm sure we could work something out." Her face reddened and her jaw clenched, and he was just beside himself with a case of the giggles threatening to escape. "You know, I collect many things in my little shop. Rare books, vintage silver, and more than a few things in the memento mori vein"—he leaned in close and smiled sweetly at her—"for those who love to walk on the dark side. Our mutual acquaintance, Miss Georgeson, is among those who visit my shop."

"I think I'll pass."

"I collect other things as well."

"Like what?"

"Secrets," he said simply. He watched her pupils dilate with understanding.

"You know something."

"Oh, Mrs. Otto, I know many things."

"You know why my husband was killed, don't you?" The angrier she got, the more her spine stiffened. He enjoyed watching simple people and their predictable behavior.

"Why don't you tell the police what you know?" she asked. "What do you get out of keeping it secret?"

There, she had it. For such an intelligent woman, it sure took her a moment to get there.

"Why, Mrs. Otto, if I gave out my client's secrets, then I wouldn't be much of a businessman, now would I?"

"This has everything to do with that Georgeson woman, doesn't it?" she asked, but Christopher simply pantomimed zipping his lips and tossing the key. Mary Otto's face bloomed crimson and purple with rage. "You know," he said thoughtfully, "if you were one of my clients, then I would be obligated to keep your secrets."

"I don't have any secrets."

"Lies don't suit you. Everyone has secrets, even you. Even that little mouse of a thing you call your friend has secrets. You and I would do well as business partners."

"I don't think so."

"Suit yourself." He shrugged. She huffed at him before stalking off to go and presumably rejoin her friend. Mary Otto was like a protective bulldog. Sometimes real life was more ridiculous than fiction, and he smiled at that. He had let himself be so distracted by Mary Otto and her drama that when Henry Williams pushed past him with a shoulder check, he was nearly caught unaware. But Christopher was sharp, whipping himself around so that Henry couldn't escape him right away. He leaned in and whispered into his ear.

"I know what you've done, Henry," he said in the silkiest voice he could conjure. Henry's reaction was priceless. The man froze, and his gorgeous blue eyes grew wide. He was a frightened animal. This was simply perfect. Christopher Blackwood purred contentedly.

"You don't know anything."

"Don't worry, love. I don't want anything from you," Christopher replied. "Well, that's not God's honest truth. I do want something from you, but I doubt you'll give it up."

"Just stay away from her." Henry's voice was laced with fear and hatred. Christopher watched the pretty man struggle against a need to cause violence against him. It would have been delicious, but he wrangled himself back and seemed to realize that a confrontation in the middle of the police station was probably not in his best interest. Instead, he sidestepped Christopher and left through the main doors. Christopher smiled. All the little spiders weaving their webs of deceit. All he had to do was wait out all the drama, and he'd have what he wanted. In the meantime, he had other business to attend to.

Christopher Blackwood smoothed down his suit jacket and unconsciously patted his silk pocket square gently to make sure he hadn't been ruffled up too much by Henry Williams' bravado. He then made his way to the long reception counter where a few officers waited behind clear acrylic barriers. One of the officers was a petite woman with dark hair pulled back into a sleek knot at the base of her neck. She wore makeup, but it was clean and simple, matching her simple and severe uniform.

"Excuse me," he announced in a softer voice than he used with Henry. "I'm here to pick up a records request I made."

She met his gaze with large brown doe eyes. "What's the request number?"

He diligently offered answers to all her questions. Eventually, she confirmed his request and that it had been prepared. She pointed to a seating area just off to the side of the large atrium. Someone had attempted to cozy up the utilitarian space, but there was no way to soften a police department. No one enjoyed spending time here. People only came here because they had been very naughty or because someone else had done something naughty to them.

Either way, he settled himself into one of the chairs, crossed his legs, and folded his hands in his lap. It was always better to wait without distraction. He'd learned ages ago that keeping a keen eye on his environment usually offered some tidbits, morsels of secrets that he could use down the road. He waited patiently for nearly twenty minutes before the officer returned with one of those interoffice delivery envelopes in her hand. He accepted the envelope without rising and waited for the woman to return to her station behind the counter before he unwound the tie holding the envelope closed.

The contents of the envelope were sparse; if he were being honest with himself, he hadn't expected much of anything at all. But he slid the tidy stack of papers out of the envelope and thumbed through them briefly. He was in luck. He wasn't at all sure that they would have kept autopsy records from such a long time ago, but here it was. Only two pages, but the information he was looking for was there.

His cherub face brightened. When the game of secrecy was played well, it offered immense pleasure. He had just the bit of information he needed to ensure that when this particular game was done, he would be the victor. He didn't like losing money on a business deal, and his opponent was wily and clever. For the briefest of moments, he was worried that he wouldn't have the tools he needed to win, but that had all changed now. He would have to do a little more investigating on this, but the plan for his final play in the game was forming in his mind. His newest client would be glad to hear it. If any-one had been paying attention to him, their blood would have curdled at the sight of his satisfied smile. Like a cat catching a mouse, all he had left to do was play with his food before he devoured every last morsel.

CHAPTER SEVENTEEN

Parish, Colorado, was a perfect little town out of place and time with the rest of the Front Range. Nestled against the Rocky Mountains, twenty minutes north of Fort Collins, it was postcard perfect. The mountains offered a cyan backdrop to the picturesque little town during the summer and a brilliant cascade of ambers and golds during the upcoming autumn. It was a small town with one church and a tiny post office. Main Street was lined on either side with giant elm trees that had grown together to form a canopy of branches and leaves. White picket fences and colorful gardens bordered the quaint streets.

Christopher was glad to be home. His shop was right on Main Street, and he parked his car in front. It had been a long day, but the entertainment had been worth it. Unlike Fort Collins, there was no push toward modernization here. Also, everyone here knew each other. It was hard to keep a secret in such a small town, so he had decided a long time ago that he would have to be particular about what secrets were worth keeping. In the end, business matters won out, and he would have to put his sexuality on display.

He'd struggled with his sexuality for most of his life until his father died. He buried his father, along with his father's judgment, his rules, and the hate he had bestowed on Christopher because his son's sexuality didn't match what he thought constituted that of a man. It was more likely that he was embarrassed to be judged by standards he didn't understand, or maybe that he was just a horrible, frightened little man. After that, he'd never actively tried to hide the fact that he was a gay man, but he didn't go around pointing it out either. He managed to find himself the occasional lover every now and again and, for the most part, didn't feel so alone. Well, that's what he kept telling himself.

The hot sun beat down against the back of his neck as he unlocked the door to his shop. He loved his shop. The large picture windows and rustic trim showcased his public collection of rare books and vintage trinkets. The oak sign swinging above the door to his shop had been lacquered in black and the lettering carved in relief, *Blackwood's Attic: Rare Books & Unique Collectibles*, was painted in gold. *It is all very classy, much like me*, he thought.

He opened the glass-fronted door, and the silver bell above the door jingled merrily. The late summer heat in Colorado was oppressive, so he left the front door propped open with a brass doorstop in the shape of a rabbit. The shop was warm, and he desperately needed a glass of iced tea. His shop wasn't filled with random junk gathered from local flea markets and garage sales; rather, it was a curated collection. The folks in town often saved their earnings to buy items from his shop. Books and paintings were kept near the back of the public space of his shop to protect them from the damaging effects of the sun, while smaller curios were in locked cabinets or displayed in the shop windows.

The glass display case he used as a cashier's desk was placed near the door to his office. He wasn't ready to get to work just yet and instead walked towards the back of the shop where a staircase led up to his little apartment. The short corridor between the shop and the stairs was decorated with a few pieces of artwork and a single unadorned door leading to the basement. He paused briefly at the door with a sigh. The only hint that something important was tucked away behind that door was the robust lock on it, but most people didn't notice little details like that. They were too busy only looking for the things they wanted. People were like that, greedy and self-centered. They just lied about it all the time. The rich donated their money to charities and claimed the benevolent act made them feel like they contributed to the prosperity of society, when in fact, it was merely a way to cheat the government out of some taxes. Middle-class folks donated their time because they hadn't quite learned the tax benefits of donating money, but they too claimed that they did it all to make the world a better place.

Christopher differed from them because he didn't lie about his intentions. He understood that society would not be made better just because of his paltry donations. Compassion didn't make the world better, and if he'd had enough drink in him, he could probably convince someone that donating time or money actually harmed society rather than promoting social prosperity.

Christopher sighed. He'd much rather pour himself a glass of wine and spend the evening in his vault, which was what he called the basement. He kept significant items in his collection here, the items that the citizens of Parish would be appalled by, at least publicly, but he knew better. Humans were curious creatures and were drawn to the macabre. He placed his palm on the door and smiled. Later, he promised himself, when the day was done, he would come and visit. For now, though, he needed to get back to work. But first, tea. Nothing good could come from trying to get himself moving again without a cup of tea first.

He let his hand drift away from the door to his vault and walked down to the end of the corridor, up the stairs, and through the door of his tidy apartment above the shop. His apartments were a curated mix of old and new, much like the items in his vault. The wood floors were rustic, but the appliances were top of the line. The furniture was old-fashioned but covered in modern fabrics, and the art on the wall was moody and secretive, just like himself. He turned on the electric kettle and stared out the little window in his kitchen while he waited for the water to boil.

Something was worrying him. It wasn't like him to worry. Christopher was a planner. He had contingencies for everything. It was, of course, how he'd managed to create his dark little empire, but this latest project was something new. Working with Verity was a unique experience. Where he would normally have to bully and threaten his usual clients, Verity was a calm, unflappable buoy amid a storm of idiots. He assumed that she'd been manipulating the circumstances lately. He didn't care about that except that it meant she was just as devious as he was. He understood people willing to do anything to get what they want. If she was like him, then he could easily map out his next steps to ensure their deal ended in his favor.

What he saw last night rattled him just a little. No, it hadn't been the grisly death of Richard Belker. That beautiful man had earned his sticky end. It wasn't that insufferable detective, Karen Parson, either. Christopher had tangled with her before, and she was exactly what she seemed. She was a woman devoted to catching bad guys. She lived her life in black and white. To that dour woman, there was nothing in the gray space where everyone else lived their lives.

The kettle boiled away happily, the switch clicking off, startling Christopher out of his thoughts. He poured the boiling water over a bag of tea in his favorite cup and let it steep for a few minutes. He realized his faith had been shaken, his faith in Verity. When he'd seen just how shattered Verity had been after that bloody ordeal, a kernel of doubt had planted itself in the back of his mind. Was she as strong as he'd first imagined her to be, or was she simply like every other person? Christopher sighed. He would have to make a contingency plan for that, too, he supposed. He brought the cup to his lips. As the soothing liquid warmed him, his nerves settled, and his brain formulated a new plan to ensure that he got what he wanted in the end. He smiled with satisfaction at his brilliant plan.

The soft tinkling of a bell made it to his ears, and he realized he had a customer. He took the cup of tea with him as he made his way back downstairs and into the shop front where he greeted one of his regulars. By the time he had finished helping the vulgar busybody, Edith Knoxburough, in finding a gift for her daughter-in-law, he'd formulated the rudimentary elements of his new plan to ensure that Verity Georgeson would follow through with their arrangement. There were just a few items he needed to follow up on.

Christopher stepped around the glass display case he used for a cashier's desk and through the door into his office. If he needed to talk with a client in private, this was where they could sequester themselves. The wood-paneled room with old, creaky wood flooring held a vintage filing cabinet along one wall, and a few of his favorite paintings, those that he was able to display, were hung on the walls. The richly stained partner desk sat in the center of the room with a few chairs for his clients, and in the corner was a ridiculously expensive leather work chair from Chesterfields in London for him to work in. The phone rang, and as much as Christopher wanted to continue traveling through his thoughts, business called, quite literally. He picked up the receiver on the desk phone.

"Blackwood's Attic, how can I help you?"

"Blackwood," the slimy voice on the other end of the line slithered. Ah, Carlton West. Not his favorite client, but a rich one.

"Carlton, it's been a while. How can I relieve you of your money today?"

"I'm bored with my collection," Carlton said. He had the kind of voice that made Blackwood want to take a shower. "Looking for something new."

"And what did you have in mind?"

"If I knew that, I wouldn't be calling you, would I?" Carlton snarled.

Christopher despised the man and his undeniable lack of culture and manners. All Carlton knew was that he wanted things no one else had. He relished his monopoly on his collection. Christopher knew exactly where this conversation was going to go.

"I see. Were you thinking of something you can display, or something for your other collection?"

"I want something special," Carlton boomed. Christopher pulled the phone away from his ear at the noise. "My collection is full of shiny baubles, they're beautiful and rare, but—"

"But you're looking for something a little darker," Christopher offered. For a moment, there was nothing but silence. He wondered if he'd lost his touch, but his doubt was only momentary.

"Yes," Carlton said eventually, and Christopher smiled.

"You're in luck. I'm working on an acquisition that may be perfect, just what you're looking for."

"Yeah, what is it?" his client barked.

Christopher leaned back in the plush leather of his chair. His eyes closed, and a faint smile touched the edges of his mouth. He wanted to tell the story the right way, but he knew Carlton wasn't sophisticated enough to enjoy the tale as it should be told. All Carlton would care about was the innate value of what he was purchasing. The only downside of offering Verity's little box to Carlton was that he wouldn't be able to keep it for himself, but he knew Carlton would pay handsomely if Christopher could verify the provenance.

"There's a little vintage box I've been trying to acquire. I've just been working through the final details of the deal with its current owner, but it would be perfect for your collection."

"A box? What sort of bullshit are you trying to pull on me, Blackwood?" Carlton bellowed. Christopher much preferred working with the likes of Verity Georgeson than the bullish Carlton, but sometimes money was money.

"I assure you, Carlton, the history of this particular acquisition is suitably macabre for what you are looking for."

"I've got a lost Monet in my basement and a diamond that would put the Hope to shame sitting in my safe, so this box of yours better be something fucking special."

There was nothing worse than a collector who bragged. Christopher had a feeling he would regret selling Carlton the little treasure, but he was a businessman, and business was business.

"I'll email you a few things. Take a look and get back to me. I'm sure you'll want it."

"I'd hate to have to look for another Blackwood."

"I shall talk to you later," Christopher said with as much confidence as he could muster. With a click, the other line went dead. A few manners went a long way, but manners were becoming something as rare as the items he collected.

He sighed again. There was nothing he could do to change Carlton, but he could do something to change Carlton's mind. He hung up the phone and opened his laptop. Twenty minutes later, he clicked the send button on an email to Carlton. A collection of newspaper articles from the 1920s, as well as a few autopsy reports from the same time, would surely tempt Carlton's interest. If not, well then, there was just no accounting for bad taste.

Chapter Eighteen

Mary's house was empty. Not empty like someone had just moved out, but empty and haunted. All her furniture was still where it ought to be. All the art hanging on the walls was familiar yet empty. Geoff's presence was so large that it would fill any space. He may have been on the portly side, but he was passionate and energetic. All that passion and energy had faded away at the moment of his death. Now, Mary was left with the empty shell of their life together.

Anita stood at her side, and Mary wondered if her friend could feel the emptiness too. She was afraid to speak too loudly in her own home, as though her voice would echo back to her. She would never hear Geoff's boisterous laugh again; neither would she hear his gruff whisperings in her ear or feel him in her arms. Mary had never thought the absence of everything could carry weight, but here she was, being crushed by emptiness.

She desperately needed something to take her mind off her loneliness and she was glad to have Anita with her, but what could her friend do to alleviate this ache she felt? She would be drowning in her own sorrow. Fingers intertwined with her own. She looked at her best friend and saw her misery reflected back at her, like a mirror in a horrific house of fun at a carnival. The two women held each other's gaze long enough to reinforce their bond. They would stick together through this, but Mary couldn't help but think that they were now bonded through more than just friendship. They were both widows now, tangled together in loneliness and horror.

"Mary?" Anita asked, practically in a whisper.

"Hm?"

"What's going on?"

Mary was still stuck in her sad thoughts, but the question caught her off guard and pulled her back to the present.

"What do you mean?"

"I mean, a week ago, life was perfectly normal. We should be at a cocktail party together or planning for a fundraiser. Instead"—Anita threw her free hand in the air, exasperated—"look at us." Mary knew what her friend was feeling. Life had gone from normal to bizarre and twisted. "How did this happen?"

"I don't know, but I mean to." Mary realized that her opportunity to let her grief swallow her up had passed. Regardless of how crushed she was, her friend needed her. She straightened her spine, stuck out her chin, and gave her friend a wicked smile that promised everything. "I know that you and I can figure out what our husbands had gotten themselves into, but we're not going to figure it out on no sleep."

The hollow look on Anita's face made her realize how exhausted they both were. They had spent the night at the police station, and it wasn't restful. The night had been full of questions and fear and horror. They needed to be rested if they were going to make any headway. "I'll tell you what. We should both take a little nap. When we get up, I'll brew us a strong pot of coffee and we'll see what we know," Mary declared. Anita gave her a weak smile but nodded her acquiescence.

"I'll admit that I could use some shut-eye."

"Good. Then it's settled. Go on, take the guest room." Mary kissed the top of her friend's head and sent her off, the slow shuffling feet against the plush carpet the only sound in the empty house.

Mary decided she should probably take her own advice and lay down for a little bit. But for two hours, she just lay there, staring up at her ceiling. Sleep would not come even though exhaustion overwhelmed her. The grief and anger she'd been carrying around with her days made her whole body ache, yet sleep would not come. She couldn't recall when she last slept. That wasn't good. A therapist would surely have something dire to say about that.

Well, if she wasn't going to sleep, then she might as well put herself to some use. Mary slipped her bare feet into her fuzzy slippers. She looked down at her feet and blurted a harsh laugh. She looked ridiculous. The contrast between her rumpled pantsuit and her fuzzy slippers was not for the faint of heart, but she didn't care.

Mary made her way downstairs, taking care to be as quiet as possible. She didn't want to wake Anita. Her friend had been through her traumatic shock, and at least one of them should get some rest. Well, that was the plan, but when she shuffled into the kitchen, Anita was already there, pouring two cups of coffee.

"Hi," Anita said sheepishly.

"Hi," Mary returned with a sigh. "Couldn't sleep either?"

"No. My mind was too busy thinking about everything that's happened. And every time I closed my eyes, I saw Richard."

"I know." Mary wrapped her arms around her friend. "I know."

"I miss him. I miss him so much. He wasn't perfect, but he was mine and I was his." Anita sniffled into Mary's ear. "What am I supposed to do without him, Mary?"

"I can't make that decision, love. You have to do that on your own."

"Okay."

"But I'll be here for you the whole time."

"Thanks," Anita said. Mary wrapped her hands around her friend's face and took a good look at her. Dark circles were framing her bloodshot eyes.

"Look at us. What a pair we make."

"Ugh, I know," Anita said, slightly disgruntled as she wiped away the fresh tears trickling down her cheeks. "While I was lying there, I was thinking about everything going on." Mary knew the feeling. The first few days after Geoff had died, she'd done anything she could to keep from thinking of him. "When I was being questioned by that detective, she showed me a photo."

"I hope it was better than the photo she showed me." Mary scoffed, thinking of the photo of her husband's hands on Verity Georgeson. Anita's face lit up, and Mary was glad to see some color return to her face. Anita handed her a mug of coffee before taking a seat at the counter. The familiar scent of roasted beans infiltrated every pore of her aching body.

"No! I mean, yes, it was better," Anita blurted out. "Well, actually, I don't know if it was better. It was just strange. The longer I think about it, the more I think it was something important."

Mary joined her at the counter. As soon as the hot liquid slid down her throat, she was instantly fortified. The tension she was carrying melted just a bit. She leaned in to listen to what Anita had to say.

"I don't want to even think about why Richard was at her house. I can't let myself think about that yet, but that detective woman said that the picture had been in his pocket. I think he pocketed it because it was important, and I'm starting to think that it might be our first real clue about what is going on."

"How so?" Mary asked.

"You wouldn't believe me. I wouldn't have believed it if I hadn't seen it with my own eyes. It was a photo of two women. They looked related, and get this, one of them was Verity Georgeson."

"Well, she's hardly difficult to miss."

"You don't understand. It wasn't Verity like we'd seen her. She looked ordinary."

"Ordinary?"

"Yeah, she had brown hair, cut short," Anita said, waving her hand around her chin to indicate the length. "She wasn't wearing much makeup, no fancy clothes, just jeans, and a T-shirt. Detective Parson said she has a daughter."

"I wish I could have seen that."

"I know, but apparently that Detective Parson had learned since the last time she'd seen you. She wouldn't let me take a copy, and she sure as hell wasn't about to leave me alone with it," Anita said. Mary had the dignity to at least look a little guilty before Anita just blazed on with her story. "The thing that was different this time, though, was that it wasn't a photocopy." At that, Mary perked up. She had an idea where this was going. "I got a look at the back of the photo."

Mary thought about the photos in her own house. In an age of social media and digital storage, it was something of significance that someone would have an actual print. "All right, I'll take the bait."

"It said, 'Louise and Jenna," Anita said with a smile. She leaned back in her chair with a satisfied Cheshire grin spread across her youthful face.

"Wait a minute. I thought you said it was a photo of Verity Georgeson?"

"It is."

"Then what does . . ." But Mary's voice trailed off as she realized Anita's point. "Oh!" Mary thought about the enigmatic Verity Georgeson. Her perfectly coiffed hair, her vintage wardrobe, and the mystery around her were all pieces of this deadly puzzle. Mary wondered how much of Verity was just for show. It wasn't much to go on, but it was something. "We may not be able to see the whole picture, but I know that Georgeson woman is involved, well obviously now, but she was involved earlier too. I'm certain of it."

"I can't help but agree with you, Mary, but what do we do with this?" Anita asked.

Mary wasn't sure where this trail would end, but she knew where to start. The corners of her lips tugged upwards.

"I think it's time we do a little research of our own."

"Where do we start?" Anita asked.

"Why don't I take Verity and you take those other two names, and let's see what the internet can find for us," Mary declared. She had a plan, a mission, a distraction from the grief and overwhelming despair that constantly threatened to overtake her.

However, an hour later, Mary leaned back in her chair and rubbed at the ache forming in her temples. "I've never been so frustrated." She sighed. "Verity is a phantom."

"What do you mean?" Anita asked, walking into the room.

"I can't find anything about her more than five years old."

"That can't be right."

"That's what I'm saying. No one just appears like that out of thin air, with no history," Mary said, but a funny sort of look rose on Anita's face. "What?"

"What?" Anita echoed.

"I asked you first."

"I was just thinking . . . What if we're looking in the wrong place?"

"How so?"

"What if Verity wasn't always Verity? What if she used to be someone else?"

"Like she changed her identity?"

"I know it sounds ridiculous and two days ago, I don't think I would've thought about it, but it kind of makes sense now. What if something truly terrible happened to her in the past and she wanted a fresh start?" Anita proposed.

Mary understood. She would have loved to run away and be someone else, someone who wasn't a widow, someone who didn't carry around this crushing grief. But grief didn't go away just because a person wanted to have a different life. She could change her hair and her clothes, but she couldn't rid of painful memories. Those would always be a part of her. Those memories made her who she was.

Mary wasn't certain she liked who she was becoming without Geoff. Maybe it was the same for Verity. Maybe that was the whole point of this crazy charade. What if Verity didn't like who she'd become and had decided to change everything about herself? But this world they lived in wasn't very good at forgetting. Everything about everything was stored on the internet for perpetuity. It would be impossible to run away completely.

"That's all well and good, but I don't care how much you try to erase your past; there's always something that can come back and haunt you," Mary argued.

"Exactly, Mary. The photo! Richard found that photo, and the detective seemed to think it was important. What if that photo is proof of her other life, her old life?"

"How do we find out? We don't even have a last name. Even the internet is going to have trouble with that search."

Anita lowered her gaze before her face lit up. "Verity's smart, or at least that's my impression of her. I have to think that Verity is smart enough to keep herself off social media, but what about the other woman?"

"What other woman?"

"The photo said, 'Louise and Jenna.' I don't know which one is which, but one of them is bound to have a social media presence."

Mary thought about it and recognized that her friend might be onto something. A half-hour later, they had their next tantalizing piece of the mystery and were determined to confront it. All Mary wanted was answers to her questions, but all she seemed to find were more questions. This time, the mystery bore the name Jenna Jones.

CHAPTER NINETEEN

The drive to find this mysterious Ms. Jones was quiet. Anita normally cranked up the radio and belted out along with her favorite songs, but today, she kept the radio turned off. She and Mary both rode in silence as she followed the directions through one of the older neighborhoods in town. This particular neighborhood was full of small starter homes and tiny duplexes, but it had been surrounded by larger, nicer homes.

Anita drove slowly, staring at house numbers until she found the one they had been looking for. The small ranch-style home was old but loved. The lush green lawn was surrounded by flowers. A little concrete porch extended in either direction at the front door, and there was even a cute little bistro set with red cushions where Anita could just imagine herself sitting while drinking some afternoon iced tea or a morning cup of coffee.

Parked in the single-car driveway was an old Subaru, used but not abused. When she had searched for directions to this place, she had done a quick reverse address search as well. She was trying to figure out if anyone else lived here since they didn't know how old this woman was or what they could be walking into. The search had provided a list of people associated with the address, many of which Anita was sure were previous tenants. The one thing that did catch her attention though was that, along with Jenna, two other people with the same last name were associated with the property. A Rourke and Louise Jones had also been listed on the property.

Anita parked the car across the street, and the two friends watched the little house for a while. It might not be grand or glamorous or even posh, but the little house was loved and cared for. She couldn't say exactly how long they sat there watching, but they were stirred into action when the shadow of a figure walked past the white lace curtains hanging in the front window.

Anita and Mary stepped out of the car. Neither of them knew what to expect, but Anita wasn't getting any less nervous by continuing to stand there like an idiot. She hooked her arm through Mary's, and together, they crossed the street devoid of any traffic, catching the sound of children laughing nearby and an ambulance off in the distance. As they approached the house, a large black truck drove slowly around the corner, cautious of the children playing in the street, and parked curbside a few houses down.

The path to the front door was paved in bricks that appeared to be dated back to the original construction of the house. By Anita's guess, thanks to paying attention to her architect husband, she estimated it had been built sometime in the sixties. On the other hand, the brick-paved walkway had been repaired over the years, as was evident by the occasionally mismatched pavers and the fresh mortar spackled into the cracks.

They approached the front door, and Anita found herself standing next to the little bistro set. She couldn't help but notice a paperback book lying open face-down on the iron filigree table, its covers flapping in the gentle breeze. She raised her closed fist to knock and was startled when the door opened before she made contact. The young woman still holding on to the door appeared just as startled as they were, since her vivid green eyes widened and her red-lipped mouth had formed a perfect "O." The woman was probably still in her early twenties. Her skin was tan and perfect, her naturally blonde hair piled high on her head in a messy bun.

Anita resisted the temptation for her jaw to fall open. The shape of this woman's mouth, the elegant arch of her manicured eyebrows, and even the expression of startled curiosity were all exact matches to Verity. Whatever it was they'd been expecting, this was certainly not it. She hadn't expected to be confronted by Verity's daughter. She hadn't actually thought that Verity was the kind of woman to have a child. Where did raising a family fit in that couture life of hers? Anita, Mary, and Jenna all stood there at the door, momentarily speechless until they all apologized over each other.

"I am so sorry," Anita said. "We didn't mean to startle you."

"Oh no, I'm sorry, I had no idea you were there," Jenna replied with a warm smile that was identical to Verity's. "I just realized I left my book out here and was coming to get it." Jenna stepped around Anita and grabbed the book she'd seen on the table. "Honestly, I'm lucky you didn't knock on my forehead."

Jenna stepped aside and, with a subtle flick of her hand, welcomed Anita and Mary into her little home. Mary gave

Anita a curious look as they entered. Once inside, Jenna turned to Anita. "What can I do for you?"

Anita faltered. She hadn't thought this far ahead. She'd thought it was going to take creative thinking and plenty of lies to get this far, but this young woman was so open and friendly.

"We're acquaintances with your mother," Anita said somewhat truthfully, trying to think of any believable lie. Jenna's face lit up in that beautiful smile that instantly reminded Anita of Verity.

"Oh, that's great!" Jenna exclaimed. "I'm sure she's got you working on some crazy project." Anita wondered what that could mean. Could it be that her daughter, living this perfectly ordinary life, knew exactly what her mother was up to?

Jenna held out her hand for a shake. "I'm Jenna, by the way, but I guess you already knew that." She laughed.

"Hi, Jenna. I'm Anita Belker, and this is my friend Mary."

"Hello," Jenna said. Anita thought she noticed a flicker of recognition in her eyes, but it faded as quickly as it had arrived. "What can I do for you?"

Anita was amazed by the openness of this young woman. She looked around and couldn't find any of the eccentricities she'd been expecting from the daughter of Verity Georgeson.

"We were just going to ask you the same thing," Mary offered. "Things have been getting a little out of hand lately, and she wanted us to check on you and make sure you were all right."

"That's super sweet," Jenna said. "I miss my mom so much sometimes, but I know that she's always got some crazy big projects going on. Come on. Why don't we sit down and have some iced tea?"

Anita and Mary followed her to the tiny kitchen at the back of the house. Everything about it was old, but it had a do-it-yourself feel about the place that made it pleasant. Anita and Mary sat down at the kitchen table while Jenna poured three glasses of fresh iced tea with lemon wedges. Jenna pushed aside a laptop and stack of textbooks so that they wouldn't be in the way and sat next to the ladies.

"What are you going to school for?" Mary asked.

"Architectural design," Jenna said, and both friends couldn't help but see the connection.

"That's adventurous," Mary said. "You don't hear about many women in the industry."

"I know. That's part of the reason I chose it, but mostly I've always just loved architecture."

"My husband is an architect," Anita said. "Was an architect."

This time, when the light of recognition returned to the young woman's face, she spoke up. "Richard Belker?"

"That's him."

"I've seen his work," Jenna said. "I like to follow the careers of local architects." She bounced up from the table and rummaged around in a nearby tidy pile of books, looking for something in particular. When she returned to the table, she held an oversized coffee-table book.

Anita recognized it immediately. Richard had been so proud of himself for having one of his designs showcased in the book celebrating local architecture. Jenna pushed the book across the table, and Anita took it graciously. She knew just which page was Richard's and turned to it. She noticed that another nearby page had been bookmarked, and when she turned to that page, she saw a glossy photo of Geoff Otto staring back at her.

"Did you ever have a chance to meet him?" Jenna asked. Anita and Mary both nodded. Anita realized the girl didn't seem to know of Richard's death. It would surely make the local news soon.

"Geoff and my mom were good friends," Jenna added sadly. "It's broken her heart to lose him."

"How long had they known each other?"

"Oh my gosh," Jenna started with a brightly lit face, "since I was seven, or so. We went on one of those historic home tours, and Geoff was there, talking about one of the houses and all the work that went into preserving a historic home. I guess you could say they started off as pen pals after that."

Anita didn't sense any deception from the girl, but she also couldn't reckon how Verity and Geoff could have known each other for so long without Mary knowing about it. She could feel Mary's growing frustration as she sat next to her.

Something didn't fit. Anita's thoughts drifted to everything going on, and she felt so lost. A moment of silence lingered before Jenna spoke up again. "I hope you don't mind me asking, but you both look like you could use a friend."

Anita leaned back in her seat, taken aback by Jenna's intuitiveness. "Who did you lose?" the young woman asked, before checking herself. "I'm so sorry. I don't mean to pry. I understand not wanting to talk about it if you don't want to."

"Thanks," Anita said. "What about you?"

"My dad died a few years back."

"I'm so sorry," Mary said. She could see the shadow of emotion flicker across the girl's youthful face.

"Don't be," Jenna said. "It was one of those mixed blessings."

"How so?" Mary asked.

Jenna seemed lost in her own thoughts and memories for a moment before replying. "Well, he was a very hard man to be around."

"In what way?" Anita asked.

"Well . . ." Jenna hesitated. "He had a horrible temper. Don't get me wrong, I loved my dad, but he could be cruel. Not to me, mind you. He loved me, I never doubted that, but he was a jealous and angry man, and he took it out on Mom. He would put her down, make her feel bad for wanting things he didn't want, and didn't let her go out and do anything unless it was his idea."

"Doesn't sound fun at all."

"It wasn't. Mom was always a tough lady, but he would lash out sometimes, and . . . Well, the marks were never where anyone would see. She believes in promises being kept, and she would have never left him unless she thought I was in danger. My mom started to get real depressed. Things got pretty bad. Daddy didn't even seem to notice that anything was really wrong. Mom just went along from day to day, she stopped daydreaming about stuff, which doesn't sound like much, but she and I used to sit for hours when I was little and talk about the things we wanted to do, to have, to experience. She went from being this free spirit sort of woman, always working on something creative, to someone who was just surviving from day to day."

"That sounds terrible." Anita could almost imagine herself in that life. Richard wasn't what one would call a kind man, but when he doted on her, she couldn't help but feel special.

She wondered what Verity was like then. "How did you discover your interest in architecture with all of that going on with your parents?" Anita asked.

"I've got my mom to thank for that," Jenna said with a smile. "When I was little and she wanted to get us out of the house, we would go for long drives through the city just looking at all the different kinds of architecture: the Queen Anne Victorians, the Tudors, and all the great buildings downtown. We would daydream about what type of house we could have and how we'd decorate it. Those are some of my favorite memories I have with her."

"That sounds really lovely," Anita said dreamily.

"It was. I wish either of us had time for that kind of stuff still, but it's almost impossible to get our schedules in sync these days." Anita could just imagine Jenna and her mom together. They would certainly be a force of nature unto themselves. "But no matter how much I miss having more time with her, I wouldn't trade what we have for anything."

Jenna got up and pulled the pitcher of tea from the fridge and refilled their glasses. Anita had lost all sense of time since she'd been so warmly welcomed by this amazing young woman. She was reminded of a younger version of herself, before she had lost identity to her own emotionally abusive husband.

"Jenna, can I ask you a personal question?" Anita bravely asked.

The younger woman sat back down and looked at her directly. "Sure."

"How did your dad die?"

Mary stiffened beside her. She was worried that this was pushing the limits of her hostess's patience, but to her surprise, Jenna answered willingly.

"He died of arsenic poisoning," Jenna answered solemnly.

"Oh my gosh!" they declared in unison. There was no way that was just a coincidence.

"That was a really hard time for Mom," Jenna said, and her expression turned sad.

"I can't even imagine," Anita said, but next to her, Mary's face turned red with anger.

"There was a huge investigation, you know. The police thought she'd murdered him."

"That must have been terrifying for you."

"It was. They wouldn't let us be together until all the charges were cleared. I had to stay with my grandmother through the whole investigation since I wasn't quite old enough to be on my own."

"I guess the police obviously cleared her of the charges, but what happened? How did he get poisoned, by arsenic of all things?"

"The police were furious. They couldn't find any of the evidence they needed to lock Mom up. I remembered having to talk to the judge at the hearing. Sometimes, I still get mad about it. My mom is the strongest woman I know. She's fierce, but she's no murderer. She's gentle and loving."

Anita was starting to think Jenna's love and admiration for her mother blinded her to some pretty obvious flaws of her mother. The police were probably right, after all. Jenna was flushed and excited. She was young and enthusiastic and had probably been used to keeping her strong ideas. This outburst seemed cathartic for her.

"I'm glad that she's got women like you to help her out," Jenna added.

"I am too," Anita said softly, not knowing what else to say. She was a little horrified by what she had learned. Anita thought about Mary and what she'd said about Geoff's death. The number of dead husbands piling up around Verity was looking more than a little suspicious. Anita's stomach turned. What had they gotten themselves into?

Anita could see Mary's jaw clench, so before Mary would give away their true motive in being there, Anita stood up and loudly admired the painted brick fireplace. Jenna got out of her seat and followed her. Arranged neatly along the mantle was a collection of photos. One of the photos looked to be of Jenna and her friends. Another was of Jenna and an older man that Anita suspected was her father. Then again, there was another photo of Jenna with a different man, still much older than her. Anita stared at the photo and realized there was something familiar about the man. He looked familiar, not like she knew him, but more like someone she'd seen recently. Then it hit her. The man in the photo was the same man she'd seen Verity with last night.

"That's Henry," Jenna said from over Anita's shoulder, "my mom's boyfriend." Jenna had a sweet look on her face as she stared down at the photo in Anita's hands.

Anita shook her head, trying to clear her thoughts, and switched her gaze to the last photo on the mantle, the one in the center of the collection of photos, in a place of prominence. It was a photo of Jenna and her mother. Anita picked up the photo tucked into a silver frame. The two women were sharing a happy moment, with their heads pressed in on each other and warm, grateful smiles spread on both their faces. The women's eyes were closed, and their arms were wrapped around each other tightly. It was enough to warm any heart, but it was a stark contrast to the fact that these two could very well be black widows.

"She's beautiful, isn't she?" Jenna asked over Anita's shoulder.

"Yes. She really is," Anita said, trying to stifle the shaking in her voice. Jenna stared down at the photo in Anita's hands, and Anita recognized the look of longing.

"You really do miss her, don't you?" Anita asked.

Jenna nodded with a sad smile on her lips. "But I remind myself that it's all for a great reason." Jenna took the photo and returned it to its place on the mantel. "Henry took this photo. He wants to marry her, but I don't think Mom will ever marry again."

"Maybe she'll reconsider after everything is all said and done."

"Maybe, I suppose. Someday, her crazy projects will be done, and we can settle down together. We agreed ages ago that the only real companionship we needed was each other. We're going to grow old together. Two old bitties with a house full of cats. Daddy hated cats, you see."

Anita couldn't erase the thought from her mind that Verity was probably a murderer. Was her daughter a victim or a willing participant?

"We really should be going," Mary said finally.

"So soon?" Jenna said. "I don't get to be around my mom's friends that much, and I want to hear all about what's going on."

"I'm sure she'll fill you in on everything as soon as things have settled down." Anita hoped she sounded authentic.

"You're right," Jenna said. "Thank you, though, for stopping by. I didn't realize how much I needed this."

"You're very welcome," Anita said.

With that, Jenna led the two women to the front. Before the door closed behind them, Anita noticed Jenna staring longingly at the photos on her mantle. Mary and Anita stood there on the cute front porch, struck by all the contrasts of late.

Anita and Mary made their way back to the car, not speaking. Anita wondered if Mary was drowning in as many thoughts of anger, conspiracy, and fear as she was.

CHAPTER TWENTY

Verity emerged from the police station. The late afternoon sun was stifling after spending so much time in the controlled environment of the station. She was drawn and spent. Every ounce of energy had been drained away. Verity had been in the same clothes for more than a day, and Richard's blood had dried a dark, crusty brown. The once elegant fabric was stiff and scratched against her skin. Verity wanted nothing more than to soak in a hot bath and drink an entire bottle of wine.

Since the police had brought her here, she didn't have her car to drive home. She pulled out her phone to call a ride home through a rideshare app, but a familiar pair of calloused hands gently wrapped around her own. Her eyes rose and met Henry's. His eyes said everything that needed to be said. She gave him a halfhearted smile, and he pulled her into his arms, wrapping himself around her.

Verity melted into him, shuddering with relief. He was, after all was said and done, a devoted man. She loved his devotion, his strength, his earthy natural scent. It was like an exquisite cologne to her senses, mixing with the familiar scent of his shampoo. He was predictable, too, but that wasn't always a bad thing. She didn't know how long the two of them stood there, but it didn't matter. Uniformed officers came and went, yet the two of them ignored the world. For this moment, everything was still and quiet, a pleasant counter to the previous night's bloody mess.

Henry released her eventually and held her out at arm's length, his face crumpling at the sight of her. She hadn't checked herself in a mirror, but she surely must have offered a frightening sight. His rough hands slid down her arms, and she relished the sensation of his touch. It reminded her of her old life, sometimes. Henry brought her hands to his lips and kissed them, but as his lips touched her hands, she noticed his brows furrowing. He turned her hands over. There for them both to see were the black smudged remnants of having been fingerprinted.

"I hate what you're going through," he said softly.

Verity reached up and cupped his face in one of her hands and smiled sadly. "I know you do, but there's nothing to do but to cooperate. It's nothing I haven't been through before."

"That's just it, V. Doesn't that detective realize what she's putting you through?"

"I'm sure she's acutely aware of what she's doing, Henry." Which was the truth. She'd spent enough time sequestered with Detective Parson to know that the woman understood the similarities between what was going on now and what had happened in Verity's past. She could feel the detective pulling on those strings, trying to push her into making a mistake, pushing her to condemn herself, but Verity was playing a long game and she knew better than to let the detective paint her into a corner. She wasn't willing to let this mess ruin her carefully laid plans. She was innocent; Verity just needed to remain vigilant and patient for a little while longer.

"I don't like it."

"I know, but if I make a fuss or do anything other than cooperate, she could take a dislike to me, and we both know how that will go."

"What can I do?"

"Just stay out of her way and don't go doing anything heroic," Verity said. She rose onto her tiptoes and kissed him softly. "The rest will take care of itself."

Henry looked at her with a wounded expression but nodded. "Will you at least let me take you home?"

"Absolutely." And with that, they rode home together, their fingers interlaced between them resting on the console in his black truck. Neither of them said a word. Words weren't needed when they were comfortable in each other's company. Verity was rather grateful for the silence. She needed time to think, and she knew that Henry's devotion to her would mean that he would be hovering for the next few days. She adored how much he cared for her, and she cared for him too, just not in the way he was probably expecting.

When they arrived at Verity's place, she stepped across the threshold of the front door into her home and wanted nothing more than to melt in a hot bath, but the reality of what she'd been through was impossible to ignore. Traces of last night's horror show were littered everywhere. Dusty patches remained on her furniture and doorways from where the police had searched for fingerprints, a single blue shoe bootie was leftover from the investigation, and the smell of antiseptic still lingered from the EMT's efforts to save a dead man. Amongst all the signs of her home being intruded upon, there was still one familiar constant. Dorian sauntered over to her from wherever he'd been lurking and wove his black body through her legs in lazy figure eights. His strong purr instantly calmed her frayed nerves.

"Hello, Dorian." She bent down and gently rubbed the space between his ears, making sure not to give him too much attention. She always had to respect the superior intelligence and shifting moods of the cat. "I missed you too." Henry followed Verity inside, and Dorian stiffened at his arrival. "Don't be mean."

"One of these days, cat," Henry teased, "we're going to have a reckoning."

"Cute."

"That's me," Henry said, kissing her on the forehead. "How about I run you a bath?"

"You're a saint."

The master bath in Verity's house was only limited by the architectural restraints of the time in which her home was built. So, it wasn't an en-suite; rather, it was down the hall from her bedroom. While it might have taken her a few extra steps to get there, the luxury with which it was decorated made up for that in spades. The classic black and white tile scheme was accented by the exquisitely deep cast-iron soaker tub. The back of the tub rose higher than the rest of the basin. She normally leaned back as she soaked, but today she was in for a special treat. Henry had filled the tub with her favorite additives, lit the pillar candles, and pulled up a small stool she usually kept at her vanity. He was currently perched at the end of her tub, patiently washing her hair. Her knees were pulled, her head tilted back, and if it hadn't been for the ordeal the night before, she would be in absolute heaven. Neither of them spoke, simply enjoying the aromatic space between them. The sensuous milky water swirled around her pale flesh as Henry rinsed her hair, sending sudsy water down her back. When her extravagant bath was done, Henry helped her out of the water and wrapped her up in a fluffy robe.

"You dry off," Henry said, "and I'll get some dinner started." With that, he left the room and Verity was finally alone, if only for a few minutes. There was still plenty to do if she was going to make a success of her arrangement with Christopher Blackwood, but for tonight, at least, maybe she could enjoy some peace. It was a luxury to have Henry cater to her, but if she were honest with herself, she preferred time alone.

She combed out the tangles in her short brown hair, patted serums into her skin, and gently massaged in some moisturizer. Verity took a good look at herself. She liked what she saw. Her straight hair cut at her chin was a soft ashy brown and showed off her slender neck. Green eyes against her pale skin used to be something she hated when she was young, but she'd grown into loving them. She was learning to like who she was becoming. It wasn't until she'd become a widow that she realized how much of the things she wanted out of life she'd pushed away to make her family happy. She was done with that. It was time to take care of herself. She smiled, and her reflection smiled back. Only a little while longer now, and she'd be done with this charade. Soon enough, she'd be able to disappear forever and live a quiet life.

Verity made her way downstairs, and the smell of onions caramelizing greeted her. She didn't know what Henry was concocting, but it smelled delicious. Still in her fluffy robe, she entered the kitchen, settled onto one of the stools, and watched him finish. Before long, he placed a bowl of savory nibbles in front of her along with a glass of wine. It wasn't fine dining, but no Michelin star restaurant could match Henry in love. He sat on the stool next to her, and together, they ate. The clinking forks, the mastication of food, the tap of Henry's beer bottle against the counter, the traffic outside, all of it was a symphony of ordinary life, but Verity's life was far from ordinary.

"I think we might have a problem with Mary Otto and the Belker woman," Henry said after pushing his empty bowl away. Verity took in his haggard appearance. He really did worry about her.

"How so?"

"They paid Jenna a visit today." She gave him a startled look. Henry was blunt, unrefined. There was no deceit about him. "They didn't stay long, but I thought you should know."

She'd already known this. Jenna had texted her while she was waiting for the detective to release her. Jenna was the only thing from her old life that she cared about, cherished.

"Do you think they mean her harm?" she asked.

He shook his head. "No, not intentionally, but if they keep digging, they might get the attention of people we don't want."

He wasn't wrong there, but what he didn't realize was that some of their curiosity was part of her plans. She needed them to be wary of her for the poignancy it would add later, but Henry didn't need to know any of that.

"Will you keep an eye on her for me?"

"Of course. She's a good kid."

"Thanks, Henry," she said.

He leaned in and kissed her deeply. "I would do anything to keep you both safe." His voice caught slightly on the words.

There it was, she thought. *That hint of fear in his voice*. He was afraid to lose her, and she knew it. That was everything she needed to know.

"I know," she said and kissed him back. "I'm exhausted. I think I'll head to bed early."

"Come on, I'll tuck you in," he said with a smile, a sad smile to be fair. Verity let him dress her in her nightgown and put her to bed. Then he lay down next to her, fully dressed, and pulled her in tight against him. His heart beating in his chest was like a metronome of sorts, slowly lulling her weary body to sleep, but her journey to deep sleep was interrupted.

"I'm sorry, V," Henry whispered. The dark room was cast in blue-gray shadows, and the only other sounds in the room were that of the distant traffic coming from one of the busier thoroughfares in town.

"For what?" she mumbled sleepily.

"This is all my fault."

"Don't be ridiculous," she replied in what she thought was a soothing voice, but Henry shifted his body against hers. Silence enveloped her again, and her body grew heavy, falling towards the wonderful descent into sleep.

"I did it, V. I killed them."

A moment dragged on before those words reached into her sleepy mind, deep enough for them to be understood. Could she have misunderstood? Her sleepiness fell away, and her brows knitted together. She turned around to face him. In the dark and the shadows, she could barely make out his features, but she felt the familiar touch of his hands on her body. His muscles were tight with tension, and he trembled slightly.

"What?"

"I killed them."

"You killed whom?"

"All of them, V." His voice was still barely a whisper; secrets like these were dangerous if spoken too loudly. "Geoff Otto . . . Richard Belker . . . and . . ." Sadness stained the melody of his rich voice, but not for the deaths he was confessing, Verity knew, but sadness for the heartache and trouble he had caused her.

"Henry, I don't understand."

"And, and Scott."

"What are you saying, Henry?" The tiredness had escaped her. Had she just heard him confess to killing all of them, including her deceased husband?

"I couldn't stand how they treated you. You deserved better than all of them." His hands tightened around her body. "Scott never appreciated how much you gave up so that he could be happy."

"I don't understand."

"Don't get me started on Geoff Otto, V. He was always putting his sausage fingers on you."

"But, Henry, I needed him."

"No, V. You didn't. You only thought you did. You're the strongest woman I know. You didn't need that pig to get a deal going with Blackwood."

He was rambling. He had knocked down whatever wall was within him that kept this gruesome secret, and now he couldn't seem to stop the tide of confession. "I wish you'd let me get rid of him too," he added coldly.

Her heart was pounding in her chest. Even in her fear of being caught in the embrace of a murderer, points were connecting in her mind.

"The photos they found in Geoff's car, that was you?"

Henry didn't answer right away. "Yes," he finally admitted.

"And Richard?"

"He broke into your house. He was nosing around everything. I'd seen how he looked at you, and I knew that if I gave him any room, he would end up just being like Otto."

"Henry—"

"I couldn't stand any of them treating you so badly. You deserve so much more. You deserve everything.

"Oh, Henry, what have you done?" She was caught in a trap, trapped by Henry's love. Her hands were shaking. What was she supposed to do now?

"I'm so sorry, V. I just couldn't let it all happen."

She reached her hands up to his face, despite the darkness in the room, and hoped desperately that he wouldn't notice her tremors. Her fingertips touched the rivers of tears streaming down his cheeks. He was genuinely sorry. She kissed him tenderly, regardless of the knot of fear cinching her stomach.

"You really do love me."

"More than anything else in the world," he whispered. His voice had grown haggard through the tears. She pulled him in tight against her. She didn't know what else to do. How was she supposed to comfort someone who had killed nearly everyone of any importance in her life?

She could taste fear at the back of her throat. Henry clutched at her like she was a life raft in a turbulent sea of doubt and fear. Was he done killing people for the sake of her safety, or were there other people in her life she needed to worry about?

He had mentioned earlier that Mary and Anita concerned him. Would their snooping into her secrets put them at risk? She couldn't have their blood on her hands either. She needed to do something, but what? This had started out as a plan to finally live a quiet solitary life, but now it had turned dangerous. How was a woman supposed to sleep with a murderer wrapped around her?

Henry had already drifted into a deep sleep in her arms. She guessed the old saying was true enough. Confession was good for the soul even if it was her soul.

Chapter Twenty-One

Verity awoke. The hour was late, and the blue shadows had been chased away by the black of night. She had no idea how long she'd been lying there with Henry in her arms after his terrifying confession before sleep had finally overtaken her. There was a decided difference between thinking that someone was dangerous and having them confess their grizzly sins. How could someone prepare for that? Now her body was intertwined with his, stiff with tension. Verity could feel her weariness deep in her bones, and all she wanted right now was sleep. So what could have woken her up?

A faint blue light momentarily appeared, briefly chasing the blackest of the night away. Then everything was cast back into darkness. A minute later, it reappeared for only a second. Then she realized it was coming from her phone on the nightstand next to her. She twisted around Henry's sleeping body slowly, so as not to wake him, and tapped on the screen. She had a text message. The glow of the phone hurt her eyes, but she read the message anyway and sighed. She supposed that when she dealt with even the most fashionable of criminals, most of the work was done in the shadows. She typed a short message back before beginning the slow process of getting herself untangled from Henry. Verity eventually extricated herself from his arms and slid silently out of bed.

She peered back at him. Henry was a beautiful man. Uncomplicated and doting, he was the exact thing she needed sometimes to counter the chess game that her life had become. She watched him sleep for a few moments, wondering how he could have done such horrible things, before she slipped into her favorite silk robe and matching slippers and padded out of the room to get ready for her unplanned rendezvous with Blackwood.

She went into her bathroom and softly closed the door before crouching down to retrieve what she needed from the bottom drawer of the vanity. She was grateful she had a spare wig; otherwise, she would have had to risk waking Henry to keep up her charade. Verity was fairly certain Blackwood knew more about her than he let on, but there was no need to be careless when she could avoid it. A cursory glance in the bathroom mirror reassured her that she was adequately dressed for the moment. She turned out the bathroom light and made her way downstairs. This was her home, and she didn't need the light to find her way. Ambient light spilled through the stained glass of her front door, casting ominous shadows that reached across the floor and threatened to engulf her. She loved the shadows, and games like this were made for the dark. But she would be a liar if she claimed to not yearn for some days in the light. Soon, she reminded herself, soon.

A band of light from a vehicle's headlights curved through her living room. Verity flicked the curtain aside just enough to see if it was her last-minute guest. It was. She went to the little table in the foyer and opened the drawer, slowly. She didn't need Henry waking up in the middle of this. He was already uncomfortable with the fact that Verity was dealing with Blackwood at all, and after the night's earlier confession, she couldn't be sure that Blackwood wouldn't make it onto Henry's list of sins.

Tucked amongst the other items in the drawer was what she was looking for. The colored light coming from the stained-glass window caught on the metal flask. When she picked up the flask, it sloshed gently. She'd been expecting it to be empty. Verity unscrewed the cap and put her nose to it. The heady scent of bourbon filled her sinuses. She was sorely tempted to take a sip from the flask, but it probably wouldn't do her any favors to drink it now. She poured its contents out into an empty crystal decanter sitting nearby on her bar.

Tucking the now-empty flask in a pocket of her robe, Verity quietly exited her house. She carefully closed the door behind her and padded out to the sidewalk where she found Blackwood leaning against his car, his suit jacket unbuttoned and pushed back by his hands, which were stuffed casually in the pockets of his trousers. He was the picture of patience.

"Ms. Georgeson, pleasure," he said, tipping his matching newsboy cap.

"Evening."

"I apologize for the late notice, but I assumed you wouldn't want this particular business happening in broad daylight."

"Neither would you, I would gather."

"We're of like minds, Ms. Georgeson." He stepped towards her and tilted his head. It was a gentlemanly gesture and out of place in the modern world. It wasn't the first time she wished common courtesies like that still existed. Manners were something that seemed to have gone by the wayside. Now, when people wanted to make an impression, it was by slapping around vulgarity and flesh. There was something to be said about the manners and expectations of the past to ensure a common set of rules to guide society. The young people of the world today were working hard to destroy all rules to reestablish new norms, but the process was ugly and painful. At least when she dealt with Blackwood, she knew the rules she was playing by.

"Do you have it?" he asked.

"I do," she said, pulling the flask from the pocket of her robe, and holding it out to him. He leaned forward, stepped away from his car, and reached for the flask with elegant leather driving gloves. As she placed the flask in his hands, a tingle of worry nagged at the back of her mind. She realized that it was covered not only in Henry's fingerprints, which had been part of her plan, but also her own. Verity wondered if he would use them against her. She hoped not but was worried that it was her first true misstep in working with him.

"Yes, this will do nicely." He turned the object over in his hands, taking his time to examine the flask in the streetlight. Verity watched his expressions change like the tide coming in and washing out again. Curiosity and intrigue fought for dominance, but it was the new twinkle in his eye that worried her the most.

"I'm curious," Verity started. "Is this for your personal collection, or is it for one of your other clients?"

Christopher Blackwood continued to admire his new possession for a moment before he answered her. "I've got a buyer already intrigued, but I'll admit that I wish I could keep it for myself."

Verity knew how he felt. She felt the same way whenever she brought out the little box from its dark hiding place in her safe. It was a little reminder that there were still mysteries in the world. This world of science and social media threw a spotlight into every crack and corner of the world, but what was the point of sloughing through this mundane, overexposed world if there were no mysteries to lose oneself in? That sense of mystery had been what intrigued her about the old house. It was like an ancient archaeological dig. Every time she went there, she discovered something new and wondrous about the place. She could hardly wait until that was what she could spend every day doing. To be left alone with the mysteries of the past, bringing it back to what it once was, and having the ability to leave behind a true legacy for her daughter. These were the things she craved the most.

Verity watched as Blackwood pulled out his silk pocket square and carefully wrapped the flask before putting it in his pocket. When he'd finished, his clear blue eyes met hers. They held no emotion. She wondered how he managed to do it. He was a passionate man, she knew, but the trick of keeping one's emotions out of business dealings was something she was still trying to figure out.

"And the rest, my dear?"

"You'll have everything we agreed to when I'm done with them," she answered, trying to keep her tone neutral, but she bristled at the accusation. She hated being hounded. It was a reminder of her old life, and she was not prepared to reincarnate those feelings.

"I know that you're a woman of your word," Blackwood soothed. "I was not questioning your competency. I was merely trying to discern a timeline for the conclusion of our current business."

"Soon." Verity was speaking the truth about that. With Henry's recent confession, all the pieces of the puzzle were finally falling into place, as long as she didn't get anyone else killed along the way. She glanced at her house as she lost herself in her private thoughts. Her eyes drifted up towards the window of her bedroom where she left Henry sleeping. There were only a few more things Verity needed to win over Mary Otto for everything to work. Mary was the key to everything.

"Is everything all right, Ms. Georgeson?" Blackwood asked her. His voice pulled her back to the present, and she looked into those piercing eyes but saw concern. She knew better than to think he had any concern for her well-being, but rather, it was most likely a concern for their business arrangements.

"I'm always all right, Mr. Blackwood." It was the truth. She was a strong woman. She'd endured abuse, shame, and loss in her tumultuous life. Yet, here she stood, outlasting them all. With a smile, she added. "Yes, I'm quite all right. Thanks to Henry, I'll be ready for the last phase of my part of our little negotiations. The rest should fall into place neatly."

"Is there anything I can do to assist you?"

"That's very kind of you to offer." She knew he wasn't offering out of the kindness of his heart. "But tomorrow will see the last of the pieces of our little game set into play. All will be well."

"Very well, then. I'll wait for you to contact me at the appropriate time." He tipped his hat to her and folded himself into his car.

Verity stood on the sidewalk, bathed in the light of a nearby streetlamp, watching Blackwood drive away. When he was well out of sight, she turned back to look at her house. Its vintage shape was outlined by moonlight, the rod-iron fence forebodingly guarding it. She loved old things, but ultimately, this house was only a means to an end. What she really wanted was the other house, derelict and decaying as it was. She wanted to breathe new life into it. She wanted to wander its corridors, to be a true mistress of the manor, to one day become one of the ghosts claiming it for her own. She just needed to be patient a little while longer.

The night air was chilly, and Verity could feel the end of summer approaching. She looked out at the sleeping block with a ping of jealousy at those people who would be content with such a life. She'd never been satisfied with the life she had been given, even as a child. Verity always wanted more. At least now she was on course to finally have what she wanted without being concerned about others' opinions. The broken house was everything she wanted, and one of these days, when she was ready, she would invite her daughter there. It was the only secret she kept from Jenna. She should have felt guilty over having kept this a secret from her, but in all her life, she'd had nothing that was just hers. So, for now, she was willing to be greedy, to keep the old house a secret for a little while longer.

Verity wrapped her arms around herself. She'd been cooking up a storm of lies and deceit to get what she wanted. She would spend the rest of her days in prison if the full extent of what she'd done was ever exposed, but she was prepared to take that risk. The identity of Verity Georgeson would only exist for a short while longer. She found comfort in knowing that this would all be over shortly. The final task would be dangerous and heartbreaking, but for everything to be convincing, it had to be done. The fear of that move crawled along her spine, and she shivered against it.

Verity turned her back on the quiet, sleepy neighborhood and padded back up to her house. The black lacquered front door with the amber-stained glass closed silently. It was going to be a busy day, and she needed to get a few more hours of sleep before she could set the last of her plans into motion.

Chapter Twenty-Two

Mary checked her reflection in the visor mirror and let out an exasperated huff. She tried to rub away the weariness and exhaustion from her face, but it didn't do her any good. Even the best makeup was having trouble concealing the deep shadows around her eyes. Widowhood wasn't serving her very well.

She'd hoped to have learned the real reason behind her husband's death, but at every turn, she was left with more questions than answers. She never thought that she would find herself tangled up in such a sordid mess. If she couldn't ever forgive Geoff for betraying her trust by consorting with that Verity woman, she at least wanted to find him some sort of justice for his cruel death. It would've been one thing to expose his dirty little tryst, she probably would have overcome it through a profitable divorce settlement, but death was something altogether different.

She slapped the visor mirror closed and slumped back in her seat. She wished closing her eyes would block out the world, but she was parked downtown. Even with the late summer sun beating down, the sidewalks were full of people, and the constant noise of traffic made it impossible to concentrate.

The only good to have out of all the mess was the reaffirmation of her friendship with Anita. The girl might have been young, but she was a constant source of strength through all of this. Well, at least until her misery reared its ugly head. Mary found it impossible to think that the deaths of both of their husbands were a coincidence. Two men from the same architectural firm, both of whom were engaged in a salacious relationship with the same eclectic woman, just happened to die in such horrible fashion. No! That was too much to ask her to believe. It didn't matter what the police said they were doing about it either. She had little faith in them, but perhaps that was because her faith in her husband had been so grievously misplaced. She didn't feel like doing anything much today. Well, getting sloppy drunk and tearing apart her husband's office sounded nice, but she knew herself enough to know that she'd regret it afterward. She got out of her car and stood in the bright light of the summer sunshine.

Like the first taste of warmth in the spring after a long cold winter, the sun's heat soaked into her, and Mary raised her face to the light. It soaked into the rich fabric of her black suit, but it didn't quite reach her broken heart. She wasn't ready to grieve just yet. There were still things to do, secrets to uncover before she could permit herself to give in to the despair clawing at her raw edges.

She forced herself to remember why she was out here today. While she might have had the strength to fight off her despair, her friend wasn't so cynical. Mary hoisted her purse strap over her shoulder and set off down College Avenue. There were never any truly convenient places to park downtown, so no matter where she was meant to be meeting someone, a bit of a walk was always involved. Her black suit, drawn eyes, and stiff spine offered a strange juxtaposition against the crowds of happy tourists and shoppers. She served as an anchor against a sea of tank tops and cheeky shorts. The familiar bouquet of bug spray and sunscreen couldn't permeate her mood. But it wasn't long before she found herself looking upon the familiar silhouette of her dearest friend sitting at one of the outdoor tables of their favorite coffee shop.

As Mary approached her friend, she was taken aback by her ambiance. Anita was usually quite poised for a young person. She would hold her back straight, the lines of her long slender neck making her look almost exotic. There had been enough of the girl next door to make her approachable. Today, though, her friend was slightly hunched, and her head hung low over a cup of iced coffee. Anita was a tender individual, and the sight of her friend aching so profoundly by all the carelessness of her recently deceased husband was taking a toll on her. Mary hated seeing her friend like this, and she felt her spine stiffen against the betrayal of people they had trusted above all. Anger and hatred were strong motivators, and Mary's momentary lapse in drive to solve this conspiracy of secrets was swiped away, replaced with love and tenderness for her gentle friend. She slowed her steps and laid a hand on her friend's shoulder. Anita jumped despite Mary's care not to startle her.

"I'm so sorry, Anita, I didn't mean to frighten you," Mary said as she slid to the other side of the round iron table and settled into the opposing chair.

"Oh, it's all right, Mary," Anita said with a hand over her heart. Mary took in her friend's haggard appearance. "I guess I'm a little jumpy. Sorry," Anita added.

"You have nothing to apologize for."

"I suppose," Anita said reluctantly.

"Anita, I mean this in the kindest way possible, but you look absolutely dreadful." Mary gave her a wry smile. There wasn't anything the two of them needed to say. They knew each other's hearts. Mary and Anita were both grieving and angry. The emotions of loss and betrayal mixed awkwardly until neither of them was certain of what they were feeling. Mary felt exposed sitting out here in the open, which unsettled her. Bistro tables were scattered around the sidewalk outside the small cafe, a small iron railing shielding them from the throngs of people walking by. The sun beat down on her and she wished that the heat could burn through her anger, but she knew that wouldn't happen until she had her answers. Anita, sitting across from her, clad all in black, a mirror to Mary, was solemn. The two women stood out from the crowd, little islands of black in the sea of skin and sweat.

"I feel like all I want to do is apologize to everyone."

"For what?" Mary asked.

"For everything. I'm so sorry my husband was a jerk. I'm so sorry that I was too naïve to know what was going on." Anita clenched a fist. "I'm so sorry I couldn't keep my husband satisfied, that he ran off with some other woman. I'm sorry that even after everything that woman has done that I still find myself jealous of her."

Anita hung her head after that last thought. Mary reached across the table and wrapped Anita's clenched fist in her own hands, hands that were a bit knobby at the knuckles and covered in a few age spots. Mary's hands reflected a life fully lived. She wasn't about to stop now, but she needed to make sure this mess didn't crush her tender friend.

"None of this is your fault."

"I know that, but I feel like it's my fault anyway," Anita said in despair. She sighed deeply, her body practically shrinking before Mary's eyes. This just would not do.

"I will not stand by while you berate yourself for your husband's behavior," Mary declared. "We will find out what's going on, and we will right this ship." She leaned forward, conspiratorially. "Now, what do you say we come up with a plan to dig up our husbands' secrets and figure out what this mess is that they managed to get themselves into?" Anita returned a weak smile, and Mary knew that her lovely friend was close to despair. She knew the feeling all too well. "I know what you're going through and I know it feels lousy, but I promise you we will get answers," Mary encouraged, "and when we do, we'll both be free to grieve."

"Mary, I don't want to grieve. I want to be angry. I want to hate him for what he did."

"I know. I feel the same way, but I'll be damned if I just roll over and let their mess ruin me. I'll not stand for that."

"I'm afraid that when this is all over that I'll . . ."

"I know. You're afraid that when all is said and done, you'll forgive him."

"I feel like a traitor to women everywhere."

"Let them think what they want. I can live with any outcome as long as I know it's the truth." Mary slumped back into her chair, crossing her arms like a petulant child. "It's the lies. The lies are digging into me, and I can't move on until I know the truth."

"What do we do?"

"Just what we have been doing," Mary rallied. "Let's keep poking the hornet's nest, turn over every rock. I will not stop until I know why this has happened."

"What if the answer is worse than not knowing?"

"I can't imagine anything worse than not knowing. I'm tired of feeling like I don't know anything about my husband. I will not be made a fool of," Mary pronounced emphatically. Anita thought about all this, and her head shook as she fought some internal battle over what direction would be best for her. Eventually, she sighed and looked her friend in the eye.

"You're right, Mary. The secrets are the worst part of it all."

Mary watched Anita, who was frail as a bird, slim, and petite; she hoped she was stronger than she looked. A dog barked nearby, and Anita jumped at the sound. Mary couldn't blame her. She was a little jumpy herself. After everything that had happened so far, it was a wonder that either of them was brave enough to leave the house. Geoff had been poisoned. It was strange to thing to think someone actively chose poison as their method of murder. Fear shivered up her spine at that thought. It was still so surreal to think that Geoff had managed to get himself tangled up in something so dark that it was necessary to kill him. Had he been a willing conspirator? Mary hoped that Geoff had just been a fool. It would be worse for everyone if he'd actually been a complicit partner in whatever this was. She gave Anita's hand another gentle squeeze, and her friend relaxed slightly.

"We *will* find out why Richard and Geoff were murdered, Anita. I promise you that."

"I'm afraid, Mary," Anita said. Her pretty face was marred by fear and worry.

"I know," Mary said, her own voice dropping into thoughtfulness. "I know." She hated to see her friend this way. Mary was old. It wasn't so long ago that she would have laughed at being called old. The older she got, the more fiercely she enjoyed life. While she was too old to care or worry about the superficial needs of many of today's young people, she understood her own mortality. Her day would come when she would have to face the end of her life, but to have it ripped away so violently as Geoff and Richard had, well, that was something else entirely. It was cruel.

Mary watched her friend's eyes as they stared blankly at the crowds passing by. Anita's eyes were wide with fear in every twitch, but it was such a juxtaposition against the bright, happy people walking by with shopping bags and street food.

The happy atmosphere of sandals and sneakers slapping along the sidewalk was subtly disturbed by the clack of a woman's heels against the concrete.

"Excuse me," a familiar voice queried, "ladies?"

Despite Mary's heart thrumming with anger, she couldn't contain her surprise. By the look of Anita's wide-eyed expression, her friend was just as surprised as she was. The two friends turned to look up at the woman who approached them.

Verity Georgeson stood there in an elegant black pencil skirt and vintage blouse. The black hat she wore had a large brim that came down and shadowed her face, but Mary couldn't help but notice something familiar. The dark circumstances that haunted Mary and Anita seemed to have taken hold of the eclectic woman as well. Her fair complexion was tarnished by shadows around her eyes. Verity wrung her hands unconsciously, her face a mirror of the very fear that Mary was struggling with.

"I'm so sorry to interrupt you," Verity started, her voice catching slightly, "but I need your help."

CHAPTER TWENTY-THREE

Regardless of the late summer sun beating down on the little bistro table outside the cafe, the aura at their table was cold enough to frost over. Mary's face turned a sickly shade of aubergine, and her mouth pursed tightly against the tirade of vulgar thoughts she didn't want to say in public. Anita's mouth hung open in a perfectly painted circle. Meanwhile, Verity stood over them, wringing her hands nervously around the handle of her handbag. Mary was the first to recover.

"You've got a lot of nerve, Ms. Georgeson," Mary managed to say. She expected the eclectic woman to fight back but instead watched the woman she was sure was responsible for her husband's death shrink right before her eyes.

"I didn't know where else to go," Verity said sheepishly. She seemed hopeful that she wouldn't be turned away, but Mary wasn't inclined to give in to her.

"And what are we supposed to do for you? We're fresh out of husbands for you to murder," Mary hissed. Anita balked, and Verity looked as though she'd been physically slapped.

"Mary!" Anita whispered. Her eyes scanned their surroundings nervously. This wasn't something done in respectable company, but Mary didn't think of Verity as respectable company.

"Is that what you think?" Verity asked.

"Are you going to stand there and tell me you didn't have anything to do with our husbands' deaths?"

"I—"

"I don't have time for your lies, Ms. Georgeson," Mary declared before turning her gaze away from Verity and taking a deliberate sip of her coffee. Verity stood next to their table, a boulder in a river of people, twitching nervously as people bumped into her. Watching from the corner of her eye, Mary saw the proud woman's shoulders slump. As Verity's fingers continued to twist around the handle of her handbag, Mary's anxiety sang in response. She knew that feeling, but she wasn't ready to forgive or forget. Verity's beseeching look was lost on her.

Anita stared at the two women as they both fought through an invisible battle, but in the end, Mary was the victor. Verity seemed to understand that she'd lost, and she turned away from the table, slowly walking away. Her steps weren't as confident as they usually were, but the more distance put between the sparring women, the more each of those steps resonated with resignation.

Mary looked up from her cup of coffee and found herself staring into Anita's flabbergasted expression. Anita leaned forward. "What are you doing?"

"I'm standing my ground," Mary pronounced. Anita huffed impatiently at her friend before springing to her feet and scampering through the crowded sidewalk after Verity.

"Verity, wait," Anita called out to her. It wasn't until she laid a hand on the promiscuous woman's arm that she stopped and turned to face Anita. Verity's face was turned at just the right angle, allowing the cheerful yellow glow of sunlight to illuminate the woman's face. Anita was taken aback by what she saw. Her skin was paler than she remembered, and her eyes were cast in dark shadows. The woman's usually enchanting green eyes were watery and rimmed in swollen lids. Whatever her preconceptions about Verity she had were thrown away by the fear and sadness caught in every hollow and fine line on her face. "Oh my!" she said softly. "Verity?"

"Mrs. Belker, I—"

"Forget that. Call me Anita, please." Anita offered a sad smile. "What's wrong?" Verity looked around them nervously before she spoke hesitantly.

Mary tried not to watch her friend, but when she saw Anita's hand cover her mouth in shock, she couldn't help but grow curious. Her face flushed. She hated how this woman seemed to infect her life. How had she let this happen? When she saw Anita dragging Verity back to their table by the hand, she clenched her fists against the rage thrumming in her heart and wanted nothing more than to stomp her feet in protest, screaming, *No, no, no,* like a petulant child. What was the foolish girl doing?

"Mary," Anita started, breathless.

"No, I don't—"

"Mary, just listen. Please." Mary looked at her friend's beseeching eyes and melted ever so slightly under the pressure. She couldn't bring herself to speak, her anger was too near the surface, so she simply nodded curtly. Anita pressed Verity into the chair between her and Mary, then leaned in conspiratorially. "Mary, just listen to what she has to say." Anita gave Verity a look filled with sympathy. "It's just horrible."

Mary didn't want to listen to Verity. She didn't want to look at the woman who had single-handedly ruined everything, but when she gave the woman her attention, she couldn't help but notice her trembling hands. Mary sighed; she could feel herself giving in to the woman. *Would she ever learn?*

"Go on, Verity, tell her what you told me."

Despite the sunshine and throngs of happy shoppers and tourists, there was a heaviness to the air hanging over the little bistro table where the three women sat. Verity sat between the two friends, the skin on her lovely face taut, she twitched this way and that at the crowd bustling past them. Verity was a wild animal caught in the grip of fear of an unseen hunter. Mary couldn't imagine what could've turned the confident, self-made woman into a frightened child.

Mary Otto listened to what her enemy had to say and her blood turned to ice as Verity laid out the frightening confession her lover offered her. Beneath the brim of her fashionable hat and painted lips, Verity's haunted eyes revealed the truth that Mary hadn't wanted to see. It was exactly what she was afraid of. She was afraid to see her enemy as anything else, but here it was. The truth staring her in the face was that her enemy was a victim too. She may have had a hand in the secrets and lies, the betrayals that all this mess was tangled up in, but something precious had been taken from her as well. She felt at odds with the world around her. The tangy scent of sunscreen, the crinkle of shopping bags, none of it could wash away the sour taste of fear at the back of her mouth. This was more than just some conspiracy, some game of chess played between opposing players. This mess belonged to something far more dangerous. Mary knew of nothing more persistent, more lethal, than love.

When Verity had finished telling her story, the three widows sat in silence. The coffee on the table grew cold. The crowds faded into the shadows, and tendrils of fear snaked all around them.

"I'm so sorry," Verity offered eventually. Mary studied the woman. It was the sort of apology that rang true; she saw the truth of it in Verity's eyes. Verity knew that no apology could bring their men back. No apology could fix what had been permanently broken. Here she was, though, asking for some sort of absolution or forgiveness, for something that could never be undone.

"I can't forgive you," Mary said. It wasn't meant to be cruel, just merely honest.

"I know. I don't expect forgiveness," Verity said. "I wouldn't be able to either if circumstances were reversed." Mary studied the woman for a moment, searching her face for any hint of deception, but there was none.

"Mary?" Anita asked gently, but Mary didn't respond. What was she supposed to say? "Mary, what are we going to do?"

"Why should we do anything, Anita? This wasn't our fault. This wasn't our doing." Mary was furious, but even though she was answering her friend, she'd directed her fury at Verity.

"I don't have anyone to go to," Verity said.

"What about Jenna?" Mary spat. It had the impact that she'd been hoping for. Verity's face twitched.

"No" was all Verity could say before she could recover. It was more than just shock, and for a moment, Mary saw something she hadn't expected. There was anger, rage even, behind those dark green eyes. Her body tightened, and Mary instinctively wanted to take a step back from Verity. She was afraid, but not about being alone or lost or grieving. She was afraid of Verity. In that split second, she realized that she might have pushed the woman too far. Verity leaned in slightly. Her hands were clenched so tightly around the handles of her handbag that Mary could see the woman's knuckles blanch. "You're not a mother, neither of you, so I know you can't completely understand where I'm coming from."

"I'm sure I can only imagine," Anita replied.

"You can't. Everything I have done, everything, has been for Jenna," Verity said. Her voice was low and deep, and the threat of stepping dangerously close to an uncrossable line was laced in every word. "I'll admit that I've done some truly awful things, but it has all been for her."

"We didn't mean to imply—" Anita started.

"Nonsense, Anita," Mary countered. "That was exactly what I was implying. Listen here, Ms. Georgeson, we are not friends. In fact, we are as far from friends as we could possibly be, but I understand that something must be done. I'm not listening to you so that we can become friends. That's never going to happen."

"Then why are you giving me the time of day?"

"Because we need to do something. I can't imagine what other damage that unhinged lover of yours could do."

"I don't have an answer for that," Verity said. The three widows fell into a contemplative silence.

"Would he hurt her?" Anita asked after a while. Verity's face crumpled slightly under the weight of that thought.

"I don't think so."

"But you can't be sure, can you?" Mary said. Fear and worry were etched into each of the fine lines around Verity's eyes, and

Mary realized that no matter what persona Verity put out for the world to see, she was a mother first. This woman would do anything to protect her daughter. Verity shook her head in response. Mary sighed. "Fine. Do we just report this to the police, then?"

"If we do that, then they're going to arrest Verity too!"

"I know that, Anita, but what else are we supposed to do?"

"I'll do it," Verity offered softly. Mary looked at her. She was defeated. Here was a woman who had done incorrigible things to ensure a legacy for her daughter, yet she was willing to risk her own life and freedom to put things right. Mary was having a hard time faulting her for her decisions. She didn't know if she would have done the same thing in her place. She and Geoff had decided a long time ago that they weren't right for being parents. The things they wanted in life weren't suitable for raising children. There were many people out there who judged her harshly for being a woman who didn't want children, but that was just another challenge to being a woman in this modern world. Women were judged for having children, for not having children, for being a career-climbing parent, and for choosing to be a homemaker. There was no way to win with today's hypercritical standards. If there was no way to win, then it was just best to live life by her own rules. Here she was, listening to a woman who had done that very same thing; it had just rippled out with deadly consequence.

"There has to be a better way, Mary," Anita said. Mary was only slightly listening.

"I don't know how else to stop him," Verity said, but Mary had already started to form an idea, a very dangerous idea. She looked across the table, taking in the impossible circumstances.

"Do we trust the police to do what should be done?" Mary finally said.

"What do you mean?" Anita asked, but it was Verity who connected the dots.

"It will get ugly, for everyone."

"Even Jenna?"

"Yes," Verity said resignedly.

"Then we'll just have to find another way to settle our problems," Mary said, admittedly even shocking herself. Verity and Anita gave her a quizzical look, but when Verity finally understood what Mary was offering, her mouth set in a hard, thin line, and she gave the woman a solitary nod. From this point forward, the three of them would be irreparably connected with a secret of their own.

CHAPTER TWENTY-FOUR

Henry sat in his truck, drumming his thumbs against the steering wheel. He was parked in front of Verity's place and knew she wasn't home. His gut twisted with worry that his confession to her the night before could have ruined what they had. She was an early riser and he was used to her getting up before him, but when he made his way down to her kitchen, he'd found the house empty, except for the cat. Dorian had hissed at him before stalking out of the room with his usual air of superiority. He wasn't necessarily against cats, but he was certain that Dorian was Verity's true secret keeper. There were things about her that only the cat knew. Maybe Dorian was upset at him for laying his confession on Verity. Had he gone too far in telling her what he'd done? Henry tried to recall her face from the night before, but nothing stood out from his tear-stained memories. He wasn't proud of what he'd done, but he wouldn't take it back either. Every cliched movie said that the first kill was the hardest and then it got easier after that. They weren't wrong.

When he first met Verity, back before she was the woman she was today, she had been timid. They had worked together for a time at the same company. Their relationship had grown out of routine and small talk, but the chemistry, the electricity connecting them, was obvious from the first moment they met. The conversations they shared were usually mundane and work-related, but as they grew closer, they shared stories of their past lives. The two of them bonded over similar heartbreak and tragedy. Over time, the attraction between them grew to where co-workers had started to gossip, but even though they shared tender feelings for each other, their emotions were never put into words. The occasional secret glance, a silent conversation shared through the ether when his brilliant blue eyes held her steel-rimmed green eyes. He knew then that they could've been something special if given the chance. He adored that precious smile of hers he'd fallen in love with. Verity's smile was open and honest. It was luminescent, pulling people into her stratosphere. Her eyes squinted, emphasizing the fine lines around them. As time wore on, he noticed she smiled less often. A cloud of remembered trauma etched her smooth skin, darkening her face, but she was always quick to swipe it away.

Henry remembered the day he'd recognized he belonged to her. It was a casual moment when several of them had congregated in the break room at work, and they were sharing some raucous joke. He couldn't remember the joke now, but she had bent in half with laughter. When she righted herself, her face was pink from laughing, her mossy eyes sparkling, and then she'd placed her hand on his arm. It was a small gesture, lacking in all sexuality, but it was like a lightning bolt had struck him right in the heart. His skin tingled, his nerves vibrated. They were meant for each other. Unfortunately, she was already spoken for by a man full of alpha male bravado and leaning towards the jealous type.

It was that very day, Henry and Verity had been in the elevator after a long shift, that he kissed her for the first time. Brief as the elevator ride down to the ground floor was, he crossed the small space and placed his lips over hers. It was a bold move, especially with today's awareness of sexual harassment, but he needed to know for sure how she felt about him. Humans were liars, but sometimes there was no way to lie. Henry believed that a kiss was one of those times. When her lips melted into his, he knew then that they were meant for each other.

Now, years later, he worried that he might have lost her. She'd left their bed in the middle of the night, and he couldn't shake the sight of seeing her standing outside, alone in front of the house. Had he frightened her? Henry didn't mean to. It was just that he couldn't stand lying to her. He wondered what his life would be like today if he would've brushed that tiny gesture between him and Verity away those years ago. Would he be with her now? Would those other men still be alive? They were assholes anyway. Some men believed the world was theirs to own or burn. It pissed Henry off.

He'd finally managed to get some sleep and a little peace of mind. Until he found himself standing in her empty kitchen with nothing but a note. *Henry, I have an early meeting, but I'll see you tonight for dinner.* It was signed with a "V". The only time she ever seemed to break character was when they were at the old house. He'd be lying if he said he understood what she saw in the place. It was a wreck. He didn't believe it could be saved, but she dreamed of living a quiet life. He just hoped she still saw him sharing that life with her.

Henry was anxious for dinner, to see her again. His twitchy paranoia exasperated when he saw Christopher Blackwood drive around the corner in his Jaguar and park on the opposite side of the street as him. The last thing he needed was that slimy mafioso shoving his nose into other people's business. He was probably here to see Verity. *Well, tough shit*, he thought, *she ain't home*. Henry watched the blonde man step out of his car; he was impeccably dressed in a surprisingly modern tweed suit.

Blackwood crossed the street with an air of such casualness that one might have thought he lived there. He made directly for Henry's truck while checking his phone. Not moving, Henry simmered with hate, his knuckles blanching as he gripped the steering wheel tightly. He simply glared at the man, who rapped on the window of the truck with a knuckle. Henry reluctantly sighed before lowering the window.

"Hello, handsome."

"What do you want, Blackwood?"

"Oh, nothing much," he said, but Henry saw mischief flash in the man's eyes. "I was just running some errands and thought I'd stop by and see if the lady of the house was home."

"I bet."

"I don't suppose she's home?"

"No, she's not, and I'm pretty sure she wouldn't appreciate you stopping by."

"In all honesty, I don't think you have the slightest idea what Ms. Georgeson would or would not appreciate."

"I think I know her better than you do."

"Are you certain of that?" It was an invitation to a challenge. "She's not who she appears to be." Henry bristled against the accusation.

"I know exactly who she is."

"Are you sure about that?" Blackwood said. Henry had had about enough of this prick and was dangerously close to losing his temper. With everything he and Verity had going on right now, neither of them needed Blackwood spreading his poison. Henry grabbed Blackwood's tie.

"Look here, asshole. I don't know what you think you are doing, but I've had enough of it." Henry snarled in the cherubic man's face, catching a whiff of his subtle musky cologne. Henry shoved Blackwood away. Christopher Blackwood stumbled and bent as though he'd been punched in the gut, but he caught himself. Slow like honey, Blackwood righted himself. He straightened his tie and smoothed down his tweed vest before leveling a cool look at Henry.

"I was willing to play nice with you, but I've realized that though you may be pretty, you aren't prepossessed of any endearing qualities."

"Whatever."

"I think she'll get the better of you in the end, Mr. Willians, and I'm going to enjoy the show," Blackwood said.

The blood in Henry's veins curdled at the smooth malevolence in Blackwood's icy eyes. "What the hell are you talking about?"

"If you know the intriguing Ms. Georgeson so well, then I would've thought you'd have figured out just how many secrets that woman keeps."

"She has to," Henry said confidently, but the damage had been done. A worm of doubt had wriggled itself into his mind. Blackwood recognized that flicker of doubt and seized it, stepping closer to Henry, yet keeping himself out of arm's reach.

"You're too far in this mess. She has you," Blackwood said. "You're just a little insect caught in her web."

"Get out of here," Henry demanded, but his body was reacting without his consent. His hands shook, and a knot bloomed in his gut.

"Henry, dear, you are only a means to an end. Think of all those nasty things you've done in the name of love. Do you really think she loves you, or does some part of you already know that you're around just to do the dirty work?"

"I won't throw away everything we have together just because of a few lies spewed by an asshole like you," Henry hissed.

Blackwood smiled, slowly, deliberately. "Suit yourself, but I'd be cautious if I were you. She's probably got enough evidence tucked away in that quirky little manor of hers to have you locked up forever." His words sounded like sage advice, but they were laced with something else. What was Henry missing?

"It's been positively lovely chatting with you, but I have other business matters to attend to." Blackwood turned his back to Henry. The man paused briefly, and Henry wondered if he was going to turn around and say something. But he continued on, making his way back to his car. Henry watched him drive off, an icy feeling of dread lingering.

He wanted to believe Blackwood's words held no merit, but when he turned to look back at Verity's house, he felt different. The house was the same as it always was. The wrought-iron spears surrounding the lawn, the brickwork, the porch, even the stained glass in the obsidian front door was exactly as it had been before, but it all felt so ominous now. Was Verity keeping secrets from him? Was she hiding evidence that could get him in trouble? He didn't think she would throw him under the bus like that, but he couldn't untie the knot in his stomach. He needed to know for sure.

Henry got out of the truck and approached the house. He put his hand on the gate, the dusty black iron cold to the touch. Sunlight beat down on him, he figured the iron would be warm too. He ignored his screaming instincts and opened the gate. The sleepy neighborhood offered a chorus of chirping birds and distant traffic to join the soft thuds his work boots made against the cobbled pathway. He traveled up the steps and through the black door that now felt far from inviting.

Henry stepped inside Verity's house and closed the door behind him. It was still the same as ever. Her eclectic mix of vintage and modern furniture, crisp colors, and worn patinas quietly watched him. If she was hiding proof against him, there was only one place she would be keeping it. He ascended the stairs. The light upstairs differed from the ground level. No, that wasn't quite it. It was more as though the light affected the space differently here. Downstairs, the brooding textured wallpapers and refurbished vintage furniture painted in vibrant colors inspired conversation and left visitors feeling welcomed. It was all choreographed with intent. But upstairs, the space was more intimate, a truer reflection of who Verity was when no one was watching. The large bed draped in fabrics mimicking the deep ocean, the antique furniture restored rather than altered, the comfort of memories on each surface, all of it spoke to the woman beneath the charade.

Henry crossed the space in a few strides and approached the desk at the far end of the room near the picture window that faced out onto the street. It was her father's desk, one of her few possessions that had belonged to him. Verity's relationship with her father was complicated. It was a story full of tears and regrets, and in many ways, it was full of foretelling. Her life had become as convoluted as his before he died, only the details differing.

Henry rifled through the contents in neat piles on the top of the desk, but nothing appeared sinister among them. What he was looking for was probably tucked in a locked drawer. Verity wouldn't be so careless as to leave something incriminating out in the open. The old secretary desk had a fold-down writing surface that could be locked when folded up. It was indeed locked and had no pull knob. He remembered all the times he watched Verity get into her desk and remembered that she unlocked it with an old iron skeleton key and used the key as a drawer pull.

Scanning the room quickly and checking the few places available to him, like the nightstands and her wardrobe, he returned to the desk empty-handed. If he tried to force his way into the desk, he would damage it, which wouldn't do him any good. If he found she was hiding evidence against him, the last thing he needed was her finding out that he knew.

What was he thinking? He knew she would never betray him. In a fit of frustration, he buried his face in his knuckles and snarled helplessly into the room empty of anyone but himself. The hairs on the back of his neck stood up, and a shiver ran along his spine. Henry spun around, certain he was being watched, but he was alone. This was ridiculous. Blackwood was trying to drive a wedge between them.

Something tugged at the hem of his jeans, and he launched himself backward, throwing up his fists, prepared to fight. When he looked down to see what had touched him, Dorian sat there, staring up at him with his head tilted quizzically to one side. "You know what, cat," Henry said aloud, shaking out his frayed nerves, "I really don't like you." The cat's shiny black tail twitched twice. "Yeah, I know. You don't like me much either."

His eyes drifted around the room as he thought. An idea came to him. He couldn't get into her desk without leaving behind some substantial proof that he'd been there, but there was still a place he could look he had access to, the painting hanging above the desk. He knew the combination to her wall safe. She didn't know this, of course, but he'd managed to figure it out over the years by just being observant. His lips curled into a satisfied smile as he swung the painting away from the wall. The safe was already ajar. *That can't be good*, he thought. He pulled the heavy door open all the way and stared into the black space. Whatever she had hidden here was gone now. He had nothing. The knot in his stomach tightened.

That might have been the worst of it, but he heard the familiar chirp of Verity's car being locked. She was home.

CHAPTER TWENTY-FIVE

Henry stood there, his feet planted to the spot by the heavy shroud of dread suddenly wrapped around him. Whatever Verity had been hiding in her safe, it was gone now, and with it, any sense of security. He had no proof that Verity was plotting to turn him in, but the empty feeling he had when he woke up this morning had returned. Was he worrying for nothing? Probably. He knew better than to let Blackwood's words get to him.

He closed the safe door and returned the painting to its original position before he scanned the room, making sure there was no evidence of his search. He hoped Verity wouldn't question why he was still in her house, but as he walked out of the room, his work boots made the floors creak, gifting him with an idea and possibly an alibi.

The smooth wood banister was neither cool nor warm beneath his touch, but something to the nature of wood emulated warmth. Everything arboreal seemed to evoke a primal sense of belonging in him. He needed a little of that warmth now to chase away the sliver of ice that had crept beneath his skin ever since his conversation with Blackwood. A key ground against the tumblers in the lock, and the deadbolt clicked over. Henry stood there at the top of the stairs when the black door with amber glass opened to Verity ushering in Mary Otto and Belker's new widow.

What the hell was she doing with them?

"Make yourself comfortable, and I'll fetch us some tea," Verity said somberly, but unbeknownst to her, the other two women were caught by surprise. They were rooted to where they stood, both staring up at him with wide eyes. Verity turned to see what had caught their attention and was startled to find Henry standing there looking down at them.

"Henry?"

"Hey, V."

"I didn't realize you were still here," Verity asked.

"I just came back to fix that squeaky floorboard in your bedroom." He hoped it would work. Verity's head tilted almost imperceptibly, like that damn cat of hers, but then her red lips curved into that amazing smile she always saved just for him, full of alluring and mischief. For a second there, he was afraid it wouldn't work.

"You're such a sweetheart," Verity said as he started down the stairs. She turned back to her house guests, and he saw the smooth porcelain line of her neck. "Ladies, this is Henry." He wanted to kiss that neck, slowly and patiently.

"Ladies," he offered.

"Henry, we've got some droll business to talk about. Do you think you could give us some space for a little while?"

"Sure. I'll just grab some tools and get to work." He was so thankful that she seemed to be buying it. He better not push his luck. Glancing at the other two women, he wasn't so sure that he had them fooled. They both looked as though they'd seen a ghost. Or maybe it was simpler than that. Maybe they looked as though they'd just been confronted by a murderer.

He tried to shake that thought loose, for it was too dangerous to listen to. The air in the room got thick and uncomfortable. This whole day was going wrong, so he needed to get himself out of there and fast. He leaned over and placed a soft kiss on Verity's temple, before making his way to the bar behind her. There was so much tension in the room he needed to cut it with something. Why not bourbon? He grabbed one of the cut crystal lowball glasses sitting there and poured himself a couple of fingers of the rich amber elixir, turning his back on the women as he took a sip. The warm hug it gave him instantly worked at releasing the tension in his body. He didn't know what was going on, but the tightness in his throat was a reminder that things were not as they should be.

"It shouldn't take me long to fix that floorboard," he started as he took another sip of bourbon. "I'll be out of your way in no time."

He gave a two-fingered salute to the ladies before turning his back to them. If his lie was going to work, he needed to go find some tools and at least look the part. Verity was a handy woman, very self-reliant, and he knew she'd have something he could work with in the shed out back. His stomach tightened. He hated all of this. He couldn't tell what was part of Verity's plan and what was just his imagination working overtime.

His gut twisted sharply and stopped in his tracks. The glass slipped from his fingers, dropping through the air silently, like the vacuum of sound anticipating an explosion, before crashing on the hardwood floor.

"Henry?" Verity inquired, but he couldn't answer her. The knot in his stomach lurched before it crawled up his throat. His left knee gave out just as his stomach gave in. The knee crunched when it hit the floor, but he barely noticed it as he folded in half. Bile and saliva frothed between his lips while he slapped his hands against the ground to keep him somewhat upright.

"Henry!" He knew she was calling out to him, but the agony writhing in his gut was blinding him to everything else. Verity dropped her purse on the ground and ran to Henry's side. She wrapped her arms around him. "Henry, what's wrong? What's going on?" She wiped the spit and sick off his face without a flinch. "Tell me what to do." Her voice broke. "How do I help you?"

But Henry was no use to her. He was completely lost in the ecstasy of his pain. In another spasm of retching, Henry folded into Verity, and she wrapped her arms around him. The couple was lost in their private world of anguish. Tears streamed down Verity's face. Her face was pale with fright and worry, while Henry's face was bloodless. His eyes were wide, his skin stretched tautly. His lips were curling back as he fought against each new wave of pain and sick. Henry tried to fight, but his body was losing and he collapsed helplessly into Verity. They tumbled off their knees and lay on the floor. Eventually, the waves of nausea came less frequently, and Henry's body twitched and jerked less.

Henry knew, profoundly, that his pain would never abate, and his body was losing its ability to fight it. The rolling waves of shakes and spasms were beginning to ease, but they were just replaced with something far more sinister. An invisible hook had lashed itself to the base of his spine and was pulling him back into darkness. No matter how tightly he clung to Verity, he knew he was slipping away. He knew the end of this story and that this was exactly how Geoff Otto had spent his last moments. The pain masked everything he saw, but he still recognized Verity's beautiful face through agony and tears, both his and hers. It was like looking through a window during a spring rain. He recognized all her features, but the pain distorted them.

His fingers dug into her pale flesh as his dying struggle against his own sticky end drew closer. Verity held him fiercely and bent down, kissing him on his sweat-covered face. Her kisses were soft and tender, but there was something else to them, with hidden meaning that he was too slow to discern.

Henry lay there cradled in her arms, both of them with their backs to the silent witnesses standing apart from them. She rested her cheek against his flushed face, and it was cool. He could draw every curve of her face with his eyes closed. Each fine line next to her eyes when she smiled revealed the depth of passion she carried with her always. Her lips brushed against his ear.

"Henry," she whispered. Her voice was soft as a fluffy cloud on a summer day. "I'm so sorry, Henry." Her embrace tightened. Her body rocked him gently, and he drifted away from her a little more as he gave in to the soothing motion. "I love you so much."

He couldn't answer her. His body wouldn't allow it. There was nothing left for him to work with. His stomach churned, his body still shook, and his throat had been burned away by the poison still chewing at him. Henry wanted to hold her tight like they would after making love. He wanted to caress her pale skin, kiss her neck, to make her forget all her struggles in those secret moments between passion and euphoria. He wanted to tell her how much he loved her, but he couldn't do any of that. All he could do was listen as her words came to him through his tunnel of pain.

"I love you so much, Henry," she whispered in his ear, "but you're a loose thread that needs to be cut."

How could she say the cruelest thing to him with such softness? He tried to twist his body so that he could see her eyes. He needed more than her words, he needed her real truth, but his body gave in to one last shiver of pain.

Chapter Twenty-Six

Detective Karen Parson had to park half a block away from the scene because of all the emergency response vehicles already parked in the area. This was twice now that she'd been called to this particular address, and it didn't bode well for her investigation. It was still early afternoon, and the sun was shining. There were probably birds chirping happily somewhere; she just couldn't hear it against the noise and bustle of an active crime scene. The blue and red lights strobed against the backdrop of the old neighborhood. She stepped out of her unmarked car and stuffed her hand into her blazer pocket to make sure she had her notepad with her. She never went anywhere without it, but it was a quirk of hers to always check, a nervous tick, one could say. Every cop accumulated quirks and habits along the way the longer they stayed in the field.

Several patrol cars were parked strategically to block all traffic coming into the street, uniforms were quartered at the front of the house, and she was certain someone was guarding the rear of the house too. She nodded to the officer unrolling perimeter tape around the front lawn to keep nosy bystanders and reporters from disturbing any evidence. The neighborhood was old, and all the landscaping was well established. Enormous oaks rooted here and there towered against the little Victorian neighborhood, and while all the homes had been well cared for, this particular house still stood out from the others. The dark paint against the red brick emphasized the curved arches of the porch, and the wrought-iron fence of spears gave the whole place a Gothic feel. It reminded her of a story she'd once read about a wicked governess trapped in a Gothic manor. While Parson carried her hardened persona around like the blazers she wore, she loved a good scary story, and whereas her life lacked romance, she could always find it in the pages of a good book. But she would deny it to one's face if confronted about it; after all, she'd worked hard for her reputation. It was tough being a woman and a detective in a field that was still ruled, for the most part, by old white men.

Parson pulled her badge wallet out and flashed her ID to the officer guarding the front door. Her black utility boots were silent as she mounted the stairs to once again enter the home of Verity Georgeson. Every day brought her another bit of insight into the eclectic woman and, along with it, her conviction that all these deaths were related to her in some way. She couldn't link the evidence to her yet, but her gut was rarely wrong. She had too many years of experience with the worst sides of people to ignore the notion that the Georgeson woman was innocent. She stepped across the threshold and noted the beautiful spray of gold and amber as the sunlight spilled through the artful stained-glass window set into the black door. She couldn't deny that the home was beautiful, full of deep colors and rich textures. Parson could easily imagine this place being plucked straight out of one of her favorite haunting books.

Parson tapped the shoulder of one of the EMTs who was crouching just inside the entrance and packing up some of the supplies. "Anything to note?"

He turned up to look at her, and she realized he was here the last time. She thought his name was Craig or Greg, or something like that.

"Nasty," he said, standing up and carefully pulling off his gloves, folding one into the other to avoid contamination before he tossed them into a biohazard waste bag. "Poison of some kind."

"Arsenic?"

"Could be. All the right symptoms, but you won't know for sure until after the coroner does the tox screen."

Parson nodded. "Anything else?"

"Yeah, just watch your step. There's glass and a lot of body fluids over there." He tossed his head in the direction of the crime scene, but she didn't need any signs to tell her where to look.

"Thanks," she replied as she resigned herself to taking a closer look. At the far end of the living room, a tarp was draped over the worst of it. The profile implied that what was hidden beneath was smaller than she knew it to be. First, she needed to take in everything, to get a real sense of what happened. There was time to look under the shroud of death later.

The last time she'd been here it was dark outside, and she found that the place had a completely different feel to it during the day. During the night, the shadows had blended with the dark colors to create an ominous scene for a murder, but now in the light, it was eclectic, yet warm and inviting. If it weren't for the multiple deaths that had occurred here, she'd feel perfectly welcome here. Perhaps those deaths were only something to be afraid of if one were a man. It certainly hadn't gone unnoticed by her that all these deaths were men.

Parson studied the space and noticed its tidiness. The nearby bar had an evidence marker on it, but the majority of evidence was in a tight radius, encircling the body tucked beneath the tarp. She walked over to the body, careful of each footfall so as not to step in anything nasty. Only a few evidence markers rested here, but she noticed a few smears of blood and some partial shoe prints. By the looks of them, they definitely belonged to a pair of heels. A few years ago, she would've carelessly declared that they belonged to a woman, but her world was becoming more diverse by the day, and now there was no way to declare gender until one spoke with the person. People surprised her every day.

With a short tug on her trouser leg, she crouched to examine the area more closely. The vomit was already drying in shades of yellow and green. Smears of blood were drying too, changing from bright red to a dark brown or black. The early reports didn't indicate a struggle, so she found it odd for the blood to be so smudged. She lifted a corner of the tarp and looked at the body beneath it. She wasn't expecting it to be Henry Williams.

For some reason, she thought he might make it out of this mess, but there was always time to be wrong. The man's body was rigid, but it was probably too early for rigor to set in. It was more likely that his manner of death was the reason for this state. His face was twisted, and his eyes were still open, holding a glassy look that corpses tended to get. One hand was clenched tightly, and the other was mostly clenched but a few fingers were bent awkwardly. She wondered what had caused the fingers to break. Sick had dried around the man's lips, which were curled back slightly in a singularly frightening expression. There was more than just pain in that haunting expression; there was fear. She supposed if she was dying as he had, she'd probably be afraid too. She examined the spread of fluids around him and noticed broken glass too. Well, that was an easy enough explanation for the blood, but other than a few smears of it on his face and clothes, he seemed to have no cuts.

The detective lowered the cloth back over the body, glad to have it out of sight again. It was a necessary part of her job as a detective, and while she was good at her job, very good in fact, it didn't make seeing shit like this any easier. She'd built up a wall of sorts over the years to keep herself safe, but sometimes, the bodies would haunt her.

Using her hands as a brace against her knees, she stood up and scanned the rest of the room. That was when she noticed the women. The three of them stood in a far corner of the room, huddled together like scared children. Mary Otto and Anita Belker flanked the Georgeson woman, whose hands were wrapped in fresh dressings from one of the nearby EMTs. So that's where the blood had come from. Death seemed to follow these women, and it was taking a toll. Dark circles around their eyes and their pale skin contrasted with the black they were all dressed in. Verity Georgeson looked worse off than the other two. Her makeup had smeared and tracks of tears marred her smooth skin, and as Parson drew closer, she also noticed that the woman was shaking, which reminded her of a frightened puppy.

When Parson approached, they seemed to pull into each other closer. *Well, shit.* What had started as something easy, a game of playing each one off the other, had taken a turn she hadn't expected. These three women were now bonded with each other. It happened, but not often enough to expect it in situations like this. There was no denying the multiple affairs of other women's husbands, but something had fundamentally shifted.

"Ladies," she said, announcing herself.

"Detective Parson," Mary Otto declared. Her back visibly straightened, and she pulled Verity in a little closer. Parson nodded her head at Verity's bandaged hands.

"Can you tell me what happened to your hands?" Parson asked as Verity looked down at her wrapped hands and stared at them as though she didn't understand. Eventually, she brought up her green eyes to meet Parson's.

"There was glass," she said in a small voice, without the confidence Parson had seen a few days ago.

"He'd poured himself a drink when he collapsed. The glass broke," Mary Otto added. Parson jotted this down in her notebook.

"It was horrible," Anita Belker said softly.

"From what the first responders told me, he was likely poisoned," Parson said. She was hoping to gauge the reactions of the three women, but at the mention of poison, their faces clouded over. Fear gripped them, and they simultaneously turned to stare at something over Parson's shoulder. Mary's jaw worked and ground away at itself. Anita shivered and leaned in towards the other women. As for Verity, shadows clouded her vibrant green eyes, which Parson envied. When she cried, her face got blotchy and her eyes just got red, making her look like an addict jonesing for the next hit, but Verity's usually mossy green eyes were vibrant like sunlight passing through emeralds.

Whatever was haunting these women was no secret. She turned around to locate what had wrapped these women up so tightly in fear and noticed the bar station. She jotted another note down and returned her attention to the trio. "I see. I'll take a look at it in a moment. I'll save most of my questions for later so that you three can have a moment to breathe, but I've got to know one thing."

Mary tightened her grip on Ms. Georgeson. "And what would that be?"

"Well, no offense, but you ladies aren't what I would call the picture of friendship with everything going on. How is it you all are here together and so"—there was no beating around the bush about it—"so friendly?"

"I was hoping you would be a bit smarter than that, Detective," Mary said. "It's hard to blame the other woman when you watch the love of her life die in her arms."

"S'pose," Parson said as she jotted a few more observations down in her notebook. "All right. I'll let some of the officers take you all down to the station and get your formal statements."

Mary and Anita nodded, but Verity was lost in thought. Parson nodded to them and went to check out the rest of the house. She left the three women huddled together in the corner behind her as she stepped over to the bar. It was all arranged in a tidy set of cut crystal lowball glasses, all set upside down and waiting for someone to pick them up. The matching decanter was filled with a small amount of beautiful amber liquid that, and if it weren't for the corpse nearby, a shot of high end bourbon would be appealing. She knew the forensic team hadn't been through yet, so she didn't mess with it. But from a first glance, she didn't see anything tampered with.

Parson let the rest of the team move about the living room, taking samples and photographs of the tragedy behind her. She pulled a pair of blue gloves out of the nearby EMT kit and put them on before she headed up the stairs. The house really was beautiful, but the difference in atmosphere between the downstairs and the upstairs left Parson feeling disjointed. It was as though two separate people lived here.

The master bedroom was old-fashioned, a striking contrast to the eclectic woman she knew it belonged to. Parson opened every drawer and door until she got to the desk. The desk was tidy, like everything else Parson noticed about this place, and locked, and she knew people only locked away the things they didn't want out in the light of day. Secrets, people locked away their secrets. She'd have to go down and ask Ms. Georgeson to unlock her desk. The woman was keeping secrets, and she would be shocked if they were all already laid bare. Parson knew somehow that Verity Georgeson could tame any trouble that came her way. So, why was it she couldn't match what she knew about her with the fragile, damaged creature shaking and in shock downstairs? There had to be more.

Her instincts were screaming at her that a clue was staring her right in the face, but she couldn't quite put a finger on it. Unless it was simply right in front of her. Parson scanned the room again, unsure of what she was looking for. Shadows spread out across the walls and the floor, reaching out like inky fingers. One shadow caught her eye. The light caught the edges of all the framed artwork in the room, but one caught her attention. The inky shadow escaping the painting above the desk was different, deeper. Parson reached out a blue latex-gloved hand to the classical landscape painting hanging above the desk and gave it a gentle tug. The painting lurched in her hand. She lunged forward to catch the painting before it crashed down on the desk below before realizing it wasn't actually falling; it was just on a hinge. She swung the painting open and found herself staring at a wall safe. It was locked, of course.

CHAPTER TWENTY-SEVEN

The Fort Collins Police Station bustled in the mundane late afternoon business. Parson was still filling out evidence forms when she saw the three women being guided into the building by uniformed officers. She stopped what she was working on and watched them. They weren't in cuffs, which didn't surprise her. Their behavior didn't indict them to being the most obvious suspects, but Parson needed time with them, especially with Verity Georgeson. She needed to get her away from the other two. How much of what she was seeing was a show, and how much was genuine shock and trauma? She watched them be led off into the elevators.

It was a long time after the elevator doors had slid shut that Parson was still standing there, thinking. Did she have this all worked out wrong? Something was missing, something she hadn't quite latched on to yet.

"Detective?" the officer on the other side of the desk queried. She shook her head free of the random thoughts.

"Sorry," Parson offered. She signed the last of her forms, collected her files, her scene photos, and the most recent tox screens, then drifted off to question the recent arrivals. She wasn't in a hurry, but her feet already knew where they were going. The regular soft thuds of her work boots against the polished concrete floors blocked out the bustle of the rest of the world. She melted into the metronome effect they offered as she turned ideas around in her head and scanned the toxicology reports until something caught her eye. *Shit*, she thought. She would never get the warrants she needed if this was any indicator. Could she have everything wrong?

Eventually, her feet deposited her at the end of the familiar corridor. The curved wall of glass facing the street, looking down at the busy traffic, juxtaposed against the neutral sparse wall. Down at the far end of the corridor, a black shapeless shadow hunched in the chairs. She knew what it was. The figures of the three women melted together into one shapeless form, but as she drew nearer, their shadows splintered off from one another.

Yet again, three women sitting neatly in a row confronted her. Three figures in black, all dressed in sorrow and suspicion. It was getting a bit ridiculous, if she let herself be honest. It was like looking at a morose statuette of "see no evil, hear no evil, speak no evil." The trick was to learn which woman was each monkey. She had her suspicions; she just didn't have the evidence to back it up.

Parson approached the women and nodded to them. "Ms. Georgeson, please come with me." Parson watched as Mary Otto and Anita Belker comforted the fragile women. She had to admit that if this was all a show, it was impressive. She knew what to look for in PTSD patients, and the signs of stress and shock were all too familiar to her thanks to her career. The Georgeson woman was either a true victim or a masterful criminal. It was Parson's job to draw out the truth, no matter how ugly it was.

She followed Ms. Georgeson into the room. Just before she closed the door behind her, she saw a few uniformed officers coming down the hallway. *Good,* she thought. She wanted to make sure the others weren't left on their own. She wasn't sold on their innocence yet either.

Instructing Ms. Georgeson to sit down in one chair at the table, Parson sat on the opposite side, taking a few minutes to arrange all her supplies. She'd learned long ago she didn't need words to intimidate and insinuate. She placed her notebook neatly in front of her with her favorite pen, the one that her dad had given to her as a special gift when she'd graduated from the academy. She placed each of the files in a neat row between her and Verity Georgeson, each folder having a different name written on the side tab in straight, tidy handwriting. The black permanent marker contrasted against the manila folder to showcase the names Geoffrey Otto, Richard Belker, and Henry Williams. Verity brought her face up from a gloomy stance to read the names on the folders. She reached out for them but quickly retracted her hand as though being confronted by all they represented had burned her.

"I know this is difficult, but we need to make sure we have all the details," Parson started. Verity nodded slowly. "Okay, let's start with why he was there?"

"He said he was going to fix something," the other woman stammered.

"Like what?"

"I had been complaining of a squeaky floorboard in my room, and he was going to fix it for me."

"You live in an old house. I would think there are a lot of squeaky floorboards," Parson asked. Verity twitched softly against that.

"I take care of my home."

"Sorry, didn't mean to imply that you didn't." Parson took notes, but she tried to not take her eyes off the woman if she could help it. "Was that something he did often? Fix things?"

Verity nodded. "He is a good man." Her words caught halfway through the sentiment. "He *was* a good man."

"Okay. Tell me what happened, then."

Verity's shoulders heaved up and down a couple of times before she collected her words. "Mary, Anita, and I were, well, just getting to know each other. We've all been through so much, and we had things in common."

"Like what?"

Verity's eyes pulled up and met Parson's. The pain in those eyes was hard to watch, but she didn't pull her punches with her answers.

"Heartbreak."

Fair enough, Parson thought, *that was easy enough to understand*.

"Is that when Henry showed up?"

"He was already there."

"Was that normal?"

Verity gazed at the wall behind Parson, then shook her head. "No. I, I remember that he caught me off guard."

"How so?

"Well, he'd stayed over the night before. I had an early business meeting, but I was expecting him for dinner. I left him a note," Verity said.

Parson flipped through the folders on the table, purposefully leaving the grisly photos of Henry's body exposed. Verity flinched away from them before Parson found the note, secured in a plastic bag until fingerprints could be taken.

"This note?" she asked, and Verity nodded. "But you let him stay. All right, then what?"

"I asked him if he could give us some privacy, and he said he would leave us alone."

"Why did you need privacy?"

"We'd been talking about . . ." She hesitated. "No, that isn't it. We were, we were sharing memories. It was heartbreaking to hear their stories, but they were so kind to listen to mine." She wrung her hands together, her eyes squinting against the pain beneath her bandages. "It's been such a long time since I've had another woman to confide in."

"What about your daughter?" At this, Verity's eyes shot across at her and Parson had to forcibly keep herself from reacting. Mothers were always protective of their children, and she was no different.

"It isn't right to ask my daughter to carry my burdens," Verity asserted.

Touchy subject, Parson thought.

"Okay, okay. What then?"

"He, he gave me a kiss." Verity's hand went to her cheek, remembering the feel of it. "Then he fixed himself a drink."

"He was having a drink before being Mr. Fix It?" Parson asked, maybe a little too sarcastically.

Verity sighed. "I keep top-shelf liquor. He doesn't spend that kind of money on his own booze, so he likes to drink mine when he's over."

"Charming," Parson mumbled, taking a few more notes. "And then?"

"And then he just dropped the glass. It startled all of us. I just thought it had slipped from his hands, but he collapsed too."

Verity's body shook with the memory of it as her face darkened with fear. It was always amazing how much fear memories could invoke. Sometimes memories were so potent that they could frighten one more than the event itself. She'd heard that over and over from the therapists and grief counselors she worked with when dealing with victims.

"Was there anything else?" she asked.

Verity Georgeson's head was bowed, and her bandaged hands shook delicately in erratic spasms. Her shoulders had rolled forward. She looked as though she was simply folding in on herself. When Parson had first encountered her, she could have sworn she was a strong, singularly independent woman. Each tragedy wore on her, abraded her, and now she was becoming nothing more than a wilted, spent flower.

Parson hated to see women crushed under the weight of tragedy. This world they lived in was brutal to women. They had to harden themselves to it. Sometimes she came across women who were works of art translated into flesh and movement. Parson thought Verity was one of those women. She was beautiful and strong and made her world into something beautiful even if no one else thought it was. Now, here she was, crushed by so much trauma. She's survived the death of a husband, nearly lost custody of her daughter in the criminal investigation over the suspicious death of that very husband, suffered the loss of a friend in Geoff Otto, and endured the death of two men dying in her arms, one of whom was a cherished lover. It was too much for one person to bear. She didn't quite realize how all her instincts could have been so wrong, but here she was, confronted by her own poor judgment.

The table between them was covered in crime scene photos from the three recent deaths, not to mention a folder of evidence she'd been collecting on the death of her husband. Not a single bit of this evidence was anything more than unsubstantial at best and wouldn't be enough to even get a judge to sign a warrant, but it had all pointed her to the woman sitting across the table. She needed more, just one more bit to piece it together.

"I know this is difficult, but you need to tell me."

"Tell you what?"

"Whatever secret you're keeping. I know you're still holding something back."

Verity shook her head. Parson wanted the woman to look up; she needed to see her eyes. Eyes revealed everything a body keeps hidden.

"I don't have any secrets."

"I know that's a damn lie. You have plenty of secrets. I don't care about most of them, but I care about the one you're keeping about all of this." Parson tapped on the table. "The only thing I've got connecting all of this together is you. Unless you want to be the one to go down for all three murders, then I suggest giving up the ghost."

Parson watched as the woman's shaking bandaged hands twitched under that brutal declaration. Was that shock or something more?

"I didn't kill anyone," Verity said.

"Then help me find the person who's responsible for all this," Parson demanded.

Then everything changed. A simple flip of a switch. Verity's hands stopped shaking, her shoulders rolled back and straightened, and when her bowed head lifted, all the anguish and pain of loss was gone. Dark circles hollowed out her eyes, but the woman sitting here in front of her was once again the empowered woman she'd first brought in when she was assigned Geoff Otto's case. There was no sign of any trauma. Her eyes were steady and calculating, which made the hairs on the back of Parson's neck bristle and stand on end.

"Tell me, Detective, why do I have to do your job?"

"Excuse me?" Parson said without thinking, which she immediately regretted. In that one stupid moment when Parson had been caught off guard, Verity Georgeson had taken her measure. The woman leaned back in her chair and settled her hands on the table in front of her. She was calm and collected and utterly unperturbed by any of this.

"Detective, if you really must know, the secret I was keeping was that Henry was responsible for it all."

"Why would you keep something like that to yourself?"

"He was a good man, respected. I didn't want to have his name smeared in the press simply for your satisfaction," Verity said calmly. Too calmly.

"You'd rather go to prison in his place?"

"You and I both know that I would never go to prison based on the evidence you've presented to me here. My only real connection to all of this was that Henry was jealous of any man whom he perceived as coming between us."

"He's a murderer." Parson was taken aback that such an intelligent woman would let a man like Henry Williams leave a stain on her life to this extent. Then another thought crossed her mind. How could she have not put that piece in place?

"He's the one who murdered your husband, isn't he?" Parson asked even though she already knew the answer to that particular question.

Verity's mouth twitched. "Yes."

"How long have you known?"

"Last night," Verity said. "He confessed it all to me last night."

"Convenient much?"

"You can believe me or not; it makes no difference to me."

"You don't seem very put out by it."

"What are you going to do, arrest me for my lover's misdeeds?"

"Keeping that kind of information to yourself is enough for me to have you arrested for interfering in an investigation," Parson shot back.

To this, Verity simply raised her hands, wrist to wrist, an offering to Detective Parson. Parson didn't know what to make of her. Was she being honest now, or had she known he was the perp this whole time? An even more dangerous thought occurred to her. What if Verity had manipulated Henry into murdering the others? Was it something as simple as jealousy, or was there still more to it than that? Could she have orchestrated everything? If so, how? How could one woman have that much of an effect to counter any semblance of self-preservation?

Lowering her wrists, Verity calmly leaned back. Parson saw everything she needed to see in Verity's eyes. Her pretty face was neutral, her mouth relaxed, but her eyes sparkled, they sparkled like she was grinning inside. Parson had come to the striking conclusion that Verity Georgeson was a Cheshire cat. Hopefully, she wouldn't disappear like one.

"Will there be anything else?" Verity asked.

"For now, no."

Dammit, Parson thought. She clicked her pen irritably.

Verity rose from her seat, smoothing nonexistent creases in her couture slacks, and walked around the table to the door. She put her hand on the knob and turned back to face Parson. As soon as the two women made eye contact, Verity Georgeson's entire physique changed. Her hands curled in slightly and quivered erratically, her shoulders rolled forward and her head bent down. The fragile, traumatized victim she'd brought into this room had returned right before her eyes. Parson just sat there mesmerized by the transformation and hated that there was nothing she could do. Without evidence, she could only watch her shuffle out of the room and be swallowed up in the tender and nurturing embrace of her new-found friends. Of course, if she confided in these ladies that Henry had confessed to all the deaths, then they were bonded in something more profound than a weak husband caught in the act of betrayal. They had all lost something dear to them, and the grim circumstances of those losses bound them to each other.

Parson watched the three women walk away, huddled together. She opened the folder in her hands and read the tox report again. There was no doubt about it. Verity Georgeson had enough arsenic in her bloodstream to imply that someone had been slowly poisoning her. If Henry had figured out who was trying to kill Verity, that could very well explain why he ended up dead. It didn't answer every question, but it did rectify one very important question. Detective Karen Parson knew without a doubt that she could never lock up Verity Georgeson for murder.

CHAPTER TWENTY-EIGHT

Anita had always thought funerals were curious things, and this one was more curious than most. Rather than being held in a church or at a funeral home, Anita Belker found herself staring at the beautiful Queen Anne Tower House belonging to Verity Georgeson. Although the house was not particularly large, it was grand and imposing. The ruddy stonework was complemented by the black painted woodwork, which formed arches around the porch and framed each of the windows. A wrought-iron fence entrapped the two-storied home, with each slender post capped at a point like an army of spears guarding the home. Anita passed through the open gate, mounted the steps, and crossed the threshold framed by a beautiful black lacquered door with an ornate stained-glass window. The window in the door was a work of art in its own right, with a bee and hive motif of rich yellows, ambers, and reds.

She'd only seen the inside of Verity's home one other time, and it was something she'd never forget. Anita had witnessed the result of gruesome deaths that not only frightened her half out of her wits but also broke her heart. It was strange to be here again under slightly different circumstances. Now, she and Mary Otto had forged a friendship with Verity Georgeson. She was sure outsiders questioned the sanity of that friendship since they'd all been entangled in each other's lives through infidelity and suspicion, but tragedy and horror could bring people together. Anita knew people gossiped about the whole nasty affair, but she didn't care. She had two friends who would walk through fire for her, and she would do the same.

Anita smoothed down her black dress and made her way through Verity's home, searching for her friends. She'd be the first to admit that she didn't pay much attention to the house the last time she was here; they were all understandably distracted. The interior held an exquisite collection of unique art and repurposed furniture. The mosaic-tiled foyer, which continued the bee theme, opened up to a gracious living room. There was an enormous Victorian curio cabinet with surprisingly delicate feet and a modern mid-century sofa. All the woodwork was stained in deep mahogany and rich walnut tones. The dark aubergine wallpaper carried throughout the hallways along with lavish rugs, elegant figurines, and the most wonderfully eclectic collections of prints and paintings.

She wasn't surprised to see most of the guests in attendance were men from the firm. They were like the old guard of the architectural industry, unwilling to relinquish their power. A few women were scattered throughout the place, most of whom she didn't recognize; the ones she did were like the woman she used to be. A show wife, an adornment to a prestigious career. While some men dispersed around the premises, Anita noticed that most were lounging near the dry bar that had been repurposed from an enormous French provincial bureau. She had no idea where to find Mary and Verity.

She scanned the room. There were three exits from the living room except for the front door. A library was off to the right. The door was ajar, and she could see a portion of a large built-in shelf of books. Ahead of her was a set of French doors open to a dining room, with another door leading straight through to the kitchen. Beyond the hallway to the left was another door, and like most of the doors in the house, the wood was old, stained a deep rich color, with a transom window above. It was actually functional and propped open slightly. Through the open doorway, Anita saw what looked to be some kind of sitting room.

She chose the dining room option and found herself in an extraordinarily beautiful room. Anita had expected this room to be as dark and moody as the living room but was surprised by the open, airy feel of the enormous ivory table that could seat at least ten people comfortably. The walls were papered in scenic florals of creams and silvery greens. Leafy branches and white peonies, delicate birds, and whimsical butterflies danced along the walls. A crystal chandelier hung over the table, which was set with expensive china and crystal wine goblets, and minty green cloth napkins matched the upholstered chairs. Instead of traditional dining chairs or even modern clean-lined chairs, the table was surrounded by channeled wingback chairs. Anita could easily imagine being a guest in this house, the delicate sound of silverware clinking against the fine china, bottles of wine opening on the cobalt sideboard, the plush upholstery enveloping her, and long conversations going deep into the night. She smiled at the notion of this being her future.

"Lovely, isn't it?"

Anita flinched at the voice. She had been lost in her thoughts and didn't see Verity approach. She wore an elegant black shift dress with a black Panama hat atop her head. Anita hadn't ever noticed Verity's figure. The woman before her wasn't particularly tall or skinny, but she was fit. Beneath the brim of the hat, Verity showcased fair skin and clean neutral makeup, which always stirred a little envy in her. Her skin was youthful and clear, but there were indications of lines at the corners of her eyes when she smiled softly at Anita. Her mossy green eyes hinted at the depth of experience that Anita was only just starting to learn about. Regardless of her natural beauty, Verity displayed clear signs of grief that even the most skilled makeup artist would consider a challenge to camouflage.

"It really is," Anita murmured.

"My cousin Sarina and I took ages to design it, but I think it came out beautifully," Verity replied. "I had always wanted a Victorian house. The amount of craftsmanship they put into them, architecture as art, don't you think?"

"I do."

Verity analyzed Anita's appearance from head to toe. "You look like you could use a friendly face."

Anita huffed out a small breath. Even though Anita and Verity had become friends, it wasn't yet to the same extent of she and Mary's relationship, and Anita very much wanted to be in the company of her best friend.

"More than you know," Anita said.

Verity's smile broadened, and she held out her arm in a sassy mockery of chivalry. Anita slid her arm through Verity's, then the hostess escorted Anita through the elegant dining room and through the doors leading to the kitchen, which was its own beautiful masterpiece. They passed through a beautiful white kitchen and into a small conservatory. The exterior wall of the room was completely framed in iron and glass, with comfortable sitting chairs and French bistro tables covered in linens. A ceiling fan made lazy circles as it circulated the air. Their heels clacked on the tiled floor as they made their way through to the backyard.

The backyard was simple and green, with a high privacy fence covered in ivy. What would have normally been open space was now filled with black folding chairs arranged in two large sections with an aisle between them. At the far end of the aisle, a black casket rested on a cloth-covered plinth that Anita was sure was only a disguised trolley to wheel the body away. A woman with her back to them stood with her hand on the closed casket. Anita knew immediately who it was. Verity patted her hand knowingly, and together, the two of them approached Mary Otto's side.

"Mary," Verity said quietly so as not to startle the widow, "I've brought you a friend."

Mary Otto turned around, and at the sight of Verity and Anita, her face stretched into a sad smile that was full of gratitude and relief. Mary welcomed Anita with a warm embrace, and Anita was rather shocked by the fierceness of the hug; to see the proper woman let her guard down so freely surprised Anita. It was a funeral, and people behaved strangely at funerals. Anita reached out an arm and pulled Verity into their hug. By the time they released each other, guests had started to file out of the little conservatory and find their seats. Mary gently patted the closed casket.

"Thank you for doing this for Geoff," Mary said to Verity.

"He was a good man, Mary."

The three friends stood side by side as guests greeted them, offered condolences, and collected gossip. Funerals were a lot like weddings in that way. People were either on their best behavior or on their worst, so they were fantastic places to spread gossip like wildfire. A month ago, Anita might have fretted over the gossip, but she didn't care about that anymore.

Once most of the guests had settled in their seats, Anita, Mary, and Verity took their own in the front row. Mary sat on one side of Anita, while Verity sat with Jenna on the other side of her. The sun shone brightly, birds chirruped happily, and the mourners nodded respectfully, but as the memorial continued, the fine hairs on the back of Anita's neck pricked and her nerves tingled. She knew with uncanny certainty that she was being watched. She turned a little in her seat and scanned the sea of black. Nothing stuck out to her as unusual, at first. Most of the guests were paying attention to the reverend standing at the front behind the onyx coffin, offering his thoughts on life and death and everything in between. She glanced in the other direction and suddenly found herself confronted by the withering gaze of Detective Parson. What was she doing here? Didn't the woman ever give up? Anita's nerves ratcheted up as she tried to ignore the piercing gaze of the detective. After everything they had gone through, the investigations, the incriminations, it was enough to drive them insane. Detective Parson had no evidence against them; otherwise, she would have arrested them ages ago, but Anita would be an idiot to let her guard down now. She offered the detective the mirror of her icy glare and returned her attention to the service.

By the end of the service, she had shed a fair amount of her own tears, and Mary and Verity were sniffling on either side of her. The three of them were ushered back into the house first, and then the rest of the guests followed. Anita shook hands, received hugs, and mingled with the crowd of people infecting Verity's home like a swarm of black ants, always trying to get where they didn't belong. Anita was usually a personable individual and liked being in a crowd, but her nerves were on edge and she wasn't comfortable leaving the vicinity of her two friends.

Mary spoke with the old boys from the firm, and Anita watched Verity make each guest feel as though all of this had been arranged for their own benefit. That woman's grace amazed her. Then Anita saw Detective Parson approach Verity. Mary made eye contact with Anita, and they shared a look that was the equivalent of, *Batten down the hatches*! Anita and Mary flanked Verity like soldiers protecting their general.

"Ms. Georgeson," the detective said.

"Good morning, Detective Parson." Verity's tone was cordial yet holding a hint of disdain. Perhaps it was something Anita imagined simply because she knew of the tension between the women. Detective Parson invaded their privacy, revealed every ugly secret, and paraded her belief that the circumstantial evidence proved the three women had colluded to kill their men. Parson believed that since they befriended Verity, they were guilty by association. She seemed to take special pleasure in tormenting Verity for weeks, and the detective's rage in not being able to pin the eclectic woman with a conviction was driving her to extremes. "I hope the service helps you find some resolution."

"Ms. Georgeson, the only resolution I'll find is when I can visit you behind bars."

"You are out of line, Detective," Mary hissed in a tone that could make hell freeze over.

"It's all right, Mary," Verity soothed. "The detective is just frustrated about her inability to catch the individual responsible for the deaths of our loved ones."

Detective Parson stepped so close to Verity that they appeared as though they were two lovers about to kiss, but there was no love lost between the enemies.

"I know it was you. You are never going to be rid of me," Parson snarled low enough that only the three friends heard.

Verity made a small move that placed her crimson lips at the detective's ear. It was a strangely erotic movement in the most unromantic of moments. Verity whispered something in the detective's ear that Anita couldn't hear, but whatever she said, it was enough to make all the color drain from the detective's face. Her pallor blanched, her eyes grew slightly wider, and her jaw worked fiercely. Rage rushed out from the woman in waves that, if not addressed quickly, could overcome everyone in the house.

"Detective, other people are waiting to speak with us, so I think it's time for you to move on now," Anita said in her soft voice. Before meeting Verity and becoming a widow herself, Anita would've never found the courage to speak to a person in authority like that, but here she was, a new woman, changed through grief and friendship. She realized she was absolutely fine with the woman she'd become. She met the detective's shriveling glare without flinching and held her ground until the woman left.

"Thank you," Verity said. "Thank you, both of you, for being such fierce friends." She wrapped them into a gentle embrace. "What would I do without you?"

"We're in this together, no matter what comes of it," Mary said with finality.

"Yes. I agree, wholeheartedly," Anita offered with a warm smile.

The three friends weathered the rest of the morning with grace. Eventually, the guests began to leave and Verity's home emptied out, but one of the last guests to approach Verity gave Anita a nasty case of the shivers. Christopher Blackwood was dressed impeccably in a charcoal gray suit with a matching vest. A pocket watch with a delicate gold chain accented his attire. He gave the women a regal bow of his head and offered each of them unique condolences. Anita felt her skin crawl. He was elegant and well-spoken, yet he somehow inspired a kind of fear she couldn't put into words. It was like being a little girl and trying to explain to her parents why she was afraid of the dark. She didn't understand why he invoked such feelings of dread, but she knew better than to ignore those feelings.

Anita pressed herself a little closer to Verity until he left. If she ever ran into that man again, it would be too soon.

Chapter Twenty-Nine

It was several hours before Verity's house emptied itself of the crowd of funeral attendees and well-wishers. She accepted each condolence and shook every hand offered to her. She was tired, bone tired. Verity had been playing this game for years, and she was so tired of it. Henry's death and her corresponding statement about his horrifying confession helped close the case as a spin of fate that the murderer had been killed by his own trick. Most of the officers she spoke to were quick to reassure her of just how lucky she was that it was he who'd drunk from the poisoned decanter. The corroboration of the tox screen revealing dangerous levels of arsenic in her own body was all the proof the chief of police needed to prove that Verity was also a victim. It could easily have been she. She was happy to let them believe whatever they wanted if it kept the scrutiny off her. Detective Parson was the only one who didn't believe the circumstances, but that was to be expected. Verity wasn't worried, though.

In a few short weeks, Verity Georgeson would fall off the face of the planet, and she could reclaim a little of that peace she'd been dreaming of for so long. She had one more appointment with Blackwood, and then she'd be free to settle her affairs and take up residence in the old house. Verity couldn't wait to surprise Jenna. She just knew she'd love the old place and they would have a blast fixing it up.

"Verity?" Anita's gentle voice pierced her thoughts, and she remembered she still needed to keep up the charade for a little while longer. Verity turned to face the woman who had been so gracious to see her as a victim. She wasn't sure any of this would've worked out without her belief in Verity.

"Anita, how are you holding up?"

"As well as can be expected." Anita looked around the place. "I miss him, Richard, you know."

Verity saw her face droop a little, and she wrapped an arm around her new friend. "I know. I miss Henry too."

"It doesn't really seem fair, you know, that we should have to go on without them when they were such a big part of our lives."

"I know what you mean." Verity was no stranger to loss. Not all the death in her life had been Henry's fault or part of her schemes. Her father's death had hit her the hardest. Just thinking about the empty space he had left in her life periodically made the grief fresh again. She rubbed at her sternum absentmindedly to soothe her jittery heart. "I would say that the worst was over, but that would be a lie."

"What do you mean?"

"She means," Mary said as she drew the two other women closer to her, "that we still have to learn to live our lives without them."

"I don't want to," Anita said.

"I know." Mary hugged her friend tightly. "We'll all learn together."

Verity smiled at the other two. They were an odd collection of women, but she enjoyed their company. It was a shame that she would have to leave them. She could see herself being loved and cared for if she stayed with them, but she needed something different. She needed to love herself, which wasn't easy to do. She had spent so much time trying to figure out who she was and what she wanted, and all the while portraying a woman who she would inevitably kill, metaphorically speaking at least.

"Now, ladies," Mary said in a brave tone and with a mischievous smile, "we've finally earned a drink after all this sad business today. What do you think?"

"I think you're an angel, Mary," Anita answered. Verity watched the tension in the woman's shoulders slough off with a full-body sigh, and she couldn't help but let a giggle slip out.

"I'm assuming you've found my wine collection," Verity offered.

"I'd keep it hidden in the basement, too, if I were you." Mary laughed as she led them deeper into the house, through the white kitchen, and out into the cheery little conservatory.

Verity had no objection because this was one of her favorite places in her home. The tiled floor had been swept free of leaf litter that had accumulated. The glass walls were slightly tinted against the harsh sun, but the sprawling plants resting happily on their ledges and in stands were content in the light. The little table that Verity loved to sit at and read was covered in linen, and three wine glasses full of blood-red liquid waited for them. She recognized the label and raised an eyebrow at Mary.

"I think I've had enough bourbon for now," Mary started, and they couldn't help but laugh awkwardly at the joke, "so I raided your wine collection."

Each woman took up a glass. Verity stared into the mesmerizing fluid and came close to losing herself. She was almost at the finish line, just a little while longer. "By the way, Verity," Mary said, "that is a spectacular collection of wine."

"I prefer wine to bourbon, always have, and now I prefer it even more."

"Well, ladies, I think a toast is in order," Mary suggested. They all raised their glasses. The summer light spilling through the glass walls caught the wine and threw crimson across the floor. "To endings and new beginnings."

"To new friends," Anita added.

"I'll drink to that," Verity added. The air rang with the chime of crystal clinking against crystal, and the three friends drank their wine in silence. They had cried together, they'd stood by each other through all the messy investigations around the deaths of the men they had loved, and here they were at the end of things but ready to step out on a new path. No one was more ready than Verity to start fresh. She was looking forward to her new project, a new adventure, and a much quieter life.

Not long after the wine glasses were empty and hugs had been shared, and with promises to check in on each other, Verity finally found herself standing on her front porch and waving goodbye as Mary and Anita drove off. A gentle touch placed between her shoulder blades reminded her to relax a little more. Jenna's arms wrapped around her from behind, and she leaned back into the comfort of her daughter's embrace.

This was home, not the house, or this moment in life. Home was wherever Jenna was.

"How are you holding up, Mom?" Jenna asked. Her voice was always so sweet. Verity closed her eyes and let the sun warm her.

"I'm all right, sweetie." She turned around in Jenna's grasp and wrapped her arms around her. "How about you, kiddo?"

"I guess I'm all right," she replied, but there was no conviction in her voice. "I miss him."

"I know you do. I do too. He was a good man, no matter what they say."

"He was good to us."

"He was," Verity said. Jenna looked up at her mom, and Verity's heart broke just a little more at the sight of her daughter's puffy eyes.

"We should do something special. You know, honor him somehow."

"I think that's a great idea," Verity said, giving Jenna a sad smile. "What did you have in mind?"

"Oh, I don't know. I'll think of something."

"I can't wait." She tightened her grip on Jenna as an old fear rose to the surface. That somehow this crazy plan of hers would crumble and the only thing she truly cared for, her daughter, would be hurt in the process. She had done all of this for Jenna, for the amazing relationship they shared. They had been through so much together, and Verity was finally looking forward to the future. "Look, I've got one more thing I need to take care of today, but after that, why don't we call it a girl's night in. What do you think?"

"Sounds great, Mom," Jenna said into her neck as she gripped Verity a little more firmly.

"Why don't you pick some takeout? Text me with the order, and I'll pick it up on my way back."

"Okay," Jenna said, dragging her mom back into the comfort of the house.

Once they were safely within the confines of the house, now blissfully empty of guests, Jenna went off to the kitchen to look through the pile of menus stashed in one of the drawers. Verity grabbed her leather tote hanging on a hook by the front door before making her way upstairs and to her bedroom.

She closed the door softly behind her and leaned back into it. Her whole body was so weary, her exhaustion running bone-deep. It took all her strength to stand up and pull herself back into motion. Verity made her way across the room to her desk, and pulling a small vintage skeleton key from her pocket, she unlocked the desk and folded down the writing surface. She set her leather tote down on the desk and pulled the painting hanging above it open like a door. It swung smoothly aside, and she faced the matte black surface of her wall safe. She entered her code on the keypad and swung open the small heavy door. Inside the safe, there were only two items. One was a large sealed envelope of paperwork she needed to drop off at her attorney's office, and the other was the velvet bag safely storing the vintage jewelry box. She pulled out both items and shoved the envelope in her tote right away. That would be her first stop.

She stood there for a long minute with the velvet bag cupped protectively in the palms of her hands. It was strange that all her hopes and dreams relied on something so small. Opening the bag, she inspected the vintage wooden box. It was elegant and rare, but she knew it was the story that went with it that made it special. This little trinket was linked to the rise and fall of another woman who had been disheartened by the way the world worked against her. Well, she was more than happy to take a man's money to secure her own future.

She closed up the bag and carefully placed it in her tote, her hands trembling slightly. There was no pleasure in dealing with Blackwood, but it was a necessary evil. She wouldn't even have gotten half the money he was offering if she'd gone through more legal means of sale. She threw the leather tote onto her shoulder and braced herself to put these last few tasks behind her. After Verity made her way back downstairs and headed for the kitchen, she found her daughter sitting at the counter with a pile of menus spread out in front of her, but her face was glued to her phone.

"All right, sweetie, I'm off."

"Where do you have to go?" Jenna asked without looking up from her phone.

"I've got to stop by Henrik's and drop off some paperwork, then I've got a business meeting that I couldn't put off any longer. Hopefully, I'm not gone too long," Verity said as she grabbed her keys off the counter.

"Mr. Henrik is a funny little dude."

"You're not wrong there, but he's very good at what he does."

"He always reminds me of that detective with the ridiculous mustache," Jenna said absently while her fingers moved across the keyboard on her phone. Verity stopped in her tracks and gave her daughter a skeptical frown.

"Did you just compare my attorney to Hercule Poirot?" Verity asked. Jenna looked up at her with a confused expression until she gave her mother a wink. "You ridiculous child. It's a good thing I love you."

"You know it."

"I won't be gone long."

"Drive safe, Mom."

"I promise." Verity leaned in and kissed Jenna on the crown of her head. Her eyes closed, and she breathed in the familiar scent of her child. Verity left the sweet comfort of her home and got in her car. She'd stop at her attorney's office first, and then she would have to meet with Christopher Blackwood one last time.

She pulled away from the curb, her distinctive little Victorian house falling away in the rearview mirror. Change was like that. Sometimes change came in great big events, like being slapped in the face, while other times it was just that some things simply fell away. Verity's future was the road ahead, and her past was falling away from her in the rearview mirror.

CHAPTER THIRTY

Verity Georgeson left her attorney's office with a smile on her face. Jenna was right. While he read through the documents she'd returned to him, it was impossible to deny the little man's similar appearance to Agatha Christie's most famous character. He was petite and round, with an egg-shaped head and a mustache. Although the man was impeccably dressed, his style sense was still stuck in the early nineties. Verity sat patiently while he meticulously reviewed everything. And she didn't leave until he was satisfied with her affairs being in order. Due to the uncertainty of several aspects of her plan, she'd made sure that there were at least a couple of safety nets in place, should her plans derail, or something worse.

Standing outside his office in the early afternoon sun, she checked the time on her watch and realized she had an hour before she needed to meet with the broker. *Perfect*, she thought. She had just enough time to stop by the old house. The drive was long, but it was dusty this time of year. A cloud of dust billowed behind her car as she drove down the familiar county roads to get to the old house.

When Verity arrived at the abandoned property, she pulled off to the side of the road and instantly regretted not having a pair of boots with her. She'd thought about it, but with all the chaos of putting her plans in motion, she'd completely forgotten to get that little thing done. She didn't feel like losing another pair of her good stockings to the overgrown field she'd have to cross to get inside, so she hiked up her skirt and, in a familiar move, unclipped her stockings from her garter and carefully rolled them off. She was grateful that no one ever came down this road, because if anyone passed this way, she'd be offering them quite a site. There was nothing like watching a woman get half-undressed in the middle of a country lane to stick in one's memory. Carefully rolling up the delicate stockings, she stuffed them into the glove box of her car before slipping her heels back on, grabbing her tote, and stepping into the overgrown meadow that was now her front lawn.

By the time Verity slipped through the ajar front door, little red welts covered her legs from the thistles. That decided it; she'd just have to clear a path from the road to the door before she did anything else. She looked out her new front door and soaked in the vast view. An open meadow sprawling out away from the decrepit home greeted her. It felt right, like home. She couldn't wait to get her hands dirty, to breathe new life into this forgotten masterpiece, and maybe breathe new life into herself while she was at it. She let out a sigh so deep and relieving that it must've been years in the making. She stepped out of her shoes and wiggled her toes in the leaf litter that had blown in over the decades. The tension she'd been keeping in her shoulders released, her jaw relaxed, and her lungs expanded as they filled themselves with the crisp air and heady scent of the field painted with wildflowers. She was home.

Verity bent down and picked up her shoes before making her way slowly through the house. Every time she came here, she would notice something new that she hadn't seen the time before. Sometimes it was a bit of architectural detail, like the sleek stylized linear shapes or the geometric ornamental elements on every bold surface, while other times it was a new animal that had found its way inside and taken refuge from the elements outside. She didn't want to evict the little critters, but she would eventually reclaim this space for herself. Maybe she would integrate something for them in the field behind the house. It was an idea that would have to get added to the absurdly long list of projects to tackle when it came to this place.

As she walked through the corridors of peeling wallpaper, cracked sconces, and missing tiles, she ran her fingers along every surface. She could feel the house whispering to her. Here, in the silence of nowhere, she wondered, if she listened hard enough, if she would be able to understand what it was trying to tell her. Then she found one of her favorite places, the conservatory. Unlike the tiny greenhouse at her other place, this space was vast. The walls of glass in Art Deco arches with the framing between the panes that had probably been painted black or green at one point were still structurally sound. Although the glass itself was caked with grime that had collected over the years, relatively few were broken. She saw heavy drapes that were probably meant to control the light and heat in this space, but after so long, they were practically disintegrating.

Her feet knew the way to her favorite chaise lounge set along one of the far walls that looked out into the meadow behind the house, but it wasn't empty as she had been expecting. Sitting on the chaise of tattered green velvet was Christopher Blackwood, the broker. With one leg crossed over the other, the broker leaned back comfortably, reading a book, her book. She'd wondered where she left it and only now realized that it had been here since the last time she met with Geoff. Of all the deaths that sprinkled her life, Geoff Otto was the only one she hadn't expected. Their friendship was genuine. He understood her passion for this place, and he was just as eager to restore it as she was. She'd been looking forward to collaborating with him on it and his death would affect her for a long time, but for now, she needed to be on her toes. She hadn't expected to see the broker here. They were scheduled to meet somewhere else entirely.

"I knew you were the sort of woman who relished a good classic," he started without looking up at her, "but I'll admit that I figured you were more of a *Jane Eyre* sort of woman rather than *Wuthering Heights*." He closed the book and set it down on the chaise next to him. By the time his eyes looked up in her direction, she was propped against the doorway with her leather tote hoisted over one shoulder and her shoes dangling from the fingertips in her other hand.

"I enjoy a story that leaves me haunted after I'm done reading it."

"Yes, I can see that about you."

"You're early."

"I assumed you'd want to be done with our arrangement as soon as possible."

"It's a fair assumption," Verity said as she sat down in one of the desiccating reading chairs nearby.

"Do you have it with you?"

Verity smiled. "You must know that I do, or showing up here in my little sanctuary would have been pointless."

"True."

"I don't even want to begin to think about how you knew that, but I'll be glad to end our arrangement a little early." She leaned back in the chair and set her belongings down before crossing her legs. She didn't realize the power her presence had over the space, washing away some of the decay just by being here.

"Is there anything to drink around this place? This feels like something we should be celebrating."

"Are you telling me you showed up early to my secret little hideaway and you didn't poke around?"

"Okay, fine, you got me." He reached down over the arm of the lounge and pulled up a bottle of wine and two glasses. She recognized them as her own. Verity had spent enough time over the years hiding here, daydreaming of the future she'd been working so hard for, that she'd managed to accumulate a small stash of niceties.

Blackwood unearthed her foil cutter and brandished the corkscrew after cutting the foil off one of her favorite bottles. He poured them each a glass, and they enjoyed the dark red beverage in silence. The afternoon sunlight pushed through the grimy windows, warming the room. Verity watched the tall grasses and wildflowers outside the windows as they rippled in the wind, little waves and eddies of motion coursing through the meadow. She was perfectly content here.

"Another?" Blackwood asked, raising the bottle in a question.

"Why not?" She leaned forward and offered up her empty glass, which he filled again. She settled back into the chair and studied the man sitting opposite her. Verity didn't want to admit it, but they were probably more alike than she preferred, and by the comfort they shared with the silence around them, he probably felt the same.

"May I ask you a personal question?" Blackwood said.

"As long as you understand I might choose not to answer."

"Fair enough. Why did you do all this? Don't get me wrong. I have been highly entertained by the story you've created. All the drama, despair, and mystery you've woven throughout this captivating tale will be more than enough provenance for me to turn a tidy profit. But there had to be more to all of this than just earning the price tag you've put on this little gem," He dipped his head to acknowledge the little box.

"It's a fair question," Verity admitted. She thought about biting her tongue, but he already knew so many of her secrets that there seemed no point in withholding it. "I wanted to have enough money to restore this place. It's a legacy for my daughter, a place where we can be ourselves, a place where we can feel the satisfaction of building something up with our own bare hands."

"She is lucky to have a mother who cares so much for her."

Verity bowed her head slightly at the compliment. "Well, shall we get the last of this business done?"

"If you say so."

Blackwood set down his glass on the floor near his foot. Verity set her glass down as well, and replacing it with the leather tote, she carefully pulled out the dark velvet bag. So much was riding on such a small package. She rose and brought it over to him, placing the velvet bag in his hands. He held it there for a moment, almost reverently, before he came back to the moment and pulled out an incriminating envelope full of cash.

She took the money without counting it. That would've been an insult in his eyes, and she'd rather not tarnish this deal at the last moment. She took her money and sat back down, eager to drink her wine and hopefully be rid of this man soon.

She watched him open the bag and carefully pull out the box. It really was beautiful, carved from wood and inlaid with ornamental metalwork in a geometric pattern that was the epitome of the late twenties. It wasn't only the delicate little box that was worth the amount of money Blackwood just paid her for but everything around it. The contents of the box, its place in time and history, not to mention the sordid details of its last owner, caught Blackwood's attention.

"I have to say," Blackwood started, "you really do fine work. I followed along with all the intrigue and was absolutely spellbound."

"Thank you."

"How did you get Mrs. Otto on your side?"

Verity laughed. "It wasn't easy," she admitted with a slight cough. "She's a bit of an old battle-ax if you ask me."

Blackwood chuckled. "You know, if this were all under different circumstances, I would have really enjoyed working with you again. I'm blown away by the amount of time and detail you put into your work."

"No offense, Mr. Blackwood, but I would appreciate never having to work with you again," she answered with a tickle in her throat. She cleared her throat as gently as she could. After everything she'd gone through to get to this point, she hoped she wasn't coming down with a cold. She didn't want to start her new life having to rest up first.

"It doesn't matter, I suppose. Circumstances being what they are." He got up and took his precious box close to one of the windows, tilting it in the light. "Do you know the story of your namesake? The first Verity Georgeson?"

"I know she was a widow like me."

"Yes," he said thoughtfully, "she was cunning like you too." Verity coughed unexpectedly and rushed to cover her mouth with her hand. When she looked down at her hand, brilliant red blood speckled it. Her eyes darted up to Blackwood. His back had been turned to her, but he straightened at the sound of another cough.

"Ah, I see it's starting to take effect. Good," he said softly.

"What did you do?" Verity struggled to say. Her throat was on fire, and her stomach turned unnaturally.

"Did you know that arsenic killed the original Verity Georgeson?" he asked as he watched Verity struggle to maintain her composure. "Apparently, the upper crust businessmen of the town didn't take kindly to her being so successful, at least not without a man to be her benefactor."

"Did you poison me?"

"Of course, dear," he offered without losing his place in his story. "Turns out that she became insanely wealthy only after the death of her husband. Society at the time had encouraged her to take another husband, but she wasn't very keen on that idea."

"I can't imagine why," Verity snapped sarcastically before doubling over in a fit as her stomach lurched and she involuntarily vomited onto the floor. This was not the way she saw this going.

"I knew you would understand." He set the box down on the chaise lounge, but he was holding something small in his hand. He raised it into the light struggling to push through the grimy windows. It was a vintage pharmacist's vial. The antique vial of arsenic, forgotten since the original bearer of Verity's name antagonized the local patriarchy. "A bit poetic, don't you think?"

She tried to reply, but another wave of nausea and vomiting twisted her body and she slid out of her chair, crumpling to the floor. Blackwood strode towards her, crouching down so that he could look her in the eye without stepping into the mess she was leaving.

"You see, I really appreciated the amount of art you put into your plan, the story you wove together, tangling yourself up with Geoff Otto and Richard Belker. You are an absolute artist." He rested on his haunches patiently as she shook, gagged, and retched. "I would have loved to work with you again, but unfortunately, one of my other clients really doesn't like you."

He stood up, dusting some invisible speck off his slacks, and gathered his belongings. "I'm so sorry, love, but I've got to go. I've got an appointment with them shortly." Christopher Blackwood gathered his precious new belongings and casually walked away.

He was nearly out of view when he stopped and turned around. "Oh, I almost forgot. My client asked me to pass along a message to you." She couldn't see him clearly through the tears of agony and fear, but his blurry figure stood there for a moment, staring at her as her body devoured itself from the inside out. "All this," he said, waving his hand absently around, implying the deadly circumstances she now found herself in, "is the perfect way to honor Henry."

Verity could only choke and wretch in response as she realized this was Jenna's doing. Her daughter had conspired to kill her.

"It really is a shame." And with that, he walked away. There was no way to call for help, no one to hear her. He simply left her here to die alone.

CHAPTER THIRTY-ONE

Christopher Blackwood pulled into his sleepy little town, eager to settle down for the rest of the day with a hot cup of tea and a good book. He pulled up to the curb in front of his shop and hesitated for a moment before getting out of his car. His business often kept him working in the shadows, but he honestly preferred the light. Despite his love of elegant fashion and the accumulation of power, he preferred the quiet life of living in a small town. Here, everyone knew everything about him, well, almost everything. They weren't required to like him, but they were expected to tolerate him.

He put the key in the lock to the shop and let himself in, rubbing the bridge of his nose. He'd never actually had a hand in murdering anyone before today, and he couldn't say he enjoyed it. He would have preferred to work with the charming Verity Georgeson in the future. This modern world didn't offer much in the way of grace and charm, and he was rather disheartened to have been a part of losing what little there was. In the end, though, business was business, and his client had paid him handsomely for Ms. Georgeson's demise.

He shut the door behind him and took the little velvet bag he'd been carrying over to the counter. He set the incrimination set of glasses and bottle of wine down on the edge of the counter before turning his attention to his latest acquisition. Eager to take a closer look at his prize, he turned on the nearby Tiffany desk lamp and opened the bag once more. He reached in and pulled it out tenderly, setting it carefully on the counter. The craftsmanship was exquisite. The hand-carved box was lovely in its own right, but the expertly inlaid metalwork was beautiful. Slowly opening the little box, he found it didn't contain much, but what it did contain was significant. A small bundle of letters belonging to the original owner of the box, Verity Georgeson, the original Ms. Georgeson, rested inside. From everything he learned about her through his research, she was every bit as shrewd and charming as the one he'd just left for dead. Blackwood removed his gloves and set them carefully aside before he took out the bundle of letters and gently untied the kelly-green ribbon keeping them together.

The paper was brittle and yellow but felt velvety beneath his touch. The superior quality of paper was instantly recognizable, and it made his heart just a little sadder to understand how far standards had fallen in today's world. People didn't put nearly the same care and attention into their appearance as they used to. He opened the first letter, taking care not to rip or stain it, and he read. His pouty mouth curled into a genuine smile, and his pupils dilated as he read the savagely penned letter. It would appear that the letter's owner was being threatened by another local businessperson. It was no new revelation, but how bold to put down a threat like that in writing. Apparently, the original Ms. Georgeson should have taken him more seriously, since she did in fact die as he had described. Blackwood wondered who had killed the woman. In all his research, which included what the police department had on file for the vintage investigation, they did not apprehend her murderer.

The shop phone rang, and he was pushed out of his thoughts. He checked the caller ID, seeing it was Charlton. The man was insufferable, and Blackwood did not possess the proper mood to deal with his blustering. Besides, he wasn't altogether sure he wanted to sell the box to a man like him. It wouldn't be honored like the delicious trove of mystery it was. No, he would have to find something less special for him. So, for now, he ignored the call, carefully folded up the incriminating letter, and rebound the collection of vintage letters together with their ribbon.

There were so many other items to inspect. The little compartments held antique jewelry that would have fetched close to the amount he had paid Verity Georgeson, but they weren't what he was looking for. His favorite item was easy to declare. Reaching into the box, he lifted out the top compartment and was relieved to see what he was looking for resting undamaged at the bottom of the box. This little item was a sprinkle of magic in the provenance of the box. He pulled out the little antique pharmacist's vial and held it up to the light. Liquid still shifted inside the vial, and he wondered about the potency of it after all this time. He smiled broadly, content with his new acquisition.

"Is that what all the fuss was about?" A voice from behind him made him startle, but he managed not to twitch in the face of his client.

"No, not really," Blackwood answered as the young woman stepped out of the shadows. Jenna Jones was much like her mother in many ways. She was beautiful but not in that classical Hollywood way. Her features were bold, she had an athletic figure, and her almond-shaped eyes were gray rather than the mossy green of her mother's. Her ashy brown hair was pulled up into a messy bun, she wore relaxed jeans and a T-shirt and sported bold red lips. "This was simply a means to an end."

"Probably not the end she expected," Jenna said, sauntering over to where he stood. Blackwood looked up from his new prized possession and took in the young woman. Her eyes were puffy and red, her brow was knitted together in a soft frown, but her back was rigid. Her fingers trailed along every surface she passed. He didn't respect anyone who couldn't keep their hands to themselves, but as he watched her pick up the empty wine glasses and raise them to her nose out of curiosity, he raised an eyebrow at the wonderment of happenstance. The young woman had no idea how he'd planned on murdering her mother, but she didn't seem care. All she wanted was her little slice of vengeance and because of her carelessness he knew that he would be able to redirect the blame of Verity Georgeson's death somewhere other than himself.

"No, I dare say she was caught rather by surprise," he replied. "Now, I'm positive that I locked the shop door when I left, so how exactly did you get in here?"

"It's done, then?" Jenna answered, completely ignoring his question.

"Yes, it's done." He didn't understand the young woman, and it was a pity. Her mother had gone to such extreme lengths to bequeath a legacy to her that would have most likely endured for many generations to come. It was hard to connect that graceful woman who had manufactured the deaths of so many people purely for the sake of giving her daughter a legacy to the young woman standing before him right now.

"Good."

"I must say, it is unexpected."

"What is?" she asked petulantly.

"I really thought that you and your mother were closer than all this." His curiosity was almost too much. But he wanted desperately to place the last piece to this little puzzle.

"You want to know why I paid you to kill my mother."

"Yes." There was just no beating around that bush. The young woman roamed his shop, running her fingers along the shelves, picking up items, and looking them over. She was trying to act casual, but Blackwood understood. She was still nervous about doing business with him. She was young and didn't have the accumulated experience that her mother had. Jenna might have been bold, but she wasn't confident. If this were any other client, he could use that to his benefit, but he was just as anxious to be done with their arrangement as she was.

"My mother was brilliant and kind. I loved her so much."

"Then why ask me to remove her?"

"She was the one person in my life willing to do anything for me, but she made one mistake."

"And what was that?" Blackwood asked.

It was a moment before she answered, and he could see her eyes cloud over with fresh grief.

"She killed the man I love."

"Your father."

"My father was a bastard. He deserved what he got. He never abused me, like he did her, but that was just because she was always there to protect me."

His quizzical expression didn't escape her notice. She put her hand on the door as she prepared to leave, but she turned back to him. "I was happy to let her do her thing. They were all jerks or cheaters, or both. I didn't care about any of that, but she went too far with Henry."

With that, the young woman pushed open the door, setting the little bell hanging over it into motion. The space filled with the happy sound of its chimes, but Blackwood's blood iced over. He stood there at his counter in shock at the realization that everything that young woman's mother had done to secure her future had been all for nothing from the very start. It would appear her daughter was her only blind spot. How strange things worked out that her last move in the game she'd been playing for so long was the one move that would make her lose it all.

Finally, it was all settled. He didn't have much in the way of things he wouldn't do for a good business deal, but murder was it. This had gotten too messy, and he didn't like the feeling of someone being out there who could pin him down to something like this. He would have to clean this mess up, but that would have to wait for another day. He was overdue for a hot cup of tea to settle his mind.

Christopher Blackwood packed up his new treasure and made his way to the back of the shop, up the stairs, and into his private sanctuary. As soon as he stepped over the threshold, he felt at ease. He walked over to his favorite chair and set the box on the nearby table before he went to his little kitchen to start the kettle. The window in his kitchen looked down over the quaint Main Street. Summer was ending, and although the days were still hot and everything was dressed in varying shades of green, the nights were getting cool. Autumn would arrive soon enough and all the accoutrements that came with it. He enjoyed the changing seasons. It was a natural reminder to reflect on his life and make any necessary changes to keep himself moving forward.

Sunset was still hours away, but the light spilling through his kitchen window was already changing. It no longer held that brightness of midday, the light no longer washed everything out, but rather, it cast a warmth on everything it touched. Gold and amber accented every surface as though a painter had gone through and highlighted everything with his paintbrush. Christopher Blackwood closed his eyes and watched the colors play across his eyelids, but visions of what he'd left behind in that abandoned house haunted him. He was a shrewd businessman, and he would be the first to admit that he could be cruel to those who got in the way of him accumulating power, but watching Verity Georgeson die in such a grisly fashion had already begun to haunt him. There was no solace to be had even when he closed his eyes. All he saw was her frightened eyes and her contorted body, and her sickness clung to the inside of his nostrils.

Blackwood opened his eyes, the vintage streetlamps and picket fences washing away the horror he would keep with him forever. Outside, a gentle breeze wound its way through Main Street. Mrs. Knoxburough, one of his little town's more colorful elderly characters, shuffled along with her cane in one knobby hand and her library book bag in the other, and a moving van lumbered by his shop. The kettle hopped and popped on the counter behind. Someone new was coming to town, and he smiled at the upcoming intrigue of getting to know someone new. It was just the sort of thing to wash away all this unpleasant business.

The End

For now.

Acknowledgments

I have always wanted to write (except for when I was a wee child; back then, I wanted to be a marine biologist). Creating this story has been such a rewarding and wild experience that would not have happened if it were not for the support of so many people.

I offer my heartfelt gratitude to my family. To Dan: You are the best husband a lady can ask for. Thank you for your endless tolerance of the mountains of unfolded laundry, stacks of manuscripts, and the empty wine bottles, and for wiping away my tears all those times I was overwhelmed and frustrated. I love you so much. To Milla: I'm eternally grateful for you. You are the most beautiful, amazing weirdo that I have ever known, and I am honored to be your mom. I couldn't have done any of this without you. I love you, kiddo. To Janet: Let's face it, life in our house when I was growing up was interesting, but I would not be the woman I am today if it were not for having such a supportive mom. I love you, Mom. To Dad: I know you'll never read these words. Your time on this planet was short, but you made such an impact on the lives of everyone who knew you. I miss you so much, and I wish you were still here so that we could celebrate together.

Being a writer is a fairly unglamorous endeavor. There are moments of self-doubt, frenzied idea sessions, and everything in between. Sometimes a lady just needs a little time with her friends to bring her back to something resembling sanity. To Sarina: I don't know how I ever lived without you in my life. Thank you for being a constant source of laughter and support in my life and for always being honest with me. You are the best bestie ever. To Devon: I remember the day we met. Sharing our unique writing journeys has been exciting and encouraging. Your feedback has shaped this story, and your friendship has shaped me.

To my amazing editor, J. H.: thank you for all the time you put into cleaning up my mess. I'm so glad we found each other.

I can't forget to thank my beta-readers: Alexia, Andra, Christopher, Lindsey and Matt (the couple that reads together, slays together), Samantha, and Sarah. Your feedback and ideas were exactly what I needed. Thank you for your time and thoughtfulness.

There's also Wilbur's Total Beverage in Fort Collins, Colorado. I wouldn't have survived the innumerable rounds of rewrites and edits if it were not for you keeping me well supplied with wine.

I also want to thank the authors who shaped the stories I can't live without; Agatha Christie, Jane Austen, Madeleine L'Engle, and Neil Gaiman. I would not be the person I am today without your stories.

And last, but most certainly not least, I would like to thank LeVar Burton. We've never met, but my childhood was enriched by your passion for reading and the literary adventures of *Reading Rainbow*. Now, as an adult, I'm honored to bear witness to the legacy of literacy you've built.

About the Author

G. H. Fryer is a nerdy pisces who spends far too much time in her head than in the real world. She lives in a small northern Colorado town with her husband (who keeps her grounded), daughter (who enables her mischievous behavior), and dog (who's afraid of absolutely everything). She enjoys coffee, tea, wine, and chocolate (although not necessarily in that order). She loves making new friends, especially the sort who enjoys a good mystery.